FINDING HOME

ERIC WRIGHT

FINDING HOME

A NOVEL

Cormorant Books

**Canada Council
for the Arts** **Conseil des Arts
du Canada**

The publisher gratefully acknowledges the support of the
Canada Council for the Arts and the Ontario Arts Council
for its publishing program. We acknowledge the financial support
of the Government of Canada through the Book Publishing
Industry Development Program (BPIDP) for our publishing activities.

Printed and bound in Canada

LIBRARY AND ARCHIVES CANADA CATALOGUING IN PUBLICATION

Wright, Eric
Finding home / Eric Wright.

ISBN-13 978-1-897151-11-2

I. Title.

PS8595.R58F46 2007   C813'.54   C2007-902751-2

Editor: Marc Côté
Cover design: Angel Guerra/Archetype
Cover image: Amelia Sourget/Beateworks/Corbis
Author photo: Valerie Wright
Interior text design: Tannice Goddard
Printer: Webcom

CORMORANT BOOKS INC.
215 SPADINA AVENUE, STUDIO 230, TORONTO, ONTARIO, CANADA M5T 2C7
www.cormorantbooks.com

For Valerie

ONE

THE FIRST EVENT THAT took me to England was my wife's announcement that she wanted her freedom. I wasn't sure what she meant, right away. "What for?" I asked her. "To play more tennis?" Always looking for the snappy response, the quick quip, that's me. My intentions are usually harmless, at least just epigrammatic, but the impulse is there, even in situations where I would do well to keep my mouth shut.

"That, too," she said, and I knew that this was serious.

"Too?" I asked.

She said nothing.

"What do you plan to do?" I asked.

She stayed silent, waiting for the right question. Then she said, "I'll move out on the weekend."

The other event that preceded this story and now begins it was my mother's funeral.

It was raining when I arrived at the crematorium, a drizzle only, but I had no umbrella or hat and I was early, so I crossed the street to take shelter in a café opposite the crematorium gates. Three elderly people, two women and a man, were sitting at a table by the window. One of the women caught my eye and made as if to rise, and I walked over quickly.

"Aunt Phyllis?"

She looked pleased. "That's right. Will, is it? I saw you across the street. I wasn't sure you'd know me. This ..." she gestured to the other woman, "is your Aunt Olive and this is Uncle Albert."

Both of the women were wearing hats, unusual for them, I guessed; they seemed to be holding their heads warily, as if recently crowned. Albert nursed a grey trilby on his lap. I shook hands with my uncle, kissed my aunts on the cheek and sat down. I guessed that the fashion of kissing on both cheeks had not yet reached the English working classes but I never knew how nephews greeted aunts. The lips or the cheek? And did funerals make a difference? Did they hug now? Perhaps at funerals. Having immigrated to Canada thirty years before, I had missed all the funerals of the older people I had grown up with. The only funerals I'd been to in Canada had been of those whose lives had been cut short by accident or disease, people of my generation.

I kept alert for any signals from my aunts that they had expected something more but they looked properly saluted. Now, what next? How much of a show of grief or sadness was appropriate?

"She had a good innings," Albert said. "None of us in the family can complain about that. Good genes, I dare say."

That was all right, then. We could move on. "I hope I inherited them," I said, with a smile to give it a light, self-mocking twist. I wanted them to know I didn't take myself solemnly. It was like meeting one's dinner companions on a cruise ship for the first time. I knew nothing about these people, and I didn't want to reveal myself until I had heard the topics to avoid.

Albert and Olive looked at each other. Albert said, "There's no particular reason why you shouldn't have inherited them, is there, that you know of?"

Before I could wonder what he was talking about, Phyllis said, "Did you have a good trip?" and gave Albert a look designed to silence him forever.

"Hullo," I thought, like Peter Cook in one of his monologues. I said, "Yes. The plane was half empty." I picked up the menu. "Been a lot of changes," I said. "I mean in London, not the menu."

"Haven't seen you for fifty years," Albert said, or rather shouted, in a conversational manner, as if he were making himself heard in a bar on a Saturday night.

"Nor me," Olive agreed, nodding. They were a raucous pair. Olive sounded like a Monty Python housewife.

"His mum was too busy," Phyllis said, giving Albert another, only slightly less violent, look.

"Too busy for her own family?" Olive asked, and I heard the rumblings and felt the tremors of an old grudge surfacing. Olive turned to me. "We had to rely on Phyllis here. She kept us informed."

"I'm grateful for that," I said. "And thanks for coming today." I watched them soften slightly, especially Phyllis, who had made all the arrangements. For it was my job she had done, my mother who had died.

"Your Aunt Lottie, my wife, sends her best," Albert said. "She'd have come but funerals upset her."

Olive and Albert had not come to my father's funeral, either. No one had, except Phyllis and the charwoman from the guesthouse my parents ran. The publican on the corner had sent a wreath as he always did when a customer died. That was all. Afterwards, the four of us — my mother, Phyllis, the charwoman and me — had enjoyed a meat tea in a hotel on the seafront. My mother was pleased that I had flown over but, a businesswoman herself, she understood when I had to return the next day. "The world doesn't stop for funerals," she had said.

"Why didn't the others come?" I had asked Phyllis then, meaning Olive and Albert.

"Your father never encouraged them while he was alive," Phyllis had said. "He choked them off when they tried to drop by, and Albert's not one who needs choking off twice. So, them not being welcome when he was alive, they let him have his privacy when he died, so to speak."

"Wouldn't go near the place so long as he was there," Albert was reported to have said. So he had taken the opportunity of the funeral to show what he thought of my father.

Now, though, it was their sister's funeral.

"How many you got?" Albert inquired, still shouting.

"Two," I said, guessing that Albert was referring to children.

Albert said, "Olive's got two and I've got three. They're all your cousins. Between them they've got seven kids, all your second, or your first cousins once removed. I don't know how that works. Any on your wife's side? I heard somewhere she was an orphan. That right? None of my business. Pity the kids haven't got to know each other, though." The remark was accompanied by a straight look that made it slightly barbed. Albert was taking the opportunity to show that any distances between me and the other members of the family was no fault of his.

I acknowledged the pity with a small headshake. At all costs, I thought, don't get into an argument.

"Time to go," Phyllis announced.

We crossed the busy road outside the café and walked through the grounds of the crematorium to the chapel, arriving ten minutes early for the ceremony. It was still raining.

There were three chapels, and cremation ceremonies were scheduled at twenty-minute intervals. We waited our turn along with other mourners, huddled in the communal porch.

The ceremony, conducted by a minister on the staff of the crematorium, was modified Anglican: the stripped-down burial service from the prayer book, the music for a stanza of "Abide With

Me," which we stood for but did not attempt to sing, a tiny eulogy honouring all mothers, their duty done. "We are here to celebrate a life," the minister said, in the modern way. One final "Lord's Prayer," which we mumbled together, and we shuffled outside. An attendant in a black suit led us along a concrete path to view what he called "the floral tributes," three small bunches of flowers lying in the rain at the end of the path: little enough tribute after eighty years, but my mother had belonged to no community beyond the family.

The others looked at me, waiting. I looked at my watch. This, too, was a new role for me, in charge of a family occasion. I had seen Phyllis only once since I emigrated, at my father's funeral. I had no memory of ever meeting Albert or Olive. "I hope you'll all have a bite of lunch with me before you go," I said.

It was the right thing to say, what they had been waiting for, their reward for coming. "Where did you have in mind?" Albert asked.

"I noticed a Tartan Steak House on the walk over. That seem all right?"

"Lovely," Olive said. "We got enough umbrellas?" The rain had stopped but the clouds seemed to be gathering for a fresh downpour.

I said, "I'll get a taxi."

"Get out of it, Rothschild," Albert said, boisterously shouldering me away from the idea. "It's only a hop and a skip. Come on. Step it out."

We left the porch of the crematorium and bustled along to the restaurant, continually making way for each other in a jolly fashion. It was an outing now.

"This is nice," Olive said, as the manager came forward to seat us. "Tablecloths. Proper napkins, too."

"They do a smashing sticky toffee pudding, this lot," Albert shouted. Some of the other customers stared at us.

I ordered drinks all round, bitter beer for me and Albert, a "drop of gin" for Olive and a sherry for Phyllis. When the food arrived I ordered a bottle of Australian burgundy.

"That won't go to waste," Albert said. "You've done all right, then?" he asked speculatively.

Now would begin the very English process of trying to find out how much money I made without actually asking me.

I tried to cut it short by describing our life in Toronto, the summer cottage we rented on the French River, the condominium in Arizona we had a share in. I did not tell them that Janet and I were separated. I would never see these people again.

"You sound very comfortable," Albert said. "When I heard all that time ago you were going to Canada, I thought p'raps you would become a lumberjack or something." He laughed. "Or running away from some girl you'd got into trouble. But you don't look much different from what you would be if you'd stayed here."

"Nothing like that," I said.

Nothing at all like that. As soon as I landed in Toronto thirty years before and started to look for a job, it became obvious that the thing to do was to find some work I knew something about, office work of some kind, and I more or less immediately became a clerk again. It was a stroke of luck that I got a job in the head office of Decker Construction, a company with contracts that ranged from building grain elevators in Saskatchewan to relocating a whole town in Manitoba when the ore that the town had been built to mine ran out, and a new seam was opened fifty miles away. I was hired as a timekeeper, the on-site clerk who kept track of labour and materials for the company. My usefulness to Decker was that, as an immigrant, I had no ties to keep me from being sent to wherever the company needed me — Medicine Hat or Loon Lake, it was all one to me — and in the three years I was with them I worked in four different provinces. It was a good beginning, for Decker paid for my room and board while I was out of town, and I got the same wage I would have earned in Toronto. Thus I was able to save a lot as well as get some very useful experience: above all, a crash course in some aspects of Canadian society I would never have got from reading the papers or watching television. After three years, though, with some money in the bank, I felt the urge to think about the future, to create a plan for myself. I quit Decker Construction on the best of terms, with a promise of being able to fall back on work in Yellowknife or South Porcupine any time I needed it, and began to look about me.

"Did you ever meet your grandparents? Do you remember?" Albert asked.

"I remember Gran. She used to come down in the summer holidays, didn't she? I don't remember my grandfather at all."

"Our dad," Albert said. "No, he didn't like being away from home."

"Did *your* dad get along with them?" Olive asked me.

"What a question," Phyllis cut in. "Course he did. He had to, didn't he? You know what Gran was like. I was there. Will was just little."

"I'm not sure that's right," Olive said, belching lightly. "There was always an atmosphere when our mother and Henry were in the same room. You said so, yourself."

Phyllis said, "Did I? Then I've forgotten. That was before Vera and Henry were married, I'm sure, and anyway, I made a little resolution before I left home today: Let's not have one of those funeral scenes, I promised myself. You remember Uncle Fred and his brother Tom coming to blows over what happened to Gran's jet beads? Our Gran, I mean. Right there beside the grave?"

The others protested. "Who said anything about scenes? We were just reminiscing," Albert said.

"One thing leads to another," Phyllis said. "It doesn't do to rake up the past. What's done is done." She stood up, stumbling slightly. "Now I'm a bit tipsy. Never mind. Your mum wouldn't have minded." She turned to me. "We should be off."

Albert said, "We'll say goodbye, me and Olive. Sad occasion, Will, but p'raps it takes that to get people together. You going right back to Canada? Look us up if you've got time. Worcester Park. Train from Waterloo."

"I've got some business over here," I said, "And I want to spend some time on my own. I've seen more of Canada than I ever did of England, and I thought I'd take the chance to see the country a little. Sort of be a tourist in my own country. I'm in no hurry to go back. I thought I might rent a car."

This was my first try at explaining my state of mind, to myself or to anyone else. I was feeling slightly giddy from being no longer anchored by wife or mother or — I'll get to this later — by job. I had been set free, mentally and physically, and I wanted to investigate my new state.

"Hire a self-drive, you mean? You can manage the driving, can you? It's different over there, I know," Albert said.

I remembered that Albert was a long-distance bus driver. "I don't know. I never learned to drive before I left home, so I'll be like every other North American tourist."

"I don't suppose the left-hand drive will bother you, though, will it? You like driving?"

"Not much. My wife says I'm a lousy driver." I smiled so he wouldn't take me too seriously, but it's true, I don't like driving, and I was distinctly nervous about driving on the left. But it had to be done if I was to see anything of England.

"What you need is a chauffeur. Best of luck, then. If you get lost give us a ring. I'll send someone to fetch you." He laughed.

Olive struggled to her feet. "You might find me on your doorstep one of these days, Will. I'm not too old to travel yet."

"Give us lots of warning, Aunt Olive. We're away a lot," I said, to protect myself from having them descend on me with plans to stay a month and expectations that I would supply daily outings. I kissed my aunt, shook hands with my uncle, and we left the restaurant, Albert and Olive heading for the Underground, Phyllis and me to find a taxi.

TWO

PHYLLIS LIVED IN CLAPHAM, in a two-bedroom flat in a converted Victorian house. "It's just a small flat," Phyllis said, as she unlocked the door. "But there's room for one more if you want to stay the night."

"I'm booked into a hotel, Auntie. I didn't want to put you out."

"I could've managed. I'm not set up for visitors but there is a spare room, now your mum's gone." She crossed the little hall and opened the door of my mother's room, pushing it back so that I could see inside the room. There was a single bed I might have used, but the room was crammed full of my mother's possessions: clothes, furniture, odd mirrors, ornaments, framed "views," all looking together, as such piles of possessions usually do, like so much junk awaiting the rag-and-bone man. (Did they still have rag-and-bone men?)

"These are the things she kept back when she sold the house in Lyme Regis, just in case she ever had to furnish a flat. They're yours now," she said.

"All the clothing can go for a start. Send it to the church bazaar. They still have rummage sales, don't they?"

"I expect so. I don't attend church, myself, though I reckon there must be something in it. I thought you might want to look her things over, in case your children are interested in a memento. They're grown up, of course, your two. P'raps a shawl or something."

"Did you notice anything like that?"

"Not really."

"What about all this furniture? This all Mum's?"

"I thought some of it might be valuable. That cocktail cabinet, for instance. I saw one in an antique shop in the Brompton Road. They're coming back in."

"Then show it to a dealer, and buy yourself something nice with the money. Take it. Sell it. Give it away. What's this?" I picked up a black lacquer box, the lid inlaid with a decoration in mother-of-pearl.

"Your mum's jewellery. That you *must* take back for your wife."

"Don't you want any of it?"

"Since you ask, there's a brooch she promised me when ..."

"Where?" I opened the box. "Which one? This? Take it. Here," I snapped the box shut and shoved it into her hands. "Take what you fancy. What's this?" I opened a small leather attaché case.

"Those are some papers."

"Her will?"

"I believe that's with her solicitor."

"I have to see him tomorrow." I lifted out a bundle of letters, about a dozen altogether, all from me. When I first went to Canada, I wrote home once a month for a few months, then only on birthdays and at Christmas, for my mother never replied. Instead, when she received one of my letters she telephoned me, wherever I was, and told me her news. She sent Christmas cards and money for my birthday (she was generous about that), but I don't think she ever composed a personal letter in her life, though she had a dashing signature which certainly looked like the product of a writing life.

Underneath the letters were two old photographs, one of a fair-haired man about thirty, with slightly prominent upper teeth, and another of a woman of the same age with a large brown, expensive-looking dog. She had the look of someone from a better class than us (though as the owners of a guesthouse, my parents, like publicans, were outside the class system), something to do with the way her hair was arranged and the lack of a necklace, or beads. I asked my aunt who these two were.

"I've no idea who she is," she said. "He was a traveller."

"A traveller?"

"Not one of those caravan people. A commercial traveller."

Her answer came quickly, automatically, accompanied by a poker face that delivered its own message — that she intended to evade any further questions about the picture. I might have attached a lot of significance to her reply and the way it was delivered, wondered at the possibility that I had uncovered some secret that Phyllis would never reveal — that the young man in the photo was actually a canker on the family tree, my illegitimate brother, perhaps, raised away from his mother in an orphanage, or perhaps a real brother who had died in prison while doing life for killing a prostitute — but he didn't look like Phyllis or any of the pictures of my mother from her youth, so I guessed perhaps he was simply an old boyfriend of my mother. And then I remembered that my mother had told me that Phyllis was a liar by nature, and that probably there was nothing more to her reply than that, for congenital liars are always concerned that the truth could on any day emerge to contradict some already forgotten lie. When in doubt, they take refuge in a pretence of ignorance as the simplest way to avoid being caught out.

My mother's casual labelling of Phyllis as a liar was uncensorious and accurate. Her sister's way with the truth was something one had to be aware of; it was even interesting, but it didn't rate a penalty. As I grew up, I heard my mother describe Phyllis so several times, usually when she was talking to my father or her own mother, both of whom accepted that my mother was not judging her sister, just describing her. The first time I heard the word applied, I was young enough to wonder if Aunt Phyllis would wake up the next day with a long nose, but I soon grew to understand what was really being said. After all, as my mother pointed out, everyone is a bit of a liar; with Phyllis, it was a habit.

Phyllis lied for a lot of reasons. The most usual reason was to boast or exaggerate. She always claimed her wages were higher at the Post Office, where she worked, than they were. She often changed the price of something she had bought, upwards or downwards, to give it a glow of interest. "They had Cox's apples on sale in Berwick Street market for a shilling a pound," she would say, when she arrived from London for the weekend. The price in the shops in Coombe Regis might be two shillings, and my mother would go about the business of making sure there was no truth in her sister's remark "You sure?" she would begin, always giving Phyllis room to say she'd made a mistake. ("Did I say a shilling?" Phyllis might be able to say, feeling the ground become slippery. "No, that was last week. Two shillings.") Usually, though, while sweating a little as she saw that she was being called, Phyllis stuck to her story. "That's what the sign said," she would insist.

"Did he actually call it out? Like, 'A bob a pound!'" my mother would ask, wanting to know, but also constructing an exit for Phyllis.

"No, he didn't call it out, not while I was listening. But it was there on the ticket, clear as daylight."

"I reckon he made a mistake. Or you did. You didn't buy any?"

"I was in a hurry to get the train."

"If you'd bought some you would have found out."

And there my mother would leave it. She wanted to satisfy herself that Phyllis was lying again, but she didn't want to be vindictive about it. She understood Phyllis's lies as she would have those of a young child, knowing her to be telling "stories"; but you couldn't say "Don't tell stories" to a woman of thirty or forty.

Exaggeration to gain attention was the main reason Phyllis told lies. Another was to seem to be in possession of private information, a holder of secrets. When this was her reason, she spoke so as to indicate that she felt duty bound to lie but she wanted you to know that that was what she was doing. To my question about the young man in the photograph, she responded with a pretended ignorance but also with a hint of hesitation and an opaque expression that demanded to be questioned.

In the matter of who was lying, my mother knew what she was talking about, for she herself was a superb liar, though of a very different kind. In fact, in calling her sister a liar she was saying not so much that Phyllis was trying to deceive but that to the trained eye and ear, she wasn't very good at it. My mother was a professional, a first-rate liar, and only when you were yourself in possession of hard evidence did you know she was lying. In her case, the lies were usually connected with concealing the details of her business as well as her private life. Once, I remember, she listed only one guest registered in the book during a period of three days. I was seven or eight at the time and good at arithmetic as well as reading, and pointed out the error. "There were six people here one day," I said. "You remember? You all played penny nap."

She didn't miss a step. "No, love, the other five were all friends, not paying guests. That's why if anyone should ask you, you tell him to ask me. I'll put them straight."

It's a tribute to her instincts that on the occasion when a real inspector of taxes registered for the night, her guest book reflected the full count for that day, and the day before. "I can smell blokes like that on the phone," she said to my father.

I picked up the photograph of the woman with the dog. "Who is this?"

"Her, I've *no* idea of," Phyllis said, again, with a believable directness and emphasis that contrasted with her reply about the young man. "I never set eyes on her, that I do know. P'raps a friend from before. You know, school or something."

"It's an old picture," I said.

"That frock takes me back," she agreed.

"To when?"

She became cautious. "A few years," she said, finally. "After the war, though."

"Where was it taken? Do you know?" The woman stood on a lawn fringed with rose bushes; a substantial house of five or six bedrooms filled most of the background. A path round one side opened to a view of distant hills.

"Nowhere your mum lived. No sign of the seaside, is there?"

I pocketed the two photographs and picked up a small key from the box. I held it up to Phyllis in a silent question. She smiled and moved to the wardrobe against the wall. There on the upper shelf, inside a picnic basket, a small cheap cashbox waited to be found.

I took out a bankbook that showed a balance of 830 pounds, almost three hundred pounds in notes, two National Savings Bonds, and a small quantity of foreign currency.

"This it?" I asked after I had gathered it together. "A bit of a widow's mite, isn't it? After fifty years of paying guests?"

This was not the first time that I had thought about my mother's estate since I heard the news. I was not expecting an inheritance that would change my life. In fact, I had assumed that anything she left would be used to take care of Phyllis. But thinking about it now, I was puzzled.

Phyllis said, "P'raps the solicitor will have some more information. But I can tell you one thing, you're right to wonder: that cash box was put there to be found, but not by you."

I waited for her to explain. Obviously this was one more creation of my mother's, designed to throw dust into the eyes of an inquirer into her affairs.

"I'm not sure if it was the tax man or burglars she was more afraid of," Phyllis said.

"Had she been audited?"

"Been what?"

"Has a tax inspector been here lately?"

"Someone was round last week. I told him you were coming for the funeral. He said he would be in touch. You could put him off, tell him you've been called away, like."

"I might as well speak to him. If he comes back, let him know where I'm staying and tell him to leave a number where I can call him."

"Think you can manage him? They're very clever, those people. I'd have a word with the solicitor first, if I were you."

Faintly patronizing, reminding me that in Phyllis's eyes, I was still her young nephew, no match for the authorities, whoever they were. But it was probably good advice. "I'll do that," I said. "Now what's this about the cash box? Who was supposed to find it?"

"Anyone, dear, anyone looking for it."

"She was only pretending to hide it?"

"That's right."

So the cash box was intended to look like her life's savings, and thus send a burglar on his way, satisfied, without tearing the place apart.

I said, "Where is the real thing?"

"The what?"

"Whatever she was *really* hiding."

"There isn't anything else here. But she thought a burglar wouldn't believe that." She beamed at me, proud of her sister's cleverness and wanting me to appreciate it.

I found the idea that we were looking at my mother's life savings hard to believe, and I appreciated that it might be a ploy to deceive burglars into believing this was all there was. A plausible enough story to account for an old lady, living with her memories, but unbelievable when you had grown up with my mother and knew how sharp a businesswoman she had been. I tucked the problem away, ready to be dealt with when I had learned more about her life since I had been in Canada. I said, "I think I'll call it a day, Auntie. Where is the solicitor's office?"

"Near the tube station. Across the common. Not far." She went to the mirror over the mantelpiece and took out one of the cards tucked under the edge. "Here's the address."

"Will you be home tomorrow?"

"I have to get my feet done in the morning."

"I'll give you a call. Here, take down the name of my hotel in case you need me." I scribbled the name on the back of one of my own cards. "I'll try to get an appointment with this solicitor and call you after lunch."

I left and found a taxi to take me to my hotel.

THREE

ALTHOUGH WE HAVE CLIENTS in London and New York, I rarely travel on agency business. When I do, I have trouble leaving my economy class upbringing behind. Once, travelling to a meeting in Chicago, I found myself as usual booked into the tourist section of the plane. Walking to the back, through the first class section, I was hailed by a partner going to the same meeting. Our secretaries had not got together on the travel arrangements.

This time, though, Grisham, one of the partners with much more experience of travel than I, had insisted on being allowed to choose the hotel. "If you want service in London," he had said, "You have to pay for it."

Urging me to pamper myself at the partnership's expense was a simple way for the partners to express their condolences, I realized, and I let him make the booking. Much later I realized that he was also happy to have me out of the way at a time of change for the partnership, change which would inevitably be contentious, for he was more ambitious for the partnership than I. In the end, I became in a mood to accommodate him but only because I had spent some time away, and I went home finally to find that Grisham's plans suited me very well.

I wasn't grieving, or not much. My mother had died quietly, in her sleep, after a full life, and lately I had talked to her two or three times a week on the phone. The matron of the nursing home where she had spent her last months had undertaken to call me when the end was near, so although I wish I had been there, it wasn't a surprise. I left Toronto for the funeral feeling properly sad but glad, too, for both of us, that her life had closed so peacefully.

I had brought no business with me from the office. I intended to take the opportunity of the funeral to take a break from the affairs of Campbell and Montague, and think about what I wanted to do with myself. Business was good: we had done well, and I could, if I felt like it, retire, selling my interest in the agency to the rest of the partners. I had enough to live on. The fact that the thought of retirement had even crossed my mind was enough to make me want to find a space to think in. Then, as I had said to Albert, there was the opportunity, finally, to visit "the old country" like a tourist, to see if it still felt in any way like home. An elderly Scottish lady at a dinner party in London, Ontario, had asked me if I didn't feel that I "stood apart from both worlds," England and Canada, and I had brooded a bit about that.

And finally, then, as if there really was some purpose directing my affairs, the week before my mother died, my wife took the occasion of our silver wedding anniversary to tell me she was leaving me.

And so the idea grew that this might be the opportunity to take some time off to think, to contemplate my navel a bit. In the middle of dealing with the death of my mother and the end of my marriage, I'd found that tiny bit of good news that often accompanies a tragedy, the graveside thought of some benefit that the sad event had brought. In my case, it was this realization that came to me in the night that

I was being presented just at the right time with an opportunity to find out how I wanted to spend the rest of my life without having to explain to anybody — wife, friends or colleagues — what I was doing. Everyone knew what I was doing — grieving, attending a funeral — and urged me, for their own reasons, some of them, to take my time. And now the one person who had the right to ask me what I was thinking had given up that right. Of course I was upset that she was leaving me; nevertheless, the fact that it did occur to me that I was now free to explore the question of what next, confirmed that the end of my marriage had not been the total surprise it might have been. At least part of my reaction to the news, any anger I showed, had an element of the conventional about it; I reacted as I supposed I should. And then, within my response, even so early, there was that small seed of excitement at the realization that I was being released.

I told the partners I would need at least a couple of weeks to sort out my mother's affairs, perhaps more, and Grisham assured me again that though I would be missed, I should take all the time I needed. Jack Masters said the same thing, then added, "When you return, let's get together before you come back to the office."

"Why?" Jack Masters was my only friend among the partners, the only one I needed, though I was on good terms with them all.

"We should talk but right now you should go to your mother's funeral."

I wondered what Jack had that he wanted to share, but not for long, because I didn't care much. I read somewhere recently a poignant description of the beginning awareness, before any words are exchanged, that a love affair is over, and now the description seemed to fit, not only my marriage, but my working life. My mother's death had undone something, created a detachment, made me aware of a declining interest in my own day-to-day world. I should say here that I am not hinting that I was about to embark on a journey of middle-aged self-discovery that would end in a monastery, or a gay Dominican brothel (i.e. a gay brothel in Dominica). I knew who

I was. It was just that the funeral was an opportunity to think about myself in a way I had been wanting to for some time. I was fifty-four, unattached, and with no obligations, now that the two children were well on their way.

The hotel that Grisham had booked me into had been recently carved out of the shells of two older buildings, and had no identity of its own. My room seemed like something in an espionage novel: rich, anonymous, secure, powered by dozens of silent engines. It was the hotel where M stayed when he was in town, known only to three other people.

This is the place to mention yet another world I had been visiting, or rather, revisiting lately. Before I became a copywriter, while I was still working for Decker Construction, I had had a bit of success writing humorous pieces for company magazines, and I had actually placed one in a real magazine. Then a pal of mine, an Englishman who worked for a wine company in Toronto, asked me to write something for him to read at the company roast of a retiring president. At the time I had just written a comic piece for an airline magazine about visiting England, giving advice on local customs, treating the U.K. as if it were a central African state with a mysterious culture. Tony had laughed when he read it, and he asked me to write something similarly light he could read at this dinner he had to go to. The piece I came up with made fun of the Canadian wine industry, or rather its pretensions. It was called "Ten Rules for Drinking Canadian Wine," mock advice for Albertan oenophiles. (At the time, advertisements for Canadian wine tended to quote presumably knowledgeable Frenchmen saying things like, "I have never tasted anything like it.")

I enjoyed writing the piece, and I assumed it would offend every wine industry CEO in the room, but one of these executives saw in it a potential for an advertising campaign. He had been looking for someone to devise a less earnest approach to his own company's products, to write copy that would "sell the product by entertaining the customer" as he put it, and he offered me a job. I knew I could go back to Decker Construction any time I wanted, so I took the job. The idea of being paid to write jokes seemed wonderful.

The work suited me; I found my niche as a creator of advertising copy with a whimsical tone, and from Jericho Wines I went to a vodka company, and on to a large furniture retailer. I soon realized that my real future lay with the agencies, the professionals, and I took my small success to one of them and was hired immediately. One of the things I was doing was shaking off another aspect of my upbringing, getting rid of the notion that one good job should last me until I retired. I worked at four different agencies in the next ten years before a group of us decided to start our own. To avoid using four names and sounding like a company of stockbrokers, we invented two more, and the partnership of "Campbell and Montague" was born.

At first, while we were scrounging around for business, everyone did everything, though it was understood that I was the writer. I did write copy for a couple of years, then headed the department, hired other writers, and then became the "money man," handling customer accounts, perfectly happily and successfully, too, until now. Now it was another aspect of my life I wanted to think about. Now that I had squirrelled away enough money to retire, and although I had no great yearning to surprise the world, I decided to find out if I still had some "real" writing in me. Most copywriters I know have the same yearning. A lot of them, having the career of Eric Ambler in mind, work on thrillers in their spare time. In my case, my modest ambition was to return to my roots and become a writer of humorous pieces, and lately I had been using all my spare time and some of the agency's to write some new ones. (I had already tried my hand at one or two more earnest pieces, and I still have the beginning of one story: *I am sitting alone in a construction shack in a field in Northern Alberta. The rain, which has been falling for three days now, continues to pound on the roof. No words of mine can describe the dreariness of this land of mud and stones, suppurating under a glaucous sky.* This must have been true, for the piece stops there, and I went back to copying bits of Thurber.)

Of course that didn't work either. Whatever knack had produced those jaunty little pieces thirty years before had disappeared a long time since. I suspect something like self-consciousness had arrived because everything I tried to write in the struggle to recapture that first fine careless rapture lay dead on the page. Nevertheless, although that particular spring had dried up, I wanted to write *something*, and I had the small advantage over everyone else who experiences the same yearning, that I had once produced some evidence that I was entitled to dream. And now I had the money to try.

But write what? Write about what you know: I was back to that. So I avoided the large canvases, the thrillers, the brilliant sitcoms, the historical novels, and, now that I had given up on humour, tried very hard to focus my ambition on the possible, to find a form that would let me discover what I could do. To state my ambition as minimally and yet as accurately as possible, I wanted to write some surprising sentences, to produce a bit of writing that could only have come from me. It was not far from there to realizing what Yeats meant by going back to "the foul rag-and-bone-shop of the heart," where all poetry must begin but I still needed to find the thread that would lead me there. I came up with travel writing. I thought I would start (and maybe finish) with a book about England — *The Emigrant's Return* sort of thing — something to get me going, and I thought the conceit of the traveller discovering his own country and thereby himself might be made entertaining enough to sustain a book. At any rate, whatever I wrote once I got going, a tourist guide or a book of travels, or a journey into the interior (my own), would be seen in the end to be what I had intended all along.

FOUR

THERE WAS A KNOCK on the door. A woman in her thirties with smooth fair hair cut square to earlobe level and with no makeup said, "My name is Cora; if you want anything, call the desk and ask for me."

She was very beautiful, although missing a small part of her left nostril, a detail which suggested an exotic past, in keeping with this hotel. (I made a note of her: if I returned to the idea of writing a thriller, Cora and the hotel would certainly have to be in it, the scarred nostril the result of an ordeal at the hands of whatever villains then in vogue — Chilean cocaine growers, perhaps. As it was, I learned from one of the maids that Cora lived with her mother near Tooting Bec Common, and she scarred her nose when she fell off her tricycle as a child.)

I said, "I can't think of anything. You the manager?"

"A host. Enjoy your stay."

The next morning I ate a delicious breakfast of scrambled eggs, chipolatas, mushrooms and fried tomatoes in my room, remembering the remark of Somerset Maugham, that if you want to eat well in England you should eat breakfast three times a day, and wondering if it was still true. I called for Cora, more to test out the services she provided than anything else.

A small Asian woman with hair tipped with yellow appeared.

"Cora?" I wondered if Cora was a name all the hosts had to answer to when on duty, the way aristocrats call their butlers by a house name, James, for instance, whatever the man's real name.

"Helen," she said, looking surprised that I couldn't tell the difference. "Cora is on in the afternoon. What can I do for you?"

I explained that I had to travel to Clapham Common and asked her what was the best way.

"I'll call you a taxi. There's a stand round the corner. Five minutes?"

I wanted to ask if the Underground would be quicker and cheaper than a taxi, but I accepted that she had done all those calculations in her head before recommending the taxi. Or perhaps it was an understood thing: guests at this hotel did not use the Underground.

Purrott and Ely occupied a suite of offices above a curry takeout on a small street behind Clapham North Underground station. Simon Purrott was waiting, ready to explain the situation. The solicitor looked freshly washed, with small wisps of white hair sprouting, uncombed, from all over his head.

He offered me a hand and a warm little smile. "My condolences," he said, then, like a clergyman, "She ran her race, and God grant her rest." He looked down at his desk for three seconds of respectful silence. "Now, about her affairs. I have a copy of what I hope is her last will. Do you have one? No? She left everything to you, of course, except whatever personal effects her sister might like — clothes, knick-knacks, jewellery, ornaments and so forth. All this she set out in a letter apart from the witnessed testament, so it isn't binding on you. Though I would think ..."

"I've already told Aunt Phyllis to take anything she wants."

"The proper thing, I'm sure. Now, the rest of the estate. Not a lot. Your mother lived on the state pension and an annuity."

"Would it have taken all her money to buy the annuity?"

Purrott gave me a considering look, as if he was wondering how much to say. "The question occurred to me. I asked her about it at the time, in case she had paid too much for the annuity, as it were, because property on the English Riviera, as they call that part of the coast, is pretty valuable. But she was very vague in her answer and I didn't press it."

"So she bought the annuity from her savings? Her profits?"

"Let's assume so."

"What are you hinting at?"

"Your mother kept her business affairs very private. She had almost no books, she dealt only in cash, and though there was a guest book, it didn't seem very full."

"Did the tax people believe her?"

"She was never audited while she was in Bournemouth or in Coombe Regis. Then she had apparently been living quietly in Lyme Regis for some time, so I wonder if the authorities remained interested in her. There's an insurance policy for ten thousand pounds left over from an earlier age, and another ten thousand in government bonds, which I have for you here. And whatever she had in the bank."

"Is it enough?"

Purrott smiled. "It's about right for the known facts: a widow who once upon a time rented the odd room but otherwise relied on her pensions and a small annuity. A careful, saving sort of woman."

"That doesn't sound like my mother, or the guesthouse I remember."

"That's my feeling, too. But the tax authorities never went behind it, and it is not my job to wonder on their behalf."

"But you think there was more to her? And maybe more money? That you didn't know about?"

"There was a lot I didn't know about your mother."

"What about the money from the sale of the guesthouse in Coombe Regis?"

"There wasn't much. There was a very large mortgage on the property. Almost a hundred per cent."

"And where did that money go? The mortgage money."

"Some to buy the house in Lyme Regis, of course. And repairs and improvements, I imagine. That's the usual reason for taking out a mortgage. I wasn't her solicitor at the time, and — well, she seemed to have almost no documents. Have you found any? No. Now I have to finish the formal handing over of the estate. No problems there. Here is the note she left."

The note read: *"Will, your Aunt Phyllis has been good to me. Let her have anything she wants, and if you feel flush, give her five thou from what's left. I would have done it myself but I wanted her to think well of you. I'm sorry we didn't see more of each other, especially lately, but there it is. We're still talking (as I write, I mean) and lots aren't. God bless."*

That afternoon, I returned to my Aunt Phyllis and sat with her in her living room, a small space with a television set, two armchairs, two trays on legs, a gas fireplace and a sideboard. It was a room for eating while watching television. There was no provision for entertaining callers.

"We kept ourselves to ourselves," Phyllis said, as usual making this drawbridge approach to the world sound like a virtue. "Your mum had no interest in the neighbours."

"She asked me to give you something from her estate," I said.

"She told me there might be something but the solicitor never said anything. She didn't *owe* me anything, mind, in case you don't want to do it. I can manage. I've made my arrangements."

"A retirement home?"

"Quite a good class of residence, actually. I'm rather looking forward to it, meeting a few people. It's been a bit close, with just your mum. On the south coast. My own room, naturally. Nice gardens. Lots of activities, not just bingo."

"You'll be able to manage, then? I thought that without Mum, things might be difficult."

"They might have been, but the reason I'll be all right is that your mum took care of me while she was alive, never mind the will after she was dead. She made arrangements so that whichever one of us went first the other would be looked after at this retirement home."

"Then why the legacy?"

"How much is it?"

I showed her my mother's letter of intent, pointing to the appropriate paragraph.

"She's written five thou," Phyllis said with a laugh. "Just like she would have said it. She had a slangy way with her, did your mum. Not common or rough, but slangy."

"If she took care of you through this retirement home, why the five thousand? I thought when I first read it that it was probably all she'd left you. It looks like it."

Phyllis smiled, ducking her head. "That's what it's supposed to look like, I reckon. She didn't want anyone knowing her business, even after she was dead, and she assumed I felt the same way. So she left it up to me whether I told you about the retirement arrangement. But I don't have much business for anyone to know.

"I was married once but it never took, no children. I worked for the GPO all my life, so there's a bit of a pension from the old Post Office that was, and my old age pension, of course, and a bit of savings. And this flat was mine before your mum came to live with me. So, what with one thing and another, it's nobody's business, but I'm all right. And I don't need to keep any secrets from you, as long as you keep my business to yourself, not go chatting to Albert or Olive. But now you know, your mum left it up to you to give me the five thou if you felt sorry for me."

"I don't follow."

"See, if I wanted to tell you about the other arrangements, that was up to me. But if she'd left me nothing, after all these years, people would wonder, and not to her credit. Even you might. So leaving me five thou would let people think she had done what she thought right and let people think that was it. She left it up to me, do you see, and up to you, too, of course. Artful cat, wasn't she?"

"Artful, that's the word."

"Close, too. Not devious. Close."

"There's something I'm more interested in right now. The man in the photograph."

"You already asked me that. I told you, he was a traveller." She pulled her cardigan tight around herself. "Are we done now?"

I had hoped to catch her out in some slightly different response, a small slip of invention that would confirm that she did know but there were reasons why she wouldn't tell me.

"No. Sorry. No, if you don't mind, I'd like to hear all about Mum."

"So what can I tell you?"

"You were the closest to Mum within the family, weren't you?"

"I would say so, yes."

"Why, then? Why did she cut herself off except for you? Why you? Why didn't she cut herself off from you, too?"

Phyllis sighed noisily. "Families. Why didn't she cut herself off completely? From our mother, too? You never knew her, did you? Your grandmother."

"I told you yesterday, I remember her from when I was very little. Like an old witch."

"Steady on! But, yes, she *was* fierce. Told your mum to behave herself. *Made* her behave herself, while she was around, right up to the end."

"Behave herself?"

"You know what I mean. Your mum knew."

"Was my father around then?"

"Of course!"

"You know, Aunt Phyllis, this is like pulling teeth. Why don't you make us a cup of tea and tell me the whole story."

"All right. It's nearly my lunchtime. How about a cheese and chutney sandwich? I've got a bottle of Guinness under the stairs, just for visitors. Then I'll tell you what I know. I can see now that it won't upset you as much as I'd thought it might."

And so I heard the beginning of the story; three weeks later in a village in Gloucestershire, again over a cheese and chutney sandwich, I heard the end.

FIVE

WHEN WE WERE SETTLED back in our chairs, the sandwiches and beer in front of us, she said, "You'll have to prompt me. I don't know where to start."

. "When did you begin visiting Mum?"

"Right from the time when she started to help her friend Flo with the guesthouse in Bournemouth. You never knew Flo, did you? She was a friend of your mother's from when they worked together in London. When she took over her own mother's guesthouse, she asked your mum to go in with her. I used to go down every other weekend to help out. I was only eighteen or thereabouts, and your mum and Flo couldn't afford regular staff, not at first, so I went down occasionally to give them a few hours off. I enjoyed it; our family was very working class and the guesthouse was a cut above that. When I went out to do the shopping in Bournemouth, the locals called me Miss Canning. That didn't happen in Tooting Broadway, I can tell you. I worked in the GPO during the week, but every other weekend I shot straight down to Bournemouth. My other home."

"Was my father living there?"

"Only every *other* weekend. The rest of the time he was travelling, too, for Crosse and Blackwell. After they got married, he stopped travelling and I stopped going down to Bournemouth regularly. See, I always shared the room with your mum. It wasn't a big guest-house; there weren't all that many rooms, so I used to bunk in with her. They moved to Coombe Regis, then, and you was born. Then your dad got a job with the council and stayed home to help out."

"When did they get married?"

"I'm not sure. No one was invited."

I thought she was lying again but I decided to come back to it later. There would be a record somewhere.

"So then, when Flo died, you and Mum ran the guesthouse together?"

"Don't keep calling it that. She never had a sign up, and we weren't listed. Your mum sometimes put a small advert in the *Exchange and Mart* but mostly we got referrals. She got to know a lot of the better-class bed and breakfast people in the area, and let it be known that she was not averse to helping them out when they were over-booked, just as a favour, and she built up a steady trade mostly with commercial travellers. She was a good cook, your mum. And then, she wasn't nosy, like some of the others. Or Methodist."

"What does that mean?"

"Some of the commercials brought their girlfriends with them for the night. She didn't mind but they had to bring the same one each time and pay for a double. Your mum used to say she wasn't running a knocking shop; she just didn't like the idea of one of her regulars having to go to one of those fleabags along the front just because they didn't have a marriage licence. Sometimes there would be three or four couples on a Saturday night, all at so much a head, of course, and your mum would stand them a crate of beer to have a bit of a social evening before we went to bed. She wouldn't allow no singing. Singing brought the neighbours and that sometimes meant the police. One chap played the banjo, but very quietly, mind. More often than not they had a game of cards before they went to bed. Some of these commercials were in their fifties, and in those days there was no monkey glands or anything like that to keep them up to the mark, and as much as anything they just wanted a bit of company, in bed and out of it. But outsiders would have thought the worst."

My understanding was growing. I remembered those Saturday night parties but cut off from everybody else as we were, I assumed that they were typical of the times. Now it sounded to me like my mother knew how to make the guesthouse pay.

"Did she give receipts?"

"Not very often. If they insisted on a receipt, they never came back. As far as they were concerned, we were always full."

"She didn't pay any income tax, I suppose."

"I believe she occasionally declared the odd paying guest, just in case someone got nasty and tattled."

"What about?"

"There was one man who just appeared on the doorstep one Saturday night with a tart, asking for a room for a couple of hours and waving a fiver. That was when a fiver meant something. She asked him who told him she let rooms by the hour, and he told her the name of one of her regulars who travelled in detergents. Your mum sent this fella packing and when her regular turned up, she sent him packing, too, and everyone else from that soap company. Her regular pleaded with her, swore he hadn't given a false impression but that his colleague had just taken the wrong idea. Vera was made of stone. 'You'll find what you want down on the front,' she said. 'Don't come back here.' The story got to her other regulars and that was the only time there was an incident."

All this was interesting enough but I wanted to get back to the money. It was clear that my mother had created a smokescreen to hang over her affairs when she died, protecting her estate from official eyes, as she had protected her affairs in life. Apparently she had left eight hundred pounds in the bank, the insurance policy was worth ten thousand, and there was ten thousand in government bonds. After running a guesthouse for thirty years while receiving various pensions? I didn't believe it.

I said, "Are there any other papers that you know of, Aunt Phyllis? Did she have a safety deposit box? Anything like that?"

I knew the answer. Already I accepted that my mother's bank was under the bed, so to speak; that is, if there was a cache somewhere, it would not be in a location where the Inland Revenue might stumble over it. But had she hidden it so well it would remain undiscovered until it turned up in an archaeological excavation?

"I don't know anything about anything like that," Phyllis said. "You've got everything I know about. I don't even know where she used to go on weekends." She put her hand to her mouth, a little half-completed gesture of dismay at what she had said.

"Where she used to go?"

She looked unhappy. She was still editing her memories as she went along, out of loyalty to my mother, I assumed, and now she had slipped. And yet it was in keeping with her way with secrets that the slip also looked deliberate. "Alive or dead, it was none of my business, but now I've said something, it was just that she used to go away for the odd weekend, not in the early days when your dad was still travelling, but later, when he gave up his selling job. I don't know where. It was just one more example of her being private. Anyway she made it clear that it was nothing to do with me, though your dad seemed to understand, and I don't think he objected."

A complaisant cuckold? I switched to another line of questions. "What do you know about my father's family?" I asked.

"I never saw any of them. I've had a long think about those days and the only thing that comes back is that he knew a lot about Oxford. I always had a feeling that that was where he grew up. If he had any family, that's where I would look for them."

"You never actually heard of family?"

"Once. He got a letter once that made him angry. He tore it up and told me if ever anyone appeared at the door asking for him and claiming to be related I should not let them in but tell them to leave their name and where he could find them. I thought that was a bit ominous but no one ever came while I was staying there."

"What did you make of it? Why 'ominous'?"

"I assumed he had cadgers or worse in the family, and that he'd heard one was trying to find him. Once he went off for the day and came back, and I heard him say to your mum, 'That's them sorted,' but he never spoke of it in front of me."

A number of questions bothered me. I wanted to get to the bottom of my mother's financial affairs, partly out of curiosity, and partly, now that I knew Phyllis was taken care of, to see if there was any real money lying about somewhere, enough perhaps to make a difference to me. Then, too, I wanted to find out about the people I was related to. My father's family didn't sound very promising but I wanted now to give my mother's family a chance, to reconnect with them to see if there was any kind of bond between us. Albert had offered as much. I never knew them because I hadn't been allowed to, but what were my cousins like? And their children? I sometimes felt the lack of relatives, not for myself but for my children. At Christmas, for instance, it was part of being an immigrant that there was no gathering of the family of the kind that other people had. Like the English, Canadian families get together at Christmas, even if only for the day, and even including the cousins you don't like. One of our partners takes nine relatives to a ski lodge for two days of eating and skiing.

Our kids missed out, not only at Christmas but in other ways, from being cut off from their "old country" relatives. From a purely practical point of view, I was sorry that when they did their obligatory year of backpacking in Europe I had not been able to give them access to a network such as other immigrants could provide for their children.

My wife's family was non-existent. She was the adopted child of a Winnipeg couple with whom she had never bonded, and when she left home for college she never returned. She wrote to them, saying she felt some gratitude, but they had never seemed more than guardians to her and they should not expect to see her soon or often. Her adoptive father, a professor of mathematics at the University of Manitoba, wrote back saying that they, too, felt it was best not to pretend to a relationship that had never been created. He and his wife were deeply sorry, feeling perhaps that they had entered into the adoption lacking the necessary willingness to give their emotions to a child, and that they felt more, rather than less, responsible for her under the circumstances. She was their heir, he said, and she should look to them if she found herself with a need they could satisfy. He enclosed a cheque to start her on her way. When we married, we invited them to the wedding, but they made excuses and sent us another five thousand dollars, repeating their pledge of support to my wife.

Such refusal to blame or praise themselves or her for a mutual failure astonished me when she told me of it. It would have been convenient for me to blame the breakup of our marriage on her possibly warped emotional development but, to be honest, I never saw any sign of it. Perhaps instead of love, she had got from her parents an example of how to behave when love fails, or doesn't arrive.

I said to my aunt, "I'm going to spend some time here and there. I'll be in London for a day or two. I'll call you before I go back."

"Eat and run, then, is it?" She was disappointed, I think, expecting my visit to be more of a diversion for her. But I felt she had told me all she knew about my mother. There was still an opaque quality to her replies, as if she knew she should be protecting or defending my mother, but she didn't know all the answers herself.

"Before I go back, we'll have a night out up the other end," I said, remembering the phrase from the past. Did they still call the West End that? "Have some supper," I said. "Go to a play."

"Never mind the play," she said. "Take me to Manzi's."

"What's that?"

"The best fish restaurant in London, your mum called it. She always treated herself to a meal there when she went up. When she took me I had fillet of plaice and a glass of white wine and a little apple tart for afters. It was lovely. It's just off Leicester Square."

"It's a date."

"A bit expensive."

"I'll pay for it out of my legacy."

SIX

THE NEXT MORNING BEFORE I had ordered breakfast, I got a call from the desk that there was a man waiting to see me. Knowing no one in England except the relatives at the funeral, I asked the desk clerk to put him on.

"Derek Merton here." The voice was cheerful, even chirpy.

I said, "You sure you want me? I'm from Canada. I don't know anyone here."

"Your mother died recently? Mrs. Vera Prentice?"

"Who are you?"

"I beg your pardon. I'm so sorry. I thought your solicitor would have told you. Her Majesty's Inspector of Taxes."

"What do you want with me? I don't pay taxes here." I knew perfectly well what he wanted, of course, but I thought it best not to give the impression that I had been expecting him.

"It's your mother's estate that interests us, Mr. Prentice. May I have a word with you about it? Perhaps we could meet in the lobby here."

"My mother? You should probably be talking to the solicitor. But stay there. I haven't had breakfast yet. Will you join me in the dining room?"

"That's very civil, Mr. Prentice. I'll wait here, then."

I am just under six feet; Merton was at least a head taller. He was also very wide across the shoulders, without seeming burly. Thick grey hair was combed straight back to lie nearly flat without a parting. He was wearing very old-fashioned glasses, half-framed in black plastic; clean-shaven, with a white, slightly knobbly face, he had a calm, sweet expression that would have suited a clergyman.

We went into the dining room where I was served the full breakfast (it was included in the price of the room, which was just as well because on the menu the price of breakfast translated into fifty dollars) and Merton was brought a five-dollar cup of coffee. I was making a note of prices because at this stage I didn't know what might be useful if I wrote that guidebook.

Merton looked around. "I've often wondered what this place was like. I think it used to be a book warehouse. I couldn't afford to find out, of course, not on my salary. You live well, Mr. Prentice. Now, I've been assigned the job of auditing your mother's income for the current tax year." He smiled and I waited for him to pull out a pipe, so complete did the impersonation of a vicar seem. "I gather you are the sole heir to your mother's estate."

"I gather there isn't much of an estate," I said.

"There never was much money, according to your mother's returns."

"How far back have you looked?"

"Seven years."

"That the legal limit?"

"That's an illusion many people have, Mr. Prentice. What you have heard is that in the case of a genuine, honest disagreement, when the taxpayer can show they believed themselves to be reporting accurately and according to the rules, and we accepted it at the

time, then we don't usually challenge if we discover a small misre-
porting much later."

"So what do you suspect, about this or a previous year's returns?"

"We, or rather, I, think that the returns have been inconsistent
with the probable income for some time."

"How are you going to prove it?"

He laughed. "It isn't often that I find myself in this situation,
talking to an apparently disinterested heir. Rather an oxymoron,
that. You understand, I don't mean uninterested ..."

"I know what 'disinterested' means. You're right, at the moment
I'm just curious but if you find some real money then I'll become
interested in every sense of the word. Now let's drop the word. It's
leading us astray."

"So it is. My fault, I'm sure. I was simply trying to characterise
your air of detachment. Now, could we make an appointment when
I could examine the books of your mother's business, and all the
records of her financial affairs, especially since she retired?"

"What I should do is find out first if I am liable for any taxes
on my inheritance, whatever it may be. And who I pay them to, you
or Canada."

"You have done a bit of thinking about it, then."

"Of course. I have a hazy idea that at one point the death duties
in this country were about 90 per cent, that there are no death
duties in Canada, but that I have to satisfy only one authority. I
mean I can't be dunned both by the Canadian government, and by
you."

"You're on the right track but I would consult Mr. Purrott before
you act."

"Now that you've appeared, I plan to."

"And I'd like your written permission to consult with Mr. Purrott
myself."

"Again, it seems an elementary precaution for me to call Purrott
first and ask him if I should give you permission ..."

"I don't *need* your permission. You and your solicitor could apply to the courts and hold me up for some months, I dare say, but I'll get access in the end, and you would be rather out of pocket. I just thought we might dispense with those negotiations and, well, co-operate."

I thought for a moment: there wasn't the slightest smell of cunning about Merton, and I considered that if he had a free hand he might come up with something definite before I had to return.

"All right," I said. "I'll send him a letter this morning."

"I have one drafted," Merton said, drawing it from his briefcase. "I could take it with me when I visit Mr Purrott."

"When is that?"

"In an hour."

The letter was simple. It asked Purrott to respond fully to any questions, written or verbal, that Merton put to him about my mother's affairs. I signed it and handed it over. "Good luck," I said.

"To both of us," he said.

We shook hands and I turned away towards the elevator.

"Mr. Prentice, this gentleman has been waiting to see you." The girl at the desk pointed across the lounge to a young man, a boy, really, standing waiting in front of a couch near the door. He had red hair and a slight scar on one side of his mouth, what remained, I guessed, of the harelip he had been born with. His face seemed slightly familiar but I didn't remember ever seeing him before.

"Mr. Prentice?" he asked.

"You've got the name right." I smiled. "Who are you?"

"Your second. Fred. My grandfather is your uncle. My father is your cousin."

"That makes you my second cousin, does it?" Once more, I had had no practice in identifying and spelling out my family relationships.

"I think so."

I put out my hand, feeling surprised and rather pleased at the appearance of my young relative but not sure what to do about it.

"Would you like some coffee?"

"Thank you very much."

I looked around to give the girl at the desk the order, but this was a very good hotel and she was already nodding to the waiter who had himself already cleared the breakfast table and now nodded back from the doorway that he understood. By the time we had chosen a couple of armchairs around a low table, he had reappeared with a tray to set out our coffee.

"So," I said, and waited to see what young Frederick wanted. I guessed he was bringing a message from Albert, his grandfather, perhaps an invitation of some kind. I remembered that Albert's last words to me were his address in case I was passing his way.

"On holiday?" I asked when nothing was forthcoming. He had not yet reached the age when he would take responsibility for doing his share in keeping the conversation going. His attitude seemed to be saying that he had done his bit just by being here; it was up to me to make something happen. At the same time he gave off an air of eager goodwill, ready to share in whatever I wanted to do or say.

"I just finished," he said, "I was at Cambridge."

I was glad I had not tried to guess his age because my first impression of him had pegged him at about sixteen. Now that I knew he was a graduate, though, he looked the part, about twenty-one.

"Ah," I said and wondered what lay between us, wondered what difference Cambridge made. I had read somewhere that it is still the case that a much smaller portion of the English go on to university than in Canada, though many more than in my day.

A man I know in Canada, a copywriter, an Englishman who emigrated about ten years before me and therefore felt qualified to offer me advice in my early years, told me that the university crowd in Canada operated like Freemasons. They all know each other, this man said, and you don't stand a chance if you don't belong.

That is how it seemed to the copywriter, who was having trouble finding work and ascribed his difficulties to the fact that he wasn't in the club. I was inclined to pooh-pooh the idea at first but he insisted that he was more and more being passed over in favour of members of the college fraternity. There was no doubt that he felt like an outsider but I don't think the reason was his not having been at a university. I've come to the conclusion that what he was experiencing was the permanent lot of the immigrant, that no matter how long you live there and however successfully you make a life, it's someone else's home, not yours. Home is where you came from. I never thought about this much but the question "Where is home" lies there, I found, waiting to surface when your wife leaves you, your parents are gone and you feel like retiring.

"What's next?" I asked young Frederick. "For you, I mean."

"Grandfather thought I might be able to show you around a bit."

"A tour guide, like?"

"Something like that. But it was just a silly idea, probably." He finished his coffee and sat upright, putting his hands on his knees, ready to leave.

I felt ashamed of myself. "Sorry," I said. "Sorry. No. No. Sorry. Yes. No. I'm glad he thought of it, and you did. Yes. Yes. Show me around London, you mean?"

"Wherever." He shrugged. "I don't know London too well."

Then I got it. "You're free, right? No job yet."

"Right."

"You could be someone for me to talk to."

"I'll do my best. I did *Talking* at university."

I smiled to show I had heard the joke. The idea was already growing within me. This could be a nice fit. I was going to spend a couple of weeks convalescing, licking my marital wounds, using the time to do some research in the big question of where I belonged, and think about this idea of a travel book. It would be nice to have young Fred along while I toured the post-Thatcher England to see if I could or should live here. And then I had this new excuse, the quest for the identity of the fair-haired man in the photograph, and the woman, too, though I was naturally more curious about him than her. And I had some childhood scenes to revisit. And then there was my father's past. And there was my mother's estate to be satisfied about. And, last, what could be a better introduction to Albert's family, my English family whom I hardly knew, to my family roots, than spending a week or so with young Fred. I had a dozen reasons or excuses to knock about a bit with Fred as companion. And it certainly beat sitting in Albert's living room, trying to learn something about the family while balancing a cup of tea on my knee and probably fending off a dog investigating my crotch.

SEVEN

THE ENGLISH ARE LESS interested in their relatives than any other nation on earth, including the French. That's what I've noticed in Canada. Young Luciano can set out from his village in the Abruzzi assured that there is a house near Dufferin and St. Clair in Toronto's Little Italy where a second cousin he's never met is waiting to welcome him, already making extra wine for his arrival. The same is true (in my experience) of Greeks, Russians, Poles, Germans, Ukrainians and the Irish. It's even true of the Scots, that professionally craggy race, more than it is of the English, at any rate. The first response of the English immigrant in Canada to the news that a relative is on his way to see them is to go on holiday, after sending a note pointing out the lack of jobs in Ontario, and recommending the much better situation in British Columbia. And if the traveller actually gets inside the house of his Canadian relative, he will get a cup of tea as he finds out that he has called on the day they had planned to visit an uncle's mother-in-law, who is in a nursing home in Barrie, sixty miles away. They will urge him to come back, and talk about his coming to supper, sometime, but all that will happen when he telephones is that he will learn how busy they still are and get a renewed invitation to supper, sometime.

The situation in my own family was exaggerated by my father's suspicion of all his wife's relatives, so that when my children reached their backpacking years, another reason I was unable to offer them a network of homes in the old country where they would be welcome was that my father had cut everybody off. At least I thought it was my father, but my mother had kept her relatives at arm's length and never shown interest in her grandchildren. We had visited my parents only once, when the children were about five and seven, and the visit had been a failure. My mother was still busy with the guesthouse, and found little room in her life for us. I think she was surprised that I had assumed we were staying with her instead of finding a hotel of our own. We were in the way, and my wife spent the two weeks carting the children off to the beach when it wasn't raining, and to the cinema when it was. The visit over, she declared that it was the last, and thereafter I visited England alone every three or four years for briefer and briefer stays, using the excuse of work to take me back to Canada as soon as possible. I adjusted to this and it seemed to suit my parents, too. Thus I was surprised and irritated after my father died when my mother emerged, in retirement, as a patriot who was critical of my lack of interest in England, remaking herself as a sentimental matriarch who had been denied the pleasure of enough time with her son and his family. When she saw my Canadian passport she said, "That's all very well but I hope you're not thinking of giving up your English one. I mean you'll always be British, really, won't you?" This from a woman who used to turn off the television on Christmas Day so the Queen wouldn't interrupt her dinner.

Because of my mother's need to keep her commercial affairs under wraps, and my father's suspicion of her family as potential freeloaders, I knew nothing of Albert and Olive, and not much more of Phyllis, although she had been around sometimes as I grew up.

But now Albert was indicating that he would find some contact welcome, and sending his grandson as a goodwill emissary it looked like. It was a nice development, and it fitted with my own impulses. I had an idea. "How long are you free for?" I asked.

"Would you like a personal secretary for the Grand Tour? I could do that." He made a flourishing gesture with his hand to show he was making a joke, doing an impersonation of a flunkey with lace cuffs.

I was pleased to see this bit of larkiness in Fred; it promised well for a journey. I said, "I do want to travel a bit, but just around here, around England."

"Anywhere special?"

"There are several places I want to see to start with. The place where I grew up, for one. Not a pilgrimage. I just want to see if I remember it right. After that, I'm not sure. I want to poke around a bit, and I thought I'd combine it with another idea." I told him about the guidebook.

He laughed. "You planning to spend a year at it?"

"Maybe a few weeks. You're probably right to be skeptical. But I want to make a start, try a sample, see if travel writing is my bag. Maybe I've just invented an excuse to ride around England for a bit. I hardly knew the place before I left it. And I have other reasons for wanting to take a look round."

"You planning on settling back here?"

This was one of those moments when you realize that, far from carefully concealing your inner life, you are naked as Adam in your intentions. So you have to go with it. "I might," I said. "I might consider it."

"What about your wife?"

"What about her?"

"I don't know. It's none of my business, I guess. Doesn't she have to be consulted?"

"At the moment she is probably in Ottawa with her boyfriend."

He blinked and widened his eyes, comically. "That sounds bad," he said.

"It is. We are separated."

"No, no. I meant Ottawa. If you'd said New York, I could imagine you meant she was having an affair. Leading a sophisticated life, sort of, like one reads about. But Ottawa sounds, like, for good."

"What do you know about it?"

"Nothing. That's the point. I've never heard anything about it, except that it's the capital, isn't it? The only reason for going there, I imagine, would be to get together with an Ottawan."

"I can see I won't have to burden you with tedious explanations. I'll tell you the story of my wife sometime, I expect. I'm not ready to right now. As for Ottawa, there is an art gallery, and there's a hockey team, or there was when I left, but not much else. Let's get on, shall we?" I drew the photographs from my pocket. "And I want to find out who this man is. A quest. At least that's my excuse."

"It's as good a *raison d'être* as I've heard. Did he kill someone?"

"Not as far as I know. You have good instincts, though. He is the plot. Find him and I'll find what I want to know."

"Oh, my. Where do we start? Perhaps the photographer's name is on the back. It usually is in these stories."

"You're a bit out of date. That used to be a staple, I agree, but this isn't one of those stories. There's no body and thus no murderer, but there is a mystery."

"Is there a treasure?"

"What are you talking about?"

"This story of yours. A mysterious portrait. A quest. There's often a hidden treasure, isn't there, in stories like this? Maybe symbolically, in your case."

"Actually, I think there may be a kind of treasure buried somewhere, and not just a symbolical one, either. Let's assume there is. Looking for it would give our travels a bit of shape, wouldn't it? We'd be guided by having a whole lot of extra questions to ask. We start by going down to the place where I grew up."

"Where is that?"

"Coombe Regis. Do you drive?"

"Of course."

"Don't say 'of course' like that. When I left England only about half the people your age could drive. Can you swim?"

"What?"

"Can you swim?"

"No. Why?"

"There, see. Why can't the English swim? In Canada, everyone can swim."

"Is it compulsory?"

"Obligatory, and easy to pick up. Most Canadians spend a good part of their summers as children near a river or a lake. Even in Saskatchewan. As I say, I couldn't swim when I left England but I realized soon after I landed and got invited to the odd weekend at someone's cottage on a lake that I'd better learn if I didn't want to look like a nerd. We'll talk more about this on the road. Here's the plan, then. Tomorrow I'll rent a car ..."

"Hire a car?"

"Tomorrow I'll *hire* a car, and for the next few weeks, you will be my chauffeur and teach me how to drive here, as well as translate words like 'rent' and 'hire'."

"You can't drive at all?"

"Of course I can bloody drive. You don't survive in Canada unless you can drive. One of the provincial capitals has no bus service at all: everything — social life, invitations to parties, visiting friends forty miles away, touring New England, you name it — all life in Canada is predicated on the car. Of course I can drive. But I've reached the age when I don't mind recognizing and admitting that I drive poorly — not badly, in the sense of dangerously, but unskilfully. I don't take it as a reflection on my manhood. The thing is, I learned too late and never caught up, never made myself at home in a car. I was twenty-seven before I got a licence — I still could barely drive but I was in Alberta at the time and in those days it was easy to pass the test — and for another five years I was timid and, well, *worried* when I was behind the wheel. You know? Then

— and I think this is a common experience among late-bloomers —
I drove to Prince Edward Island, which is about two and a half days
away from Toronto. That trip to PEI and back finally grew me up,
car-wise. Finally, I was totally at home behind the wheel. Friends
noticed it, and commented. I realized then that I had got rid of the
late-bloomer's habits. I no longer stomped hard on the brake at
the first sign of something on the road, or just coming up to a corner.
Driving with a late-bloomer is like a kind of dodgem car ride, stop/
go, stop/go, you know? Irritating enough in the city, but on the
highway it can wear you out. Now, if you're lucky, as I was, you
have to take a long cross-country trip at just the right time, a trip
that can make up for your lack of adolescent experience."

"Are you leading up to an analogy?"

"I wondered myself for a minute. No, still on driving. What I was
going to say was that unfortunately it's not permanent. Gradually
over the next couple of years after your trip, you revert to the jagged
responses of the badly synchronised late bloomer and then you need
another long trip, to Moose Jaw, say, to sharpen your reflexes."

"Why Moose Jaw? Where is Moose Jaw?"

"I'll get to that. Now, I have this quest to undertake, more than
one quest, perhaps, for which I am not equipped. To start with, I've
never driven on the left-hand side of the road and I have one
Toronto friend who advises me not to try. So, since driving at all
is not second nature to me — that is, I am kept busy all the time
making conscious decisions that other people make instinctively —
I'm going to have to have a lot of practice to feel safe here. Have I
made my point?"

"I'll say. I should do all the driving."

"That's it. So, I will hire a car ..."

"I have a car."

"You do? How does a brand new graduate without a job have a
car? None of my business, of course, but ..."

"It's my auntie's car."

"You have permanent access to it?"

"No, Grandad suggested it when he told me to come and offer my services. She doesn't use it much. Grandad said those car-hire companies charge a fortune."

I heard there or was reminded of our family's version of the Woody Allen line: "The worst sin in our family was buying retail." My mother was involved in a network of local merchants and providers with whom she expected to deal at a different rate from that quoted to the public. In return she might supply accommodation to their visitors at a large discount. All this business was done in cash, of course. To take one example, if she bought a piano, privately, she never consulted a directory to see who moved pianos. She let it be known that she had a piano that needed moving and soon the local builder's merchant offered to take care of it the next time he was returning to his yard from a delivery, empty. For that she paid cash, but only half the rate that a moving company would charge. (She inherited some part of her instinct in this area from her grandfather, a legend, who, as a youth, around the turn of the century, acquired one of those two-wheeled costermonger's carts with which he handled the moving of light furniture, working on weekends.)

"All right," I said. "Then take out a little extra insurance to cover me in case I want to have a go. What kind of car?"

"It's a Mini. Pretty old, but she keeps it serviced."

"A *real* Mini? Perfect. I'll supply board and room and expenses, then; you supply the car and drive it. A deal? Meet me here in front of the hotel tomorrow at the same time."

"We could leave today."

"I have something I want to do today. Tomorrow, then. But first, I'd like you to show your grandparents these pictures." I gave him the two photos. "Ask them if they know who they are. All right? See you tomorrow, then."

Fred didn't move off immediately, but stood there, giving off signs that he had something delicate to say. "What's the problem?" I asked.

"The problem, uncle, is that I haven't worked since I came down."

"You don't have any money. Don't worry, I'll pay all expenses and provide a bit of walking-about money to keep you from being embarrassed. Here." I gave him fifty pounds. "Will that do for a start?"

"That'll do it. I'll see you tomorrow."

It was the first chance I'd had to play the rich uncle who had made it big in the colonies. I enjoyed the feeling very much, glad that Grisham had put me in the right hotel for the part.

EIGHT

I WAS SHY OF telling young Fred what I was going to do with my day because to him it might have sounded silly. I wanted to look at Hampstead Heath and drink a pint of beer in Jack Straw's Castle.

When I was growing up in Coombe Regis, I rarely went up to London because I didn't like it much. School outings had taken care of the chief items — the Houses of Parliament, Westminster Abbey, St. Paul's, and a couple of visits to the theatre, Shakespeare inevitably, and just as inevitably *Macbeth* and *Romeo and Juliet* because they were set books. The major sights made no impression on me — they looked just as I expected them to; I was fourteen or fifteen but tall for my age and I wanted to look at the prostitutes in Soho and try to get a peek in some of the dirty book shops before the proprietor threw me out.

The plays were all right but neither one really overcame the gap between the Elizabethan age and me at fifteen. I've seen some Shakespeare since at Stratford, Ontario, and a couple of times I've actually forgotten where I was — once especially when I had a good seat to watch Maggie Smith pick her teeth at the front of the stage — and I've come to the conclusion that performances of Shakespeare's plays should be restricted to people over eighteen, to avoid putting off the young for life.

In the thirty years since then, I have developed no great desire to see more of London, with the exception of Hampstead Heath. Once I learned to read, I devoured everything in print I came across, spitting much of it out and digesting the rest. I can't keep much poetry down, especially the recent stuff. My experience of unrhymed verse is not good. The trouble is that when I was seventeen I underwent the usual levitation when reading "The Love Song of J. Alfred Prufrock," and I feel obliged to keep my eyes open for another such moment. I didn't get much farther with old T.S. (except the "When Lil's husband got demobbed" bit, and the line "The river's tent is broken," which is worthy of Tennyson.)

I've had some luck since then with appreciating the more classical poets; except in Browning, I've found little bits of gold everywhere. But my real discovery, unaided, is Keats. I came across "The Eve of St. Agnes" when I was in a shack on a construction site one rainy afternoon, and I subsequently read all the rest. The early long poems are just knife-sharpeners, but the odes, especially "To Autumn," are as good as Beethoven. They made me wonder, that afternoon, if I'd missed much by not going to a university, and when I got back to Toronto, I took a couple of books of Keats criticism out of the library, but I couldn't follow them, and since then I've managed on my own.

But I'm digressing. Having come across Keats's poetry, I read his letters and even a biography — my first literary biography. I made up my mind this was one writer who I'd like to know more about. I've since read most of the stuff that's been written about him, except for the criticism, and accumulated a lot of references to Hampstead Heath. (Not just from reading about Keats, of course.

I would say that Hampstead crops up in book reviews almost as often as Bloomsbury: everybody seems to have spent time there.) So I had a pilgrimage to make.

First, the next morning I walked over to Trafalgar Square and called in to the National Gallery. Paintings are not my bag; I never know how long to stand in front of them but some biographer had said that Constable's *Hay Wain* lies behind "To Autumn," and I wanted to see if I agreed.

It could be. What I really found out, though, was that the cafeteria of the National Gallery, like the restaurant in the Royal Academy, is a great place to get out of the swarm of tourists, a place where you can get a cup of coffee and read a book quietly for an hour if you feel like it. They serve a good lunch, too. I made a mental note to give it a tick in my travel guide.

I left the gallery, walked over to Leicester Square tube station and travelled up to Hampstead. I walked about the heath for an hour, had a pint and ate a pork pie at Jack Straw's Castle, feeling self-conscious, but not foolish, and returned to Covent Garden, having got what I came for, a memory of a place to refer to when I read the letters again.

It's hard to tread in the steps of the famous on your own, not part of a guided tour. Once, as an adolescent, I slipped away from the school party and visited St. Paul's cathedral, looking for God (I was about sixteen at the time). I found my way to a pew and saw above me someone in a cassock talking to a party of visitors.

"You there," he said. "Join this group. Come along." It was an order.

I said, "That's all right, thanks."

He got into a nasty temper immediately, right there in his cassock. "Either join the group or go outside," he said. "This is the Whispering Gallery, and I am about to start the next demonstration."

"I just came in to pray," I said, thinking that would shut him up.

"Then go into one of the chapels. Now."

I still felt I was in my rights to try for a bit of private meditation but it was obvious God had left me to sort it out with this officious sod, so I clattered my way down to the main part of the cathedral and out the front door. I felt like the caretaker when the monk told him to piss off. That was the last time I gave Him a chance to notice that I was listening.

I considered paying a duty visit to a museum but I like museums even less than art galleries, especially the ones where they have lowered the lights. I understand the reason but the effect (for me) is to create an atmosphere like a Victorian Sunday with the blinds drawn. Oddly, the only time I have been charmed in a museum was in the Victoria and Albert on a rare business trip, in late September. They have an outdoor café out back, surrounding a shallow pond where the young Brompton Road matrons bring their preschoolers for a paddle while the mothers drink coffee. You just need a warm sunny day, after the tourists have gone and the older children are back in school. If you are lucky enough to be walking down the Brompton Road on a day like that, treat yourself to the V and A garden café. The museum doesn't make a big deal of it; you go through a quiet door marked "Garden" and find yourself leaving the gloom of a Sunday-in-the-parlour for the sunlight of an Impressionist painting. And the wonderful thing about English museums and art galleries is that it is all free.

In the afternoon, having no great desire to sightsee on foot, I bought a seat on one of the boats at Westminster Pier that does the tour of the Pool of London all the way out to the Great Flood Barrier and back, ending with a little jog up river to give you a view of the Houses of Parliament from the water. The weather was being a nuisance; in fact, as we climbed on board there was a shower which had everyone scrambling for seats inside, under cover. I decided to gamble since I was carrying a raincoat, and the gamble paid off because as soon as I was settled in the best seat on the upper deck the sun came out and stayed out all afternoon. I enjoyed the little tour of London's waterfront, and thought it was well worth a tick; I even thought I identified the place where Pip rowed Magwitch out to meet the ferry. The only flaw in the afternoon was the head tax we were asked to pay before we left the boat. It was called "showing your appreciation of our services," a ritual in which the boat driver's assistant came round with his cap, seeded with a few one-pound and two-pound coins to show us what was expected, shaking it in front of each passenger until we showed our appreciation. It's a racket, of course, and they get away with it because all of the passengers are tourists from abroad or (a few) other parts of Great Britain. The tourists, including the Americans, are easily bullied into accepting that this is a standard custom in England and they pay up. I cannot imagine that they would be so meek if the deck hands on those cruises round Manhattan Island tried it. They (the Americans) would tell the deck hand to stick his cap up his arse, and they should do the same thing on the Thames boats. No service is provided beyond what is covered by the fare.

The whole phenomenon of English tipping practices is interesting and worth a chapter to itself. A variant of the bullying tactic is carried out on all excursions or outings involving a driver and/or a guide; on the other hand, the English abroad, or at home in different circumstances, are notoriously the worst tippers in the world. My daughter in her waitressing days on her way through college frequently experienced parties of English tourists who collectively ate a three hundred dollar meal and gave Zoe two dollars, for herself, to show their appreciation.

This time, I decided, I was not going to give in. I did, though, in the end, wilting under the pressure of the held-out hat and the "sailor," holding it, saying "Mersee, m'sewer" and winking comically until I understood.

Young Fred was waiting for me, looking at a road atlas in the lobby, when I went down for breakfast the next morning. He'd had breakfast, he said, but I guessed that was his English way of being polite and I easily persuaded him to keep me company in a second breakfast of sausage, bacon, eggs, mushrooms, fried tomato and potato pancakes, and we talked about the best way to start the trip.

"What about the pictures?" I asked. "The photos. Uncle Albert know them?"

"No luck," he said, his mouth full of toast and marmalade. "Though Grandad said he thought the man in the picture looked a bit like you."

"Did he? Which bit? The hair? The teeth?"

"He didn't pin it down." He started to crunch up the seeds of the grapes that had come on the breakfast salver.

"Grandad was probably just being agreeable. On the other hand ..." I put the photos in my pocket. "We'll go to Coombe Regis first. That's where I grew up. I could start my travel journal from there. Let's have a look at that road atlas you're sitting on."

"This isn't the one you want." He took the atlas from underneath him, reluctantly, and brought it up to eye level. He was embarrassed, and when I got a look at the atlas I saw why. It was a Rand McNally atlas of North America, including Mexico and Canada.

"That's not much help on this trip," I said, waiting for an explanation.

"I've got a confession to make. First of all, though, what am I going to call you?" He didn't sit up as straight as he had when I first arrived. The breakfast had relaxed him, much as, later in life, a large whiskey would do.

"Will's the name, Will Prentice if you have to introduce me to anyone. What do you mean, what are you going to call me?"

"I can't call you Will. It feels funny."

"Well, you can't call me second-cousin-twice-removed, can you? You could try just 'Cousin' but I don't think even the English use that any more, do they? Anyway, I think it might only have been used among women, as a term of affection."

"What about 'Uncle'? Would that work?"

"If you like. Sure. Does it matter?"

"When I was leaving here last night I asked the doorman where I might park my car when I picked you up this morning. He said that, as a guest, my father, you, would have access to a parking space, and I should just let him know when I arrive. I realized I might spend all my time correcting people who make the same assumption, and I thought "Uncle" would be a simple solution. It's sort of true. You do feel like an uncle."

"Ask Grandad. Maybe he could find a slight resemblance, there, too. Be my nevvy, then."

He laughed. "Uncle Will it is."

"Now, about the atlas."

"Hear my confession first. I have a hidden agenda, like you. While I'm showing you round, being the family host to the Canadian cousin, you could tell me what I want to know."

"Which is?"

"I'm thinking of er — doing Canadian studies."

"Studying Canada? Which bit? It's a big country."

"I mean some aspect of Canadian history."

"Do you plan to come over? To have a look, like, at what you're studying?" I was surmising that he was probably preparing to put the bite on me for a place to stay.

"Not immediately, no. At some point. When it's convenient."

"You mean you plan to have a chat with me while I'm here, go back to your college, take out a library card and become an expert on some aspect of Canada *without* taking a look?"

"Not my college, no. Actually there are at least ten centres of Canadian studies in England. I plan to base myself in London. I haven't found a focus yet but whatever I concentrate on I understand there is a lot of material in the British Museum. Most of it concerned with events before 1924."

"I see. Ten centres, all staffed by people who have never been to Canada?"

"No, the point is ..."

"The point is as long as you confine yourself to pre-1924 history, you won't have to leave Bloomsbury. No need to look at the Plains of Abraham, things like that?"

"Well ..."

"I've never heard anything like it," I said, affecting outrage. "Can you imagine how the Scots would react to the news of Scottish history being written by someone who has rented a room in Ottawa for the purpose? Jesus Christ, is this typical of history studies generally? Enlighten me. I never went to university."

"You don't have to study the past on foot, do you?"

"Oh, that's very good. Write it down. No, but you can check the places where history occurred and make sure you haven't created a theoretical Canada by accident. The last book I read about Canada written by an Englishman had the hero buying gas on the Don Valley Parkway. Look, I'm prepared to bet that you are full of assumptions you aren't even aware of, but which will get into your thinking when you start to write this essay about us. For example, have you any idea which government was in charge in Saskatchewan during the dust bowl era?"

"During what? Oh, yes. *The Grapes of Wrath*. Oklahoma."

"No, not fucking Oklahoma," really outraged now. "Weyburn, Saskatchewan, if you need a location."

"Uncle, Uncle, don't shout at me. It's just an idea I've had. I promise you, if after a week with you I still like the idea, I'll save up and buy a plane ticket to Toronto. Okay? Are you always so chauvinistic?"

"No, I'm not usually so Canadian, either. It takes a young English nevvy to bring it out. So this is why you offered to guide me? To pick my brains?"

"No, that's just a bonus. All right, yes. I was thinking of trying Canada, and your being here now, someone I can quiz about the place, seemed fortuitous. You are sort of a role model, anyway. A family legend." And then he was off. He said, "The fact is I'm bored stiff by the prospect of any future I can see. I want a distraction. I've had three interviews, with an oil company, with a national grocer, and one with the civil service."

"But no offers."

"Oh, yes. They all offered me a job, and they all stressed how soon I would be eligible for a pension. In only thirty years, in one case. Thirty bloody years! That's what I mean by bored. It's the prospect of being bored for the next thirty years that is so, well, boring. I don't want a career with a pension. I want ..."

"Distraction?"

"I suppose so. It sounds trivial put like that but that's what I want. To be taken out of my mind. Maybe Canada will do it."

"Nothing's changed, has it? People thought I left England to forge a new destiny in the colonies but I just wanted an excuse to quit my job, and to get away from my dad. I was bored with the one and tired of being badgered by the other. You know, if anyone had asked me when I woke up this morning I would have said that one advantage of a university education must be that it fills you up with such interesting stuff that afterwards you can amuse yourself for life. And here you are, just as bored at the same age as I was."

But I didn't feel the parallel very strongly. Fred, here, was on the brink of his career; all he had to do was choose it. A guy with a second from Cambridge must have a lot of options, and have been considering them for some time. I, on the other hand, had been in a dead-end low-level job, and entitled to be bored.

Then he said, "Had your girlfriend just walked out on you, too?"

"Ah. When did that happen to you?"

"The day I left Cambridge."

"Was there a good reason?"

"She said there was no future in our relationship. I said I liked the present just fine, and *carpe diem* ..."

"What's that?"

"*Carpe diem*. It means 'Seize the day' ..."

"I know what it means. It was just your pronunciation that threw me. A lively row seems inconsistent with being bored, though."

"My point was that the only time I wasn't bored was when I was with her, and even then I was bored some of the time. But she said it wasn't good enough, and what was wrong with thinking about the future, and on and on and on, and I realized we'd been down this road too often. I ..."

"Was bored with it?"

"Sort of."

"As I said, we do have something in common, but I'll tell you my story later. Why Canada?"

"I have relatives there." He grinned to show what he meant. "You seem to like it from what I've heard."

"I've been lucky. You wouldn't be an immigrant, of course. They aren't so keen to have English immigrants as they used to be, especially ones without any skills. You don't have any skills, do you?"

"No, my degree is in history and philosophy. I suppose I could teach."

"I don't want to depress you but without qualifications you might just get a shit-job in a bad private school. A supply teacher, maybe. But not in Toronto. Everyone wants to come to Toronto."

"I don't know if *I* do, Uncle. There's not much cachet about Toronto, is there?"

This needed sorting out. "Tell me, what's 'cachet' in this context? What is it Toronto doesn't have?"

"All the other places I've heard of in Canada have some kind of glamour. British Columbia has the Rockies, Montreal is sophisticated, Quebec City is historic — as you say, Plains of Abraham and all that — even the Prairies sound as though one should drive over them once, all those wagon trains, trudging west, forming a circle at night. But Toronto. I think of it as a kind of Birmingham or Swansea. Not too exciting, or interesting."

"Exciting? I guess not. The joke is I could take you to a place just outside Toronto where it's illegal to fish. It's true that I never invite a house guest to stay for more than three days. I have this schedule for visitors: Day One, downtown and the CN Tower; Day Two, Niagara Falls and the wineries; Day Three, a drive to Stratford and a look at the Mennonite villages where they still use horses and buggies. On Day Four I put them on a bus to Vancouver."

"How long does it take to get to Vancouver by bus from Toronto?"

"I'm not sure. About four days if you don't sleep, I think. I'll look it up."

"Let me get used to the idea first."

"So be it. Let's go. I'll get my bag while you bring the car round to the front."

"Should I — er — tip the doorman?"

"Probably."

He took out the fifty pounds I had given him. "How much?"

He had me there. In Toronto, a couple of dollars would be accept-able, but here? I remembered Grisham's advice: 'Treat the pounds as dollars and add a bit,' but just doubling was as far as I could go so early in the trip. "Give him a couple of pounds," I said. "Get change from the desk."

I was having a lot of trouble thinking, or rather not thinking, about English money.

Grisham's law was a starting point; it worked for a lot of things like hotels and meals but you needed experience to know how to read prices that didn't make any sense even when the formula of "think-of-pounds-as-dollars" was applied. If the waiter in a two-star hotel charges you four times the Toronto price for a cup of coffee, is that the going rate? Or is the hotel overcharging, or the waiter swindling you? You needed the experience of living off the land for a year or so to create the instinctual knowledge that you were being taken for a sucker, or not. Young Fred, I decided, was going to be a great help in this area. He couldn't have earned a High Second on a tight budget without developing a keen appreciation of prices and values.

In fact, it wasn't just the money: it was everything. Nothing made sense as I tried to understand the changes that had taken place in thirty years, tried to understand from the employment advertisements if, for instance, the teachers were badly off compared to their friends in, say, the civil service, and their colleagues in Toronto. London was full of beggars, but what did that mean? Toronto has its share. Country solicitors in England charge a hundred and fifty pounds an hour, the weekly wage of an office cleaner in Birmingham. So, are all the lawyers in Warwickshire sharks? Shakespeare thought so, but he was milking a popular sentiment. Gradually, or, if you looked at it in another way, quickly, I realized that as far as understanding English society, its domestic economy, its values, what, as they say, it all meant, I was at a disadvantage compared to Grisham. I had brought with me some thirty-year-old baggage which kept me from experiencing properly and simply the country I was travelling in — an emigrant's palimpsest? — some completely out-of-date experience which I was trying to bring to the surface to understand the England I was now trying to get a handle on. Thus I made up my mind, as far as I could, to wait — to wait until I had two similar experiences on this trip to compare with each other before I judged whether I was being swindled, or if Kleenex really cost six dollars a box here.

NINE

FRED DROVE SHARPLY AND expertly with the reflexes of his youth. I felt as if I was in a space ship; all the other celestial objects whizzed towards us and slipped by as I closed my eyes, waiting for the moment of impact that would turn me into a handful of stardust. We were also on the wrong side of the road. I said, "Allocate every necessary scrap of concentration required for the driving, and if there's anything left over, tell me where we are going."

"I thought you grew up here."

"I grew up in Coombe Regis. Where are we now?"

"We're in the Strand, passing the Old Bailey. Rumpole's turf. This is Waterloo Bridge now. See the river? That is the Thames."

Later, "Now we're on our way round the Elephant and Castle en route to Kennington."

We made our way south, passing nothing of interest until we saw a sign for Kingston. "This is where *Three Men in a Boat* starts," I said.

"Is it? Who were they? Now we're going down the A3 to

Guildford and then down the A31. There's a map in your glove compartment. It looks tricky going around Winchester, then it's a straight run all the way.

"Now. Canada," he continued. "Start with Newfoundland. How do you pronounce it? I don't want to go around in Canada like an American calling Shakespeare's county *War-Wickshire* and the next one *Glowsester*."

I said, "Let's agree, though, shall we, that there'll be no patronizing of North American accents on this trip, especially the accents of Texas and the South? The bleating noise of the English fox-hunting class is no closer to purity than the dialect of the Kennedys. I won't go on about it, but to go back to *War-Wickshire* for a moment, how do you pronounce Arkansas and Tucson and Yosemite?" (I spelled them out.)

He got Yosemite, and failed the other two. "There," I said, correcting him. "I've made my point. Have you really never read *Three Men in a Boat*?"

"I've *heard* of it, of course. But not actually *read* it, no."

"Jesus. What's England coming to? All right. Newfoundland. It's a very tricky one. The English would say *Newf'ndl'nd*, with an accent on the first syllable and the second and third syllables swallowed. I always knew that was wrong, and I used to think New-*found*-l'nd, accenting only the second syllable. But I've heard a former mayor of Toronto say it's *New*-f'nd-*land*, equal accents on the first and last syllables, swallow the second. It doesn't feel right but I'd trust my source.

"The natives are called, though not by themselves, Newfies. We make jokes about them. Like Polish jokes. You don't hear the jokes much lately, so maybe the Poles have been displaced by newer arrivals. I never understood why the Newfies were targeted as hicks, anyway. The only one I knew well was an erudite carpenter who built us a bookcase. He had a funny accent, of course, and he had the biggest yellowest boots you've ever seen, but he could argue the fallacies of Christianity or Marxism with all comers. When he saw we had books in the house, he wanted to engage me in the great questions but I wasn't up to it."

"That's very droll, Uncle. What kind of funny accent? And what about accents? Does every province have a different accent?"

"Up to a point, starting with Newfoundland until you get past Ontario, going west. Then the accent stays more or less the same all the way out to Vancouver. I don't know why that is but I can't tell the difference between an accountant from Calgary and one from Hamilton, Ontario, except that Calgarians talk more slowly. There are class differences, of course, but the differences show up in the same speech patterns from eastern Ontario to western British Columbia. A farmhand from Alberta and one from Ontario will both say "I woulda went" instead of "I would have gone," and there's no difference in dialect or accent, not that I can hear, anyway. I've heard it said that the reason that the original accents in the Maritime provinces have survived is because they haven't had the same waves of immigrants as the rest of Canada. The idea is that the original accents, Irish in Newfoundland and Scottish in Nova Scotia, were strong enough to survive being transplanted."

"Have you ever been to Newfoundland?"

"Yes, I have. I should tell you, my boy, that you are in luck because I've at least visited every province in the country, and spent time in several, though I didn't stay long in New Brunswick. My work took me to several of the provincial capitals, and before I got married I used my vacations to see as much of the country as I could. Yes, I've been to St. John's, the capital of Newfoundland, and took a bus ride to Come-by-Chance, a town along the shore, just because of the name. On the harbourfront in St. John's, an old sailor scrounged a beer off me as he told me the story of the White Fleet. You know about the White Fleet? Think of it in capitals. The White Fleet was the fleet of Portuguese fishing boats that used to cross the Atlantic to fish for cod off the Grand Banks. See, I'm full of information."

"Didn't the Canadians object?

"I believe not. There was enough cod for everyone then. Now it's a delicacy. Makes you wonder what unemployed Newfoundlanders eat. I also wonder what the Portuguese eat now on Christmas Eve. Did you ever visit Portugal? Our cleaning lady is Portuguese. She told us that back home they dry and salt cod, a practice they share with Newfoundlanders (calling them Newfies may be derogatory but it's certainly easier), then bring it back to life for the Christmas Eve feast by soaking it in lye for three days. Then they eat it before they go to church. Hard to believe, but there it is.

"But the other reason that Canada didn't object to the White Fleet fishing their coast is that it wasn't their coast. Newfoundland was a British colony until 1949. A man named Joey Smallwood took it into Confederation. The tenth province. Want to hear about Joey Smallwood? I just thought I should identify each province with a great figure. Sometimes it will be a hero, sometimes a villain, but the great man or woman would help define it, don't you think? The provincial *geist*. You could look them up on the Internet. So, Joey Smallwood was ..."

"Perhaps later, Uncle. Should I visit Newfoundland?"

"Of course. They have a phrase to describe visitors. 'From away.' 'He's from away,' they say. And they still sometimes talk of Canada as another place. I have never had such a strong sense, even in a Quebec village where no one spoke English, that I was 'from away.'"

"What about the culture?"

"Culture. Yes. There's fiddling. They play the fiddle a lot on Saturday nights and drink a local rum called screech, which I kind of like. I think there's more fiddling and more local songs in Newfoundland than anywhere else in English Canada."

"English Canada? What does that mean?"

"We do have a lot to talk about, don't we? English-speaking Canada, as opposed to French-speaking Canada, I mean. There's a lot of Irish in Newfoundland's history, too, which you can hear in the accent, and in the songs, and in the fact that they tell good stories."

"A strong folk culture, then?"

"They've been branching out recently, writing novels. Most of the best novels lately were written by people from Atlantic Canada: Newfoundland, Nova Scotia, New Brunswick and Prince Edward Island."

"I was looking at the map this morning. What's that big bit at the top of Newfoundland?"

"That's Labrador. I've never been there and I've never met anyone from there. I think it is technically a part of Newfoundland now."

"I suppose I ought to read up on Newfoundland."

"Better yet, read up on Come-by-Chance. I'm sure you know your way around the Web. Try that. Type in Come-by-Chance. Try to find out what it must have been like in the nineteenth century to be part of a tiny community with, for much of the winter, no contact with the outside, no roads, no railway and too much ice for boats to get in. Why did they settle there? How did they get there? What did they eat in the winter? And when you've found out about Come-by-Chance, extrapolate your findings to start to understand that whole coast"

"Have you done that, Uncle?"

"Not enough. One thing, if you go, beware of the moose."

"Beware of the *moose*?"

"Yes, a huge, cow-like animal with gigantic antlers. They don't attack so much as just stand in the road, and they infest the island so if you drive across the province at night you are almost certain to hit one. If you do, you'll come off second best."

"Anything else I should know about driving in Newfoundland?"

"Only that drivers from the rest of Canada find it a very backward province. It was the first jurisdiction to make it illegal to call your broker on your mobile phone, turn a corner, drink coffee and try to respond to whoever is talking to you from the back seat. All at the same time."

"That's legal in the rest of Canada?"

"In Toronto, it seems to be one of the tests you have to pass to get a driver's licence."

We stopped for lunch at Winchester, where I ordered fish cakes. When I tasted them, I was transported to a little café on the Coombe seafront where my father sometimes treated me to fish cakes in the school holidays. I hadn't eaten them since.

Fred said, "You know, it sounds odd that you should want to go on a tour like this after your mother's funeral, and — er — your wife's defection."

"Does it? Hard-hearted, like? Perhaps this is my way of dealing with those things. Don't forget the other reasons. The treasure, for instance. I think there's some money missing. I think my mother squirrelled away some money, and I'd like to find it."

"That's what this is all about, then?"

"Partly. Yes, grief and buried treasure."

He waited for more. "And? The man from Ottawa?"

"You want to know the whole story?"

"Am I old enough to understand?"

"Probably not. I'll tell you sometime. I'm just about ready to tell it to someone, but not yet."

TEN

WHEN SHE MADE HER first try at explaining, the idea that she had been living for some time in a parallel world, a world that I had had no suspicion of it, so upset me that I cut her off.

"The children?" I asked. Scott, the boy, was twenty-four, single and living by himself; Zoe, our daughter, was married and two years older.

"I told them," she said.

"Christ. When? Last month? Last year? Before you told me, at any rate. Who else knows? The cleaning woman? Your hairdresser?" The anger allowed me an outlet for my emotions. I went into the spare room, slamming the door.

"Do I know him?" I asked her the next day. I had spent the time thus far trying to avoid the question, not wanting to know the answer. But one by one, I had considered all the possibilities until I was sure I could face whatever the answer was.

"I'm moving to Ottawa," she said.

Of course. I wouldn't have guessed it in a dozen tries but as soon as she said "Ottawa" I knew it. Patrick Foley, painter, mainly of figures caught in everyday acts — mailmen, bicycle police, gardeners raking leaves. On the move upward, I'd heard, into the real money. I knew him well.

She'd met him ten years before at a show of his works in a gallery in a converted warehouse on Spadina Avenue. They got on well at that first meeting, and the next time he came to Toronto he let Janet know ahead of time and she brought him to dinner. I was fearful that this artistic leprechaun of Janet's would be out of the first act of *La Bohème* — beret, cloak and a lot of attitude towards the philistines who made up the public and didn't buy his work, something like Bertram in *Lucky Jim*. Or he would be doing the paddy-whackery thing — all suede boots and begorrahs and "have you any more of that Black Bush, me old darrlin." Even though I knew he came from the Ottawa Valley, not the "ould sod," and had an MFA from Carleton University, he would be some kind of charlatan, I was sure.

So when he came in the door in a lightweight grey tweed suit, with a waistcoat, a suit of the kind I'd been looking for ever since I'd seen it on a client from Edinburgh — a suit that I wanted to buy off him — and with a perfectly normal haircut, a clean simple handshake, introducing himself in standard Canadian vowel sounds, I was so relieved and pleased that it never occurred to me to wonder what effect he was having on Janet. I did wonder how he was so well turned out but that was soon explained; he was also a civil servant in Foreign Affairs, a job that paid very well and left him plenty of time and energy for his avocation. In no time Janet had become his agent. Periodically, about once a month, Janet found it necessary to travel to Ottawa to see what he had accumulated and assess his readiness for the next show.

"How long have you been sleeping with him?" I asked her now, wanting to get it all over with.

She said nothing.

"Who else knows about this — affair?"

She shrugged. "Who cares?"

"Ask the man who's been cuckolded for ten years; ask the dumb tit whose friends have been chattering about it among themselves for ten years. *He* cares, for Christ's sake."

A few minutes passed. Before I could ask her again, she said, "A couple of years."

"And I never noticed."

"You could say that was part of the problem."

"What the hell does *that* mean? Whose problem? Never mind. Now what?"

Janet waited, then said, "I'm going to stay with Cathy Brooks until you want to talk."

All the time we were talking, I was aware that I wasn't totally surprised; when it came, I knew it had been coming for some time. Nor was I totally dismayed.

Fred said, "So you are taking time to get used to the idea? That's also what we're doing now?"

"More or less."

"Did you get very angry?"

"We didn't have a great big knock-down, drag-out row," I said. "The first reaction was none at all. I mean nothing seemed to be happening in me. I suppose that was shock. Then I thought, I have to go somewhere, but I couldn't think of anywhere to go. I felt very vulnerable, not at all like sharing it with a friend, yet. I felt only like getting out of the house, walking the streets, but you can't do that for long without winding up on a public bench. What you can do, and what I did, is ride the subway all night. Then, when the subway closed down, about two o'clock in the morning, I went home, let myself in and went to sleep in the spare room. When I woke up, Janet had left for the day. I saw four movies that day and three the next day, and then on the third day, we met. She was waiting up for me when I got home. So finally we talked a bit. She was in misery and so was I, but she was still leaving me, so from then on it was a done deal."

"Was it a real shock?"

"Look, Fred, I have the feeling right now that you're comparing notes. If you want to talk about your situation, I don't mind."

"I was a bit. But the situations aren't really alike."

"No? Good. In answer to your question, then, I think I had already noticed that she was more content than she used to be, so it wasn't a huge shock to find out that there was a reason why. She hadn't just taken up with a fancy man — she wanted a change in lifestyle, as they call it, so she made me wonder if I was due for one, too. I'd become dull, and our life had become dull, she said. "Look at yourself," she said, in enough different ways for me to try, and I wondered if she was right. Not for her, of course, there was no doubt about that. Maybe not just relative to her, either, but in absolute terms. Maybe I wasn't thinking enough about my options, letting them disappear, one by one. In the course of our little farewell chat — as I say, there was no shouting, or not much — she said that I was still so goddam English, sometimes. She's pure Canadian. She'd said it often enough before, jokingly, but this time she was serious, making that one of the reasons for whatever it is about me that had got on her nerves. She made me wonder about that for a start."

"About?"

"Where I belong. Where I want to live for the rest of my life. They say you can't go home again but I'm wondering if you can ever leave it. Where is home?"

"You mean here or Canada? What about your job?"

"I'm tired of it. And I don't have to work any more."

"So, Uncle, let me get this straight. You're using the excuse of a quest for missing gold to find the answer to the riddle of who is the stranger in the photograph, or the other way round, we're having a look round to see if you like it enough to divorce your wife and come home?"

"Oh, I'm divorcing my wife, all right. And before you ask, I'll say of that that one side of me found life after Janet, at first, bleak and awful, lonely and miserable, frightening, even."

"One side of you?"

"Yes. See, at the same time, or in alternating periods, I found it exhilarating. In giving her her freedom, I'd found mine."

"Er, sexually, you mean?"

"You think I'm too old for that to be an issue? I hope I'm still around in thirty years time to ask you the same question. But no, I don't mean that. I mean I was free to do what I liked without consulting anyone or explaining to them. For instance, I could talk on the phone without someone in the room having the right to know who I was talking to and what the conversation was about. I was free to have a private life. Not a secret life, I'd always had that, of course, but a life of my own. I was free to go to the movies if I felt like it without worrying if she didn't want to come. Gradually, as I got used to the *loneliness*, I found the *aloneness* of it full of good things.

"But to go back to your question, I want to find out if I'm English or Canadian, more one than the other. Let me try something. I've lived in Canada for thirty years. I've knocked about a bit, as they say, seen all of the provinces, and most of my friends are Canadian. I say most, because once in a while I'm with an English friend — I have two in Canada I've known a long time — and we start talking, sharing signals, talking in a kind of shorthand that I can't use among our Canadian friends. Once in a while we go into stage cockney. The language of our roots, you might say. And it makes me curious about what I'm doing the rest of the time. I don't want to get poncey about it but am I cutting myself off from my living language, sort of thing, like every other foreign immigrant?"

"Are there many people like you there back there? Is it a standard immigrant condition?"

"I don't know. It doesn't get talked about much and certainly Wasps don't come in for much scrutiny. Whenever the stories about roots are told, they are always about the others. Their children write novels about what it was like for their parents to leave Italy, or Greece, or Hungary, or China or wherever, back then. I've talked about that to some of them, people my age who came from some other European country and never really learned English. They can't take me seriously as an immigrant: I arrived speaking the language. They're only comfortable on the weekends when they can play bocci in a Sicilian dialect. It must make for a different life from mine, consigned to be outsiders for the rest of their lives, relying on their children to interpret for them."

"It's still like that?"

"There are still lots of immigrants coming from the poorer parts of Italy and Greece. Something like a quarter of the people in Toronto were born in Europe or Asia. Many can't speak English. I communicate with our cleaning woman in one-word shouts. You know, 'No Windex! Buy Windex!' For her, I'm a typical Canadian."

"You seem very Canadian to me. You know, sort of imitation-American. I think if you settled down here again with someone local, there's a good chance in a few years she'd accuse you of being too bloody Canadian. My tutor talked about the Brits who've moved to Tuscany to live and to places in France like the Tarn district. They seem a bit pathetic to him. There's no doubt the climate's better, and the food and wine, of course, but these people spend a lot of their time looking for Branston Pickle and reading yesterday's *Observer*, and complaining there are no proper sausages to be had in Toulouse. Speak me some cockney."

"What?"

"You say you and a pal sometimes speak in cockney. Speak me some cockney."

I said. "Wodjer want me to say? Ah cahn't just make somethink up, can I?"

"You think that's cockney? I've heard Americans do it better. If you came back here, you'd better not try that kind of chat. People will think you're taking the mickey."

I couldn't think of a response, then or later. The idea that I could no longer imitate my cockney grandmother accurately, a routine party piece of mine at home in Canada, implied something disturbing, that I had lost my roots in that area, and thus, without roots in a language, I might find returning to that "rag-and-bone-shop" impossible. Perhaps "you can't go home again" was true of language, too.

Fred said, "What about your children? My cousins. Wouldn't you miss them?"

He had put his finger on the one element in my situation that I hadn't been able to think through. I said, "It's the condition of the age, isn't it? I know lots of people at home whose children now live in Singapore or Norway or someplace, having met someone on holiday and married them. It's something you have to accept."

"That's not quite the same. In your case you are choosing to separate yourself. How many do you have?"

"Two. A boy, and a girl."

"Married?"

"She is. He isn't."

"What do they do?"

"She's a gardener, a high-class one. He's on Bay Street, what you would call 'Something in the city.' Not a wheeler-dealer, but he's where the money is."

Being in a car together, embarked on a voyage, sort of, was a bit like being on board a ship; it allowed for an intimacy that understood that in two or three weeks we would separate and never see each other again. So Fred's next question didn't seem as personal as it might have on dry land, so to speak. He said, "Are you close to them?"

I paused long enough to realize, and thus to show Fred, that I had never considered answering this question except at a fairly superficial level, when it meant no more than "Do you see much of them?"

I said, "Actually, yes. When I see one of them across the street, unexpectedly, I'm surprised by joy. But remember, we are each other's only blood relatives. When trouble comes, we have to take each other in."

"How did they take the news?"

"I told you, Zoe is married. She has her own world. And she's tougher than her brother. She made sure that we, her parents, were both all right, I mean, still functioning, then went back home to cook dinner. Scott was more of a worry. Because he's making a lot of money, he thinks he's very — well — worldly, but he's still a bit of a kid. He was the one who cried, not his sister. In fact she took me aside and told me not to worry about Scott; she'd look after him. There are only two of them but I feel very lucky, nonetheless. But that's enough of that. You, on the other hand, have a whole gang that gets together for feasts and so on. Right?"

"More or less." And then he was finished with the topic, and returned to the thing that was on the top of his mind. He said, "Have you ever been unfaithful, Uncle?'

Given the difference in our ages, almost a cultural difference, the short time we had spent together and our family relationship, I found this question shockingly personal, in spite of having invited it by my own confessional. This should have been a time for us to ask little friendly questions, of the "What's-it-like-in-Canada-at-this-time-of-year?" kind. But this was a two-o'clock-in-the-morning question to an old friend. I was aware, too, that just possibly young Fred might be trying to go behind my story of my wife's change of heart to see if there was a reason I hadn't mentioned.

That was my immediate reaction. But then I felt liberated from whatever was holding back my reply. I could hear the child in him, still able to ask such things. "To my wife?" I asked. I was still thinking.

"Well, yes. Who else?"

"I don't know. Perhaps you meant some abstract vow to a liege lord involving sword-kissing or some such." I nearly had my wits back. "Look, Fred, so far this is working out far better than I would have anticipated. This trip, I mean. No, this relationship in a Mini. I mean, I'm thirty years older than you but we seem to have found ourselves with enough in common to make the talk savvy and enjoyable. Right? Why? Because I haven't assumed anything on the grounds of your age, and you haven't presumed by ignoring mine. But if you really are going to question me about my sex life, we'll get into trouble. Because that's something one can only share with strict contemporaries. Male ones."

"Why? Why only male?"

"Because women are only curious but one's pals are vitally interested in comparing what you say to their own experience and in judging whether you're telling the truth to see if it would help them understand themselves. Women believe every word you say about the subject, because they don't care much, and anyway, they have their own evidence or the subject wouldn't crop up."

"It sounds as if the answer's 'yes.'"

"What was the question?"

"Have you ever been unfaithful?"

"I thought I had answered it."

I hadn't, of course, and I had postponed answering until I didn't intend to. I was back to seeing Fred as my newly acquainted nephew. I cast about for a way to shut him up and I remembered Guy Crouchback's Uncle Peregrine in the same situation, and decided Fred deserved his reply. "However, since you've trapped me, I'll tell you. Yes, twice."

"Early in your marriage?'

"The first time was on a cruise on the St. Lawrence river, two years after we got married."

This was fun. Did they have cabins on those boats? Or did she raise her knees supine on the floor of a lifeboat on a St. Lawrence cruise ship?

"And the second time?'

"In a Toronto hotel, twenty-five years later."

"You resisted temptation for twenty-five years?"

"I was never tempted, except for those times."

"The lady then must have been extraordinary. The second lady."

"It was the same one."

There was a silence for some seconds, then, satisfyingly, Fred roared with laughter. "Ah, Uncle." he managed to say.

I said, "Can we talk about you, now, because that's what this conversation is about, isn't it? You've been unfaithful to ..."

"Daisy."

"Daisy. And she's found out. I thought with you lot none of this mattered, or am I lumbering along, ten years out of date again, addressing a member of the new celibate generation?"

"It wasn't me. It was Daisy."

"Daisy!"

"Yes, she thought it unfair to me for her to go into marriage without experience."

"I can't get my head around that one. So how did you find out?"

"She told me, right away."

"Don't say any more. Because at some point you agreed to be absolutely honest with each other, didn't you? And you told her about all the girls you've slept with."

"Yes."

"And now she's told you she's had an 'experience,' and you can't handle it."

"Yes."

"Shut up now. I'll do my Dutch uncle number later, when the answer comes to me. Change the subject and let me concentrate on the driving."

I nearly wiped us out on the road coming in to Coombe Regis. We were talking about our relatives and I got my first whiff of the sea. We hadn't really got close to the sea until now, and then, driving along the coast road, I suddenly got a lung-full and it made me dizzy. I never realized how much I missed it. No, I *hadn't* missed it, but the smell of it was so strong that I had to wonder if I had been repressing it for thirty years, not the sea, but home. Was I homesick, finally?

I've been totally happy all the time I've lived in Toronto. In the summer we have the tennis club, which has a pool, and then in the winter, as soon as the snow flies, there's the ski club. And in March, while we're waiting for the summer, we generally have a week in Arizona. A perfect life, I thought, until Paddy the painter came along. But now I smelled the sea and I wondered if I was getting a message. Was I just being sentimental?

I grew up by the sea, so it's the smell of my childhood. That smell has been lying in wait for me since the funeral. Let me see if I can get at it a bit. When I crossed the Atlantic for the first time I felt free, and I've always credited my freedom, my new life, to Canada, where all my adult experience has taken place: marriage — good while it lasted, i.e. until last month; two kids who are as Canadian as Molson's Ale; generally a nice life all round. So, is one whiff of the sea telling me that it is all pretence, that I belong here in England, and always will? Am I ethnic, then? And would I have realized it without the funeral?

Lately, whenever I came home, I felt her pulling me back, and I always took off from Heathrow with a feeling of once more having escaped. But this time it would be different. This time the funeral had set me free. This time no one would try to keep me here. Then I smelled the sea, and it took me by surprise. Now that I'm really free, where should I be? Is thirty years only skin deep after all? Are the Catholics right about the first seven years? Where do I belong?

The breakup and my mother's death had combined to set me adrift, and that's what was in my head when I went the wrong way round that roundabout. I wasn't being forgetful. We don't have roundabouts in Toronto — well, maybe a couple of toy ones, painted on the road. No, I was totally disoriented, knowing I was in England and feeling therefore that I had to do the opposite of what my Canadian instincts were telling me. So I turned right because in my daydream, as I came up to the roundabout, I remembered to go the opposite way to what I was familiar with, but somewhere in there my old English instinct got in the way. Something like that. I didn't go right unconsciously, but deliberately.

Fred was good; he talked me down like a stewardess handling a deranged pilot, no panic at all as he guided me into a lay-by, and took over the wheel.

"Before we go much further," I said. "I want to go in there." I pointed at the shimmering waves.

ELEVEN

WE PAUSED IN THE main street of Coombe Regis, high above the sea. Signs ordered us to a parking lot on the right. As we paused, traffic immediately piled up behind; soon they started sounding their horns.

I pulled out my wallet and gave Fred some pounds. "Go and buy us a couple of cheap swimsuits," I said. "Size thirty-eight for me."

"I can't swim. I told you."

"As I remember, you don't have to. This is the English seaside. You just go in up to your waist and then jump up and down, shouting."

"I'll just watch you. Do you mind? What kind of swimsuit?"

"One with stripes. I've never had one with stripes."

He took us into the parking lot, and set off to buy the swimsuit.

"Lovely day," the attendant at the parking lot said. He nodded towards the sea. "Freeze your balls off, though, that would."

The beach was sharply angled from back to front and shingled with smooth stones the size of grapefruit, an obstacle course for the bare foot that might have been invented by the municipal torturer. All the other people on the beach, shod in black rubber beach shoes, watched me pick my agonized way to the strip of sand at the water's edge.

I checked to make sure I was not bleeding from the arches, then said, "Here goes," and ran forward to fall into the surf.

"Jesus Christ," I said, when I could speak. "Talk about freeze your balls off."

"It's always best to get your head wet," Fred shouted from where he was sitting, dry and warm in the sun. "Duck under."

"In a pig's ear," I shouted back. "You live here. Why didn't you tell me?"

"I thought you knew. It's the English seaside. It's always like this."

I was standing up to my shoulders in frigid salt water so full of sand it seemed to be scouring me from head to foot with each ripple. I swam a couple of strokes, choking.

"That fun, uncle?" Fred shouted.

"It's smashing, and I got what I came for. Now I have to get out." I looked up at the obstacle course they called a beach.

"If you walk along the edge of the sand you can climb up to the path on that wooden ramp without having to crawl up the beach."

All the other people on the beach nodded in agreement with Fred's suggestion.

"Crawl is right. I think I broke both ankles coming down."

Twenty minutes later I was inside the municipal bathing hut, hosing off the salt. When I came out I was maniacally hungry. "Tea," I said. "Tea and a great big cream bun if they still make them. I'm starving."

In the café, he said, "What made you feel like paddling in the sea?"

"I'm getting to the point with a lot of things where I'm wondering if this is my last chance. Today it was paddling."

"Come on. What are you? Forty-nine?'

"Well done. I'm fifty-four, and there are a lot of things I won't do again, like go on a rollercoaster, or drink absinthe, things I'm glad to have left behind. Something was bothering me in the car, looking at the sea. When I was a kid, my dad sometimes took me in the water. I remember seeing the sea round my dad's head. I remember how he used to swim out with me on his shoulders — quite dangerous, really — but it was terrific. I don't remember it being so bloody cold, and wet, but that's all right. I enjoyed it and I don't have to wonder if I'll ever do it again. I know now. No. Know what I mean? I couldn't swim when I lived here, in spite of being by the sea. I learned as soon as I got to Toronto. My first girlfriend was a physiotherapist, and she got me into the pool up at 999 Queen Street, the local mental hospital. They have a very warm pool for the patients' therapy, and she had access to it. She dragged me along and taught me in a week. I'm still not as comfortable in the water as my kids were when they were six but at least I can enjoy the summer."

"A lot of people over here don't think you can swim outside in Canada."

It wasn't the first time I'd heard this from an English person. I said, "It's true that from January through March, the French river is frozen solid enough that the locals drive snowmobiles across it but it's also true that all through August, at least, it is as warm as soup. Compared to this, it's like the Mediterranean. But I like the sea, looking at it, sailing over it, smelling it, listening to it."

"You do miss it, you mean?"

"Yeah."

"Why don't you move back, then?"

"I'd miss the French River more. You want some more tea?"

"No thanks, Uncle. I was still wondering ..."

"When I was going to do the Dutch uncle bit? All right. Here is how it comes to me. I think you should go back to the fair Daisy and get on your knees and apologize."

He shook his head. "Forgive her, you mean?"

"I mean *apologize*. You."

"For what?"

"For being such a dickhead. Here she is, offering you her all — in a funny kind of way, agreed — but it sounds authentic, even to someone of my generation. What's the problem?"

"She's been unfaithful."

"Oh get a life, as my daughter would say. She's been *faithful*, for Christ's sake. Weird, but faithful."

Fred twitched a couple of times like an engine trying to spark, then he was silent.

I had no idea whether my advice would pass the test of any lonely hearts columnist, or get the approval of that old lady who gives sex advice on television, but I was quite sure that Fred wanted to go back to Daisy, and that it couldn't be anything but productive if he started by abasing himself. She sounded to me like what the English call a right case, but that was Fred's problem.

The guesthouse overlooked the sea about a mile along the cliff road. An Edwardian house, built for someone's private use and turned into a guesthouse during the slump before the Second World War, it stood in a quarter acre of grounds, one of seven or eight houses along the cliff road.

The sign on the gate said "No Vacancy." The door was opened by a fat, unhappy-looking man in his forties, dressed in a white knitted cricket sweater, yellow under the arms. He said, or rather chanted, each phrase rising at the end, "The sign told you 'No Vacancies'; if you're selling something, we don't want it; if you're estate agents, we're not selling; and if you're preachers, take your bibles somewhere else."

"I used to live here about thirty years ago. I was trying to see if it was as I remembered."

"Oh, yes? We've thoroughly redecorated, so it wouldn't be familiar to you, would it?"

"Do you think I could have a look at my old bedroom?"

"It's occupied. They're all occupied, so it's not convenient."

A voice, a woman shouting, started at the back of the house and came towards the door. "Let them in, you miserable bugger. They only want to *look*. Come on in. Which room was it? Dennis, get out of the bloody way. Let them in." She gave Dennis a hard push, dislodging him from the doorway.

"You can't let in every Tom, Dick and Harry that comes knocking at the door!"

"Shut up, you daft sod. How many are you expecting? When was the last time someone who used to live here came to see his old bedroom. Eh? When?" She smiled brilliantly at us. "Come on in. Up the stairs. Dennis, stay where you are. Close the door to keep the crowds out. Which room was it?"

"Under the roof. Overlooking the sea."

She led us up one more flight and opened a door. "Dennis is right. It is occupied, but they won't come back yet. Go on in. Have a look out the window. Moved away, have you?"

"I immigrated. To Canada."

"Well, then. Seen enough? See, Dennis, they didn't try to interfere with me, or steal the bed linen, or set fire to the curtains. They just wanted to have a look."

"One last thing." I took out the photos. "Do you remember ever seeing either one of these?"

He shook his head without looking. She said, "Wait a minute. This was before our time. Let's ask Digger. We inherited him. Come on through to the back."

"Digger'll be no bloody use," her husband said.

"What a pessimistic man you are," she said. Then, to me, "Come on through to the back. Digger is sort of the gardener. We call him Digger because he asked us to. His real name is Aubrey. He came with the house when we bought it."

In the back garden we found Digger, a very old man, bent over a spade, thinking. She showed him the photos. After a while, Digger said, "Don't know him. Her, though, she married royalty, didn't she?"

"Never mind," she said, and turned to me shrugging. We walked through to the road. "Some days he's clearer than others. I thought we might catch him in a lucid moment. Sorry."

As we were leaving, she said to her husband, "Hold on. I think he should know ..."

"It's none of our business," the husband said. "Leave it alone."

She said, "I'm going to tell him." She turned to me. "We had a man inquiring a few days ago. From the income tax. Mostly he wanted to know how much we paid for the house."

I waited. She continued. "Not very much as it happened. It was 95 per cent mortgaged, and we just took over the mortgage."

"How much cash was involved?"

"That's more our business than yours," said her husband, and started to close the door, while she struggled to keep it open.

I thanked them and we left them shouting at each other and drove back to the parking lot above the town. Fred said, "Do you think we interrupted an argument or something. She was determined to go up against him."

"I think there are some people who thrive on hating each other. Keeps them lively."

"You'd think they'd see a marriage counsellor."

"You missed my point. If those two started to see each other's point of view, they'd be dead in a week from boredom."

TWELVE

"I USED TO CYCLE to school. Most of us did, except the local kids who lived close enough to walk. The grammar school in Sefton, I mean. I went to junior school here in Coombe Regis. A school bus picked us up and brought us in but when you went on to grammar school in those days you had to find your own way."

We were sitting in the dining room of Appleton Manor, Coombe Regis's three-star hotel, after dinner. Our table was next to a window, overlooking the sea, and there were enough unoccupied tables that we felt no pressure to leave.

"It's funny, you not having any mates here," Fred said.

"I could probably find a familiar face in one of the pubs. It's forty years since I was in the junior school here, and my chums at grammar school came from all over. I never stayed in touch. I was isolated as a kid, living in the guesthouse. There were a couple of grammar school kids from here, and we used to get together a bit, but my parents never encouraged me to invite them home."

"Didn't you find that a bit peculiar?"

"No, because it really wasn't. Maybe things have changed but when I was a kid here, there were lots of people whose houses you never got inside. One of the first things I noticed about Canada was that everyone gets invited in: friends, neighbours, people collecting for charity — everybody. Over here, you do all your socialising on the doorstep, or you used to."

Fred said, "Generally, they're just trying to make sure that the dog doesn't get out. Did you like the school?"

"No."

"Why not?"

"It was a rotten school, that's why. The real problem was that it tried to be a minor public school, when it was really just a former second-rate grammar school where some of the duller boys paid fees."

"I would think that applied to a lot of schools then. Why did this one get up your nose?"

"The thing it did best was make me ashamed of my family, turned me into a snob, or tried to. That was the headmaster's mission. I'd like to think he didn't succeed, or rather that he nearly succeeded but Canada straightened me out."

"All water under the bridge now, though, isn't it? Hardly worth brooding about."

"That's the conventional wisdom but it's not true. By brooding about it I came to realize what a rotten school it was. For example, it encouraged bullying."

"Ah, that's the problem."

"Don't 'ah' me. I never got bullied myself because I gave as good as I got, and the thugs learned to leave me alone. There were one or two real victims, though, whose lives were made miserable."

"That wasn't uncommon, was it?"

"Maybe not, but in our case the headmaster encouraged it. Oh, he didn't order the bullies to beat up the weakies, but he made the bullies, or too many of them, prefects, gave them the power to make their chosen victims miserable. That's what I realized by brooding about it."

"I think things have improved since your day, Uncle. So, not much more to learn about your origins around here, is there? How often did you make the trip back from Canada?"

"It took me ten years to make the first one. After that I came every two or three years, just for a few days. See, some years after I left they sold this place and moved to Lyme Regis, where they bought a little house in the middle of the town and rented the top floor as a holiday flat. Mum didn't want to wait on anybody any more but she still felt she ought to have something coming in, as she put it. When they knew I was coming, they kept the flat for me, but if it was already booked I slept on a pullout couch in the sitting room. Sometimes I felt I was a bit of a nuisance, until Dad died, then she became more glad to see me."

"She wasn't hard up, though, ever, was she?"

"She said she always liked to know she could earn a few bob if something went wrong. Nothing could go wrong and I think she had more than a few bob that the tax man didn't know about. When Dad died she sold the house at Lyme Regis and she and Phyllis moved into the flat in Clapham. Mum bought places for her and Aunt Phyllis in a good nursing home to see them out, and otherwise there was about twenty thousand pounds, according to the solicitor. It isn't enough. There's some money somewhere."

"So where to now?"

"I'd like to find out about my father, Henry Prentice, who his family were, because legally they are my relatives. And I'm going to visit your grandad again, just to sort of plant the flag, mainly to be able to tell my kids what their second cousins are like, and if they should stay in touch themselves."

"How many second cousins do they — we — have?"

"Just two. I was an only child, and a mistake at that, probably. But they didn't take it out on me. No, I have two, as I told you, my son, Scott, twenty-four, and his sister, Zoe, two years older. All Zoe cares about is that she doesn't have a boss. Scott is the one who likes having a boss, belonging to an organisation. A real corporate type."

"Are they married? Both of them?"

"She is, to a musician. Chap who plays violin in the symphony orchestra."

"How about if they want to visit you? Your English relatives, I mean."

"That's another reason for having a look at them first."

He laughed. "There speaks the Englishman. So what's the itinerary?"

"Oxford first, I think. Try to find Dad's brother. Tick that off. Then back to London, see Aunt Phyllis and meet your folks."

"Is there enough time?"

"I've got all the time in the world. I'll phone my partners and tell them I'm taking a vacation. They'll manage. If they object, I'll offer to leave the partnership."

"Really?"

"Yes. I've thought about it ever since we left London. I'm starting to have a good time, and I'm going to let it take its course."

"You mean stay here for good?"

"You already asked that. I mean wait and see. I'm enjoying myself but I don't know how much is being here, and how much is, well, being free to do what I want, and how much is the society I've been keeping lately. How about you?"

"Me?"

"Yes. Can you come along for the ride? Do you have to find a job soon?"

"Excuse me, I've been watching you from across the room. Aren't you Willy Prentice?"

There was no mistaking John Kingsley, the biggest turd in the school, the bully who regularly, with the help of his fellow thug, Jack April, bicycled Billy Plaxton into the ditch on his way home from school. After two pints and a glass of the house red, I, who had seen him across the room, saw no reason to pretend those things hadn't happened.

"Yes," I said.

Kingsley went through several paragraphs of body language to show his pleasure, surprise, and eagerness to claim a rapport with his old school chum. "John *Kingsley*. Remember?"

"It's coming back to me."

"My wife and I are sitting over there. Would you like to join us?"

"Not much."

Kingsley started, began to smile in case it was a joke, saw that it wasn't, blushed, started to say something, turned and left.

"God Almighty," Fred said. "I'm glad I'm not one of your old school chums. Why are you being such a prick?"

I told him about Kingsley. "He's forgotten all about it now. I haven't. Our conversation reminded me. I should have gone further. I should have told him to fuck off. Fuck off, Kingsley, I should have said ..."

"He's coming back. Watch it, Uncle. He's bigger than you are."

"I just wanted to say, Prentice, that you were a slimy little wanker who always let the school down then and you haven't changed a bit."

"You've got that wrong," I said. "The wanker bit. That was you. 'Ninety-nine change-hands,' we called you. Remember? The old air-raid shelter on the cricket pitch? You know, where they stored the cricket nets."

Kingsley would have shot me then, if he had had access to a gun. He looked about for a weapon, and Fred moved our beer out of his reach. Kingsley said, "I've got my wife with me, Prentice, or I'd teach you some manners. If I ever see you again, I will." He looked at us for a few seconds, shaking with rage.

"Righty-oh," I said.

His wife appeared and grabbed his arm to haul him away, and Fred stood up to do the same to me.

"I thought you were the quiet type," he said as we left. "He wanted a fight. Did you?"

I said, "I was just faking it, enjoying myself, see how far he would go. I wish I knew how to get hold of Billy Plaxton, to tell him about it. He would appreciate it. Little fat kid, he was, with asthma. Played the piano."

"If you ever plan to enjoy yourself like that again, Uncle, let me know beforehand, will you?"

It was an interesting scene, as much because of Fred as the appearance of Kingsley. Young Fred, as I had so far thought of him, grew up a little at that moment. So far he had been unthinkingly accepting of my role as wise old uncle, authority on all matters within his experience, especially Canada. But that was the point, I realized, looking back, when he put a small critical distance between us, not much, but from then on, I treated him more seriously.

THIRTEEN

BEFORE WE RESUMED OUR journey, Fred rooted around in his bag and brought out what looked like a notebook. When he saw I was watching, he tried to hide the notebook under the atlas.

"Keeping a diary are you, Fred? Not too personal, I hope."

"Someone else did, Uncle, a long time ago." He retrieved the notebook and handed it across the table.

It was an old stenographer's notebook from the pre-technology days when they took notes in shorthand, then typed them up. It was about an inch thick and bound in hard covers like tiles which opened away from the user so as to lie flat when the notebook was in use. A band of cloth-covered elastic was attached, to be used like a garter when the book was stored away. Altogether it was a very satisfying writing tablet, with a feeling of heft and solidity, which may have been why it was still around. Writers, all writers, not just the maestros, are very sensitive, even quirky, about the pens and paper they use. This notebook looked like something chosen to record a journey.

"It's a nice book," I said. I opened it a few pages in. It was written in the careful script of someone putting his best foot forward, a real self-conscious beginner, as concerned with the look of his writing as much as with the content, someone "Keeping A Journal." "Where did you get it?" I asked.

"Grandad found it on a shelf in the Lost Property office of his bus company; might have been there for years. They were painting the office and chucking out the stuff that was unclaimed and not worth trying to sell. Grandad got this out of a box of rubbish, he said."

"What a cliché. Isn't there a story called 'The Old Notebook' by somebody? When did he give it to you?"

"He gave it to me when I was at school. A few years ago."

"Why did you keep it? Whose was it? What's it about?"

"Read the first page."

The first page was headed, "An Account of a Journey Across Canada by Bus and Train."

"Well, well." I flipped through, looking for a date. "Any idea when it was written?"

"Apparently at the same time as the Festival of Britain. When was that? The Crystal Palace exhibition?"

"For Christ's sake! You are about a hundred years out. The Festival of Britain took place in 1951."

"Yes, of course. I knew that. He talks about the Second War being not long over. There are lots of references to the fact that food was still rationed."

"It sounds like meat and drink to a history student."

"It isn't, though. It's a bit dull, really. But I remembered it when Grandad said you were coming over, and things sort of came together with some other things, and I thought if I read it again as you were telling me about Canada, it might be a bit more interesting."

"Let's see how it reads, then, as we go along. *I landed in Montreal on Queen Victoria's birthday on my way to visit my sister who is married in Vancouver. She was a war bride and her husband is a fruit farmer in the Okanagan valley. A very prosperous one, I should think, because the fare costs a lot of money. I'm not sure whether to go by train or bus.'"*

"What's Queen Victoria's birthday?"

"A Canadian holiday, when people in Ontario open up their summer cottages." I read a page more. "Now he seems to be walking around Montreal, listing the sights. Not too lively. I'm beginning to see where you're coming from, Fred. You are presently at a loose end; you have a second cousin from Canada who needs a guide; you think you might want to emigrate yourself, and, on the other hand, you might find something to write a thesis about if you decide to remain a student. Tell me, how much did you know about me before yesterday?"

"Hardly anything. They used to talk about you a lot, of course, 'The one in the colonies,' but the only real news we got was from Great-Aunt Phyllis. As I said, you are a bit of a legend, a small one, but I was intrigued."

"And here I am to satisfy your curiosity. And Grandad's, when you report back."

"The whole family's, actually."

I handed the notebook back. "I'll let you edit it," I said. "Just read out the interesting bits. Now, Oxford first, but I want to stop at Lyme Regis on the way. They were there for about ten years, first Mum and Dad, then, when Dad died, Mum and Aunt Phyllis. I went there about three times, I think, before they moved to Clapham. I never talked to her about why she moved but I think it was simply finding situations appropriate for their age. By the way, how was your room?"

"Fine, I think. Tell me, Uncle, I haven't travelled much in England, or stayed at many hotels. There's been no need because I'm always staying with friends. Do all B&Bs have their own bathrooms?"

"Not all of them. That's why I booked us in here." "Here" was a guesthouse above the town. "The word, or phrase, is *en suite*. Means room with bath. They used to say 'Room with bath' but they decided *en suite* sounded more genteel. Now, of course, to your generation 'Room with bath' sounds like an attic with a tin tub you fill up with a bucket. Or a room that carries with it the privilege of access to a bathroom along the corridor."

"Was it so bad?"

"We didn't think so, then. But there comes a point where, after three or four pints of Guinness, you don't want to find yourself at three o'clock in the morning in your raincoat and bare feet shuffling along a corridor just ahead of someone also in bare feet, holding up his trousers, trying to beat you to the only lavatory on the floor. I think prosperity struck. If you had the money you started to go *en suite*. And then, suddenly, guesthouses caught on, and rooms without bathrooms were the exceptions. Funny, I've just thought, in the old days most rooms had a wash basin with hot and cold running water, but no toilet. See, you didn't have to enclose a wash basin, no need to be shy about being seen shaving, and you didn't have to hook it up to the toilet drain, so it was cheap to install. So if I was alone, I used to pee in the sink. A lot of people did, including one of the leading gynecologists in Edinburgh, according to a man I know in Toronto who shared a room with him at an academic conference."

"Why the raincoat? Couldn't afford a dressing gown?"

"Bathrobe? Takes up too much room in your carry-on luggage."

Fred said, "While we're on the subject, what's a 'private' hotel? Sounds like a contradiction in terms."

"An oxymoron? I've often wondered. I've never stayed in one. I asked a friend in Toronto who has lived over here a lot. He said he couldn't define it but you always know you are in one because the landlord wears a blazer and is on the wrong side of the bar."

Fred considered this, then changed the subject. "How old was your mother when they moved from Coombe Regis?"

"About seventy-five. The reason they moved was that they took Dad's driver's licence away because of his eyes. He'd lost his distance vision: he could read but he wasn't safe at more than two miles an hour. So the guesthouse was too far from the town for them. The bus only ran about four times a day. It was time to wind down, and anyway, the house was too big for them to manage without help. In Lyme, they had everything they needed within fifty yards, and nice places to walk to."

He started the car and put it in gear. "It's a straight road," he said. "I've been looking ahead. Tell me about Nova Scotia. The atlas is in the pocket of your door."

"Have we finished with Newfoundland?"

"I thought we had. You should know."

"Right you are. Nova Scotia. What does your diarist say about Nova Scotia?"

"Nothing. The journal doesn't begin until he docks in Montreal."

"Nova Scotia, then. A very driveable province. You have to avoid the crowds around Peggy's Cove but the rest of the coast is magnificent. I'm told that Cape Breton is the best bit. I'm not much for scenery, myself, nature, that sort of thing. For me it's just background. I enjoyed Halifax but the most interesting thing that happened to me there was a chat I had with a rabbi about the history of the black population. I never thought of blacks in connection with the Maritime provinces, or in connection with Jews, either, for that matter, but the rabbi introduced me to a few of his friends and now the only people I know in Halifax are black or Jewish.

"They still keep Gaelic alive in some parts of the province, I believe, and they have festivals where they nurture a sentimental attachment to Scottish culture; you know — they get married in kilts and do the highland fling and toss cabers at each other. Again, there's a lot of fiddling goes on, and step dancing, both at the festivals and at home, on Saturdays. See? I don't know much, do I? It's a very pretty province but I don't find it too interesting. And so we come to New Brunswick."

"Hang on, Uncle. Who's the great man?"

"Sorry, yes, that's easy: Robert Stanfield, one of those rare birds who temporarily lifts politics out of the shit that the rest of them wallow in. Look him up."

I continued. "Now, New Brunswick. *There* is an interesting province. Not so much to look at — it's nearly all trees — although a trip I took once along the Saint John River stays with me — but it has a history. I think, probably, to an Englishman and a history student, New Brunswick will have the most interesting and unknown history of all ten provinces. I had a girlfriend once, for a few months, who came from Edmundston."

He squinted sideways at the atlas. "Could you circle Edmundston? I'll look it up"

"Right. When you do, see how close to Quebec it is and you'll see why more than a third of the people in New Brunswick speak French as their first language, and I think even more claim French origins. I'll write in a couple of words you could look up on the internet. One is 'Acadian,' the word for the French culture in the Maritimes — I think it comes from 'Arcadian' — and the other is 'Cajun.' Those two should lead you down a very interesting path. You'll find out how badly the French were treated in the eighteenth century, and what long memories they have."

"By the English?"

"Who else? How the English exiled the French to places like Louisiana — hence the word Cajun — to preserve their own position, and how the French slowly came back. If you spend any time in New Brunswick, you will feel a hostility towards the English that I never felt in Quebec, except from the intelligentsia. My Acadian girlfriend made it clear that I was associated with the enemy she had learned to hate. I, on the other hand, liked her a lot, but the strain got too much. She brought the quarrel with the Anglos into everything, even bed. Still, her consuming dislike of my kind energised our relationship, and I found her the liveliest, most interesting girl I've ever had. Except for my wife, of course, he added loyally."

"That's a bit patronizing, Uncle."

"Is it? Who am I patronizing, my wife or my old girlfriend? Actually it was my wife who defined her. She said that she guessed that Nicole had the same ineradicable antipathy to me as the English have to Germans. Made me think."

"Great man?"

"Louis Robichaud, the first Acadian premier, who gave the French a voice they badly needed, I'm told. Look him up."

We stopped for coffee at a hotel fronting the sea. "Black or white?" the waitress asked.

"Black," I said, "But I'd like a little jug of cream on the side."

"That's white," she said.

When she had gone, I said to Fred, "You still never know what you are going to get if you ask for coffee in this country."

Fred was reading the atlas, waiting for me to finish complaining. "What's this?" he asked. "Which province is this part of?"

"It's its own province," I said. "Prince Edward Island, famous for Anne of Green Gables, and the reason why there are so many Japanese tourists. There's a whole industry grown up around Anne, but the rest of the island is nice. The lobsters and oysters are terrific. If you decide to visit the island, go up to the French end, up towards Tignish, away from the Disneyland stuff around Charlottetown."

"Is there a French end in every province?"

I gave it some thought. "I can't speak for British Columbia or Saskatchewan," I said, "but otherwise, yes. As for Prince Edward Island, I spent a couple of weeks in St. Louis about 1975. We were doing an ad for a pharmaceuticals company, which involved filming the seaweed harvest. When the tide is right, the Irish moss — the seaweed — comes close to shore and they ride out with horses and harrows and rake it in."

"What do they do with it?"

"Apparently seaweed is where some cosmetics start. As you might guess, the tide never came right while we were there but we got some terrific footage of beautiful deserted beaches, far nicer than the crowded beaches around Cavendish. You used to have to get a ferry to the Island from New Brunswick but they've built a bridge now, more's the pity, so I doubt that the shore has stayed unspoilt. But I think that end of the Island is probably still more interesting than the tourist end."

"Did you get to know any of the local people? Did any of them speak English?"

"We'll talk about this when we get to Quebec. For the moment the quick answer is that in Canada even the French guys mending the roads speak English, so the Anglos don't have to learn French. On this trip, there wasn't enough room in the town's motel for the whole crew so I roomed with an old couple who used to farm in the area, a piece of luck for me because they told me stories of the way it was for them. For instance, when their son was ready for high school, the nearest school was in Tignish, fifty kilometres away. They couldn't afford to pay for his keep in a boarding house, so she rented a room in Tignish and stayed there with him, cooking their meals from Monday to Friday, when the husband came in the farm truck to take them back to St. Louis for the weekend. They did that for four years and then he went to the University of Montreal where he took a law degree. He's practising now in Montreal, or he was when she told me the story. She showed me their farm; they had sold it in the sixties to a professor from Toronto who wanted a holiday place."

"Hang on, Uncle. How far is it from Toronto to Prince Edward Island?"

"About a thousand miles."

"Three days drive?"

"You can do it in two."

"This is common in Canada, is it? A weekend cottage that takes two days to get to? Tell me how that works."

"I didn't say 'weekend.' I said 'holiday.' This man was a professor, I said, looking for a holiday place. He only worked in the winter. He wanted somewhere to sit and think for four or five months in the summer. Even so, he couldn't manage it. He stayed for three years then sold the place. Apparently he couldn't find anyone to cut the hay, and the grass around the farm buildings had turned into a hayfield, waist high. It must have been like the beginning of "The Sleeping Beauty." He offered the use of the land — he had about a hundred acres — free to anyone who would cut the grass around the house, but land there was very cheap then, and no one wanted it. So he sold it for what he paid, around seven thousand dollars including all buildings, this old lady said, but I don't think I can be remembering that right. Ridiculously cheap, anyway, by Ontario standards.

"We drove out to look at it one day. It was on a side road off the Palmer Road, and I remember being surprised when the paving on this side road turned to gravel after two miles. She said they got a mile of paving every three or four years, as long as they voted for the party that won the election. It was my first lesson in Canadian politics."

"Did you like it? Prince Edward Island. The French end?"

"I loved it. I had my first lobster supper there: clam chowder, lobster and strawberry shortcake, all for about five dollars. I asked if I could buy a bottle of beer to wash it down but it was a church supper and they didn't have a liquor licence. As a guest, though, I was given a complimentary glass of ginger ale. The man who gave it to me had to go behind a curtain to pour it, and I thought at first it was homemade and he didn't want me to see he was pouring it out of a big enamel jug or some such.

"It was very pleasant, sweet and soft. I had three or four glasses of it and the square dancing began. At some point I tried to teach my landlady the tango, while they all clapped. I sat down then, and watched the room revolve around the dancers. After a bit of singing I took my landlord and his wife home, holding them by an arm each so they didn't fall down."

We were silent for a few minutes, while Fred worked it out. "How come you couldn't tell?" he asked. "What was it, whiskey?"

"I would have recognized whiskey. This, I found out, just before I

left St. Louis, was screech, the very soft sweet rum from Newfoundland that I told you about. It's very hard to find on the mainland. In
Ontario, anyway. Yes, I had a good time on the Island."

"Did you visit any other parts of the province?"

"My landlord drove me around a bit on the Sunday we were
there. It's pretty, of course, very pretty. What else? Lobsters, oysters,
strawberries and potatoes. They play a lot of golf there. Now, I like
hitting the little white ball as much as Tiger Woods, but I've never
settled to it. It's a game in which you can't conceal your incompe-
tence and I don't like that. I mind feeling like an asshole when I
miss the ball completely with two couples watching, waiting to
play. There's not much else there, just church suppers, beaches and
golf."

"Great man?"

"Woman. Lucy Maud Montgomery. Look her up."

Fred studied the map for a few minutes, then asked, with a ten-
tative note in his voice, "Do you think you're a very reliable guide,
Uncle? I only ask because ..."

I cut him off. I had been expecting this for some time and I
was ready for him. "You're a historian, aren't you? I thought it was
accepted doctrine these days that what we used to think of as history is just the particular story the particular historian has decided
to tell. There's no such thing as the true history. Right?"

"Sort of. But where did you hear that?"

"I picked it up in a bar somewhere. I never went to a university,
did I tell you? I suppose what I'm telling you is a kind of oral history,
the place where all history begins."

"That would be all right if we were Vikings or something, but
this is the twenty-first century and there are such things as records,
lots of them."

"Not about the way people in New Brunswick, for instance,
feel about people with accents like yours. That's still off topic.
And that's what you'll need to know about when you visit New
Brunswick, or when they decide to separate."

"Now you are just being provocative, right?"

"Go and see for yourself."

We were on our way to Lyme Regis. Fred said, "Indians, uncle. Tell me about the Indians."

"I was afraid you would ask about them. Tell you what: we could pretend this is an interview; you ask questions and I'll try to answer them. But we should start with a few generalisations. Mine. Here goes, then, 'Everything I know and have thought about the Indian question:'

"First of all, we have marginalized a people who were doing just fine before we arrived in the seventeenth century, 'we' being the French and the English. We came looking for furs, and the result was the Hudson's Bay Company, still in business but now a department store. See, I'm off track already. So the Indians were already there, hunters and gatherers, mostly, I think, and we moved in. We gave them guns and whiskey in exchange for furs, and the decline began. Read all about it. Every province in Canada has something to be ashamed of in its relations with the Indians they found when they arrived, starting with Newfoundland where they used the indigenous Beothuk people for target practice and wiped them out.

"Fast forward three centuries. Slowly we have developed a conscience, as we accept the fact that a huge proportion of the people adrift in our slums are Indians, too many of them living from drink to drink, who are that way because of us, our traders and our missionaries. So it's our fault and we don't seem to know what to do about it. You can't give them back Canada, and short of that I don't know how the problem will get resolved. When I hear the Québécois singing songs like "Mon pays," I can't help wondering what the Indians are singing because Quebec has taken its full part in screwing the Indians. Whatever you do, Fred, I urge you not to come to any conclusions about the Indians until you have met some and spent some time thinking about nothing else. One of our great drawing-room topics is the question of whether the Indians are physiologically capable of handling liquor. People I knew in Winnipeg who have lived and worked with the Indians all their lives, and in some cases preferred them to white people, told me that the Indian has a gene missing, the one that we white men use to control our response to liquor. On the other hand, I had lunch one day with a group of intellectuals in Toronto who assured me that it was quite untrue, the theory having been disproved in an article they had read, and by their experience on a two-week canoe trip on the Spanish River when they met a lot of Indians. These were liberal people who wanted the idea to be untrue, who were ashamed of the idea on behalf of the rest of the white society. But several Indian reservations that are self-administered have banned liquor because of the problems it causes. On the other hand, I met a lot of white men working in construction camps with the same gene missing.

"I once heard a lawyer in Toronto, on a television panel, put forth the idea that it took us (white men) several million years to develop the computer, and it will take time for the Indians to catch up. He seemed to think that the Indians would first have to evolve — their brains, anyway — to the point where they could invent the wheel, and go on from there. Fortunately there were people on the panel who knew Indians who actually owned laptops.

"There have been some well-meaning attempts to do something for the Indians, starting with the church missions, who took away the children and put them in boarding schools and tried to make them into imitation white folks by denying them their language and culture. Nowadays the missionaries are seen as the villains, but they meant well, I'm sure. On the other hand, oh, Christ, let's change the subject."

"One more question, Uncle: how many Indians are there?"

"I think I heard somewhere between a half and three-quarters of a million. I should know, shouldn't I?"

We were silent, respecting my frustration, and Fred said, "How are you getting along with the guidebook, Uncle?"

"As you well know, I haven't written a word, so it might turn out to be a pamphlet after all."

"Too much work?"

"Much more than I'm ready for yet. I may not be the right person for the job. I thought I would dash off my impressions of England after thirty years, but, as you say, that might just add up to an article, an article which has probably been done. To do anything useful, I should trot around places like Coombe Regis, taking notes, awarding stars. But I'm not on for that."

"Do you have any actual impressions, yet?"

"Actually, I do. First of all, remember my little book will be addressed to North Americans. Now, have you noticed any Americans or Canadians on our travels so far?"

"Not around here."

"Right. They don't come here because the books don't mention it. They go to London; they go to all the cathedral towns; they visit castles; they see the Lake District, the Yorkshire moors and Cornwall. But they never get guided to Brighton, for example."

"Why should they?"

"Because that's where they'll meet the natives. Right now, visiting Americans find themselves elbow to elbow with the people they left Boston or Toronto to get away from. They should come to the south coast, to Bognor Regis, Eastbourne, Bournemouth." I consulted the road map of Great Britain. "Then they should visit Llandudno, Blackpool, Scarborough, Lowestoft, Southend and Margate. Here you will find the English at play, taking their traditional seaside holidays."

"I think you're pushing it a bit, Uncle, extrapolating too widely from the experience of a single night in Coombe Regis."

"You think so?"

"None of your English relatives would be seen dead in those places."

"Where do they go? My relatives."

"Spain."

"There were people on the beach when I went into the sea. Who were they? Where did they come from? France?"

"Most of them came on a coach from Lancashire. They were on a Short Break, a kind of mini-holiday."

"So they weren't foreigners."

"No. I didn't hear any of those."

"But a New Yorker, visiting here, would assume he was among the natives?"

"I suppose so."

"Then my point is made. I still haven't written a word, but the idea is looking better and better. Now, I want to stop at a bookseller and buy a good atlas. Like you, I'm going to circle every place I want to mention, and perhaps even make a note, right in the atlas. I can turn it into a text at my leisure."

FOURTEEN

IN LYME REGIS WE parked the car in the yard of a pub where we had lunch, and walked into the town, finding the main street where I remembered it to be. I located the house easily, but standing across the street from it, I was at a loss to know what to do next.

What did I want Lyme to tell me? I'd visited it half-a-dozen times but the town only came alive for me when I saw the film of *Persuasion*. My experience began with the scene in the drawing room at the end when Captain Wentworth is writing his declaration of love, seated at the desk, while Anne is listening to Captain Harville describe what love is for a man who will not see his wife again for months, if ever. The scene is like an operatic trio in which three voices blend in a single theme. I have watched the movie half a dozen times, and know the scene by heart. That scene takes place in Bath, of course, but there are some poignant moments earlier in the movie which derive some of their power from the background of sea and rocks and beach which finally made Lyme Regis, especially The Cobb, memorable. I gave Lyme Regis a tick.

"Did they have any friends, your parents?" Fred asked.

"As far as I know, only Phyllis. They never went in for friends much; the guests were their social life, especially in Coombe Regis. She hardly missed me when I left, not until after my father died, when she started to come on to me more, acting as if we'd always been close. She believed then that she'd always missed me."

"She got lonely."

"I suppose, but I'd always thought of her as tough. It was strange to have her speak, well, sentimentally. It sounded artificial, coming from her. By then I was just flying over as a duty. I didn't miss her."

"Maybe she had solved all the problems she had to be tough about."

"Like what?"

"Running a guesthouse. Keeping her relatives at bay." Fred put his hand on my arm and pointed across the street. "There's someone over there waving at you."

Across the street, next to my parents' old house, a woman had come out of her front door and was coo-eeing us.

"She seems to know you."

We crossed the street to her, a small woman in a large apron, her grey hair braided around her head, her feet in carpet slippers.

"I bin lookin' at you. You'm Vera's boy, aren't ye? I've seen you once or twice over the years, and I heard Vera had died. She held on to the house, you know, rented it to tenants like, so when I saw the "For Sale" sign go up I inquired and heard she'd gone. So I thought then that you might be back yourself to settle all the bits and pieces and I weren't surprised to see you across the street. I'm sorry about your mum, but she had a pretty fair run and there wasn't any pain, I heard."

"Were you friendly with her?"

"As much as anyone was, which was not very. Come in and have a cup of tea. Who's this?"

"This is Fred, my nephew."

"I call meself Mrs. Gough. I was never married but a lot of landladies who were really single called themselves Mrs. when I first started. It stopped people wondering. Come on in, then. The curtains are twitching all down the street. They think I'm sweeping paying guests in off the pavement."

Settled in a tiny front parlour that smelled strongly of ironing, a cup of orange-coloured tea and a ginger biscuit in hand, I told Mrs. Gough what we were doing in Lyme Regis. "I just want to get a feel for what their life was like after I left," was how I put it.

"I hardly know, dear. She was always very agreeable to me, and he often did little jobs for me, but we weren't in and out of each other's houses, like some. She told me who you was, after you went back one time. Otherwise we never sat down once for a proper natter. Mainly it was a matter of handing on people to each other, people looking for accommodation if we were full up ourselves. Mostly from me to her, because she got less of the passing trade. She never put a sign up."

"Why?"

"She said she couldn't be bothered and she didn't want people all the time, but she was pretty taken up all summer from my overflow. My boy reckoned it was to do with her income tax."

"Did she ever talk about her ...?" Here I was stuck. I ended, "other friends," aware of how lame it sounded.

But she was a knowing old biddy. "Before your father came along?" she said.

I took a breath and jumped in. "Or after," I said.

You could see she was making up her mind which way to respond, whether to be shocked, or offended on behalf of her old neighbour, or at me for insinuating things about my mother. In the end, after a couple of seconds, she decided I must have my reasons, hers not to inquire, something like that.

She said, "Never. Not ever. Mind you, she was a very private person all round. She used to go away a lot on the weekends, mostly every other, but she never said what for. If she was a bit younger I would have guessed she had a friend. You see a lot of that in the B&B business. But her husband was very agreeable, putting her in the taxi and all that."

"Every other weekend?"

"Quite a lot of them. She had a taxi pick her up on Friday and bring her back Sunday night. Being nosey ..." now she winked at Fred, "I was often sweeping my step when she pulled up, and I'd ask her if she'd had a nice outing, like, and she just said, very nice thank you, Mrs. Gough, so I got the hint. Don't ask."

"Her husband, my father, never went with her?"

"Not that I ever saw. He'd hand her in the taxi and wave to her as she turned the corner. I asked him once or twice about the weather where she was going, but it never led to an address."

"What did she tell the driver?"

"She didn't have to say anything. She always used the same one, and he knew to take her to the station."

"Always the same taxi?"

"The same *colour* taxi. Brown, but for all I know there might be twenty brown ones flitting about. I don't know whose it was because I never take a taxi. If I have to catch a train I get a lift with the greengrocer."

"A whole new quest," I said, when we were out on the street. "All we have to do now is find a brown cab."

"Let's go along the seafront," Fred said.

A little rank of taxis waited outside the grand hotel. Fred tackled the last in line. "My mother left her handbag in a taxi," he said to the driver, who was reading a newspaper.

"People always say that when they've lost sunnink. Gets on my fuckin' wick. They lose their 'andbags or someone nicks their wallets and every time they go, 'I must have left it in that taxi.' When it's not here they think I've stole it. I don't remember her or her hand-bag, so when was she ever in this taxi?"

Fred said, "I'm not talking about *your* taxi, mate. If you'll let me finish, I'll tell you. It was brown. All I want to know from you is who owns a brown taxi. That too much trouble?"

"Bonnycastle. Works out of Benson's garridge, mile and a half along the road."

"Good. Now, take us to Benson's garridge."

"You have to take the first in the queue." He pointed to the cabs in front of him and picked up the paper.

"Prick," Fred said as he rejoined me on the sidewalk.

I could only nod, lost in admiration of my new hard-case relative.

"You're her son, are you?" Bonnycastle said. "Yes, I can see the resemblance. She often mentioned you, when you were coming. I'm sorry about your mum, Mr. Prentice. She was a very nice lady. Always treated my driver right."

"I'm trying to put together a little account of her life, for my children. I'm spending a few days talking to the people who knew her. Did she ever talk to you about herself?"

"Not me. Probably Trevor Lee, her regular driver."

"Could I talk to him?"

"You'll have to go to Norfolk to do that. I've got his phone number. And his address if you want it." He thumbed through a book on his desk, and copied some information on to a slip of paper. "There," he said. "That should catch him."

Outside, Fred said, "There's a phone box if you want one, but why don't we go to Norfolk and talk to him? You might get more out of him, that way. And that way you would see a bit more of the country and visit one of the areas least known to Americans, I would think. It's exactly what you want, surely." He said this as if he had been seized by an exciting new idea.

"You ever been to Norfolk?"

"Of course. I went to Cambridge."

"That nearby?"

"Close enough for an outing. I did several. Shall I point us that way?"

It wasn't hard to put Norfolk and Cambridge and the mysterious phone call all together and come up with Daisy, the girlfriend, now back in the picture. For the moment, though, I let him have her in private. He would tell me when he was ready.

"All right. Norfolk it is. First, though, Bournemouth."

"Why Bournemouth?"

"Because we aren't far away, and because it's where they lived until I was born. Why did they move? It occurs to me that though I have no memories of Bournemouth myself, there might be someone still around who remembers my parents. I'd like to see."

In Bournemouth we picked up the trail at the tourist bureau. My mother's papers gave me the street and the number of the house, which was listed at the bureau as a guesthouse. We were directed to an area up behind the town, a district of streets wider than most, with houses that had probably been built a hundred years before, with four or five bedrooms and a room or two under the roof for the housemaid and the skivvy. Most of the houses had since acquired names as well as numbers, revealing their commercial nature, but not brandishing it with a B&B sign. These, as the bureau said, were proper guesthouses, not B&Bs.

"Posh," Fred said, looking at the street. "I always understood that our family was cursed with 'umble origins."

"My mother's generation — your grandparents — were working class. My mother went a couple of rungs up the ladder with this, I guess." I pointed across the street to the house I had now identified as theirs.

"How did your mother get this, then?"

I told him the story of "Aunt" Em and my mother's inheritance.

"You remember living here?"

"They left here before I was born."

"They might have sold it just to turn a quick profit."

"It's possible. Let's go and ask."

The man who answered the door had a hotelier's smile ready, a thin, fair-haired man about the same age as me.

"We were wondering if you have any vacancies." I said.

"A room?" His glance flickered between us as he assessed what he was seeing and hearing.

"Two rooms"

"For how long?"

"Just for the night. I'm on a bit of a pilgrimage, you see. I'm from Canada, and I'm doing some research on my family. This is my nephew."

"Lived nearby, did they? Yes, I think I can fit you in," he said, eventually. "Not for dinner, I'm afraid. We aren't opening the dining room tonight. Why don't you get your bags and park the car properly. That's it across the street? You can't leave it there. Put it in the yard of the pub. I have an arrangement with them. Here." He stepped back inside the door and re-emerged with a business card. "Put this on the dash and they'll know not to have you clamped."

"Is there a fee?"

"Not as such. But at some point you should go into the bar and identify yourselves as the owners of the car, and at the same time buy yourselves a drink. *That's* the fee." He laughed briefly, jerking his head back. "Scratch my back, eh? In the meantime, what about a cup of 'char?' I was just about to have one."

"We'd love one," I said.

He threw open the door and pointed inside. "Ten minutes then, in the lounge?"

FIFTEEN

"SO, A QUEST FOR our roots, is it? Where will you start?" He had seated us around a small table in the lounge.

"I already made a start in the town where I grew up, Coombe Regis. Then it seemed possible that, though I never lived here, there might be something to learn by coming back here."

"To Bournemouth?"

"To here." I pointed to the floor.

I waited, allowing Fred to dispel completely the possibility that might still be in our host's mind. "My uncle's parents owned this place once," Fred said.

"Really? Are you sure? I only query you because I was born here, about fifty years ago."

"May I ask?"

"Actually fifty-four."

Fred looked at me. I said, "Quite a coincidence. Were your parents on holiday, staying here?"

"Not exactly. You see, this was their house. *They* owned it then. They must have bought it from yours."

"As a guesthouse?"

From the back of the house there came the noise of a dish breaking. The host excused himself and disappeared. A sound of voices, then one voice, male, hysterical, rose up. "I'm *trying* to cook your fucking dinner. When you've finished charming the guests, perhaps you would do *something* about dessert. And not those sodding baked apples again."

A door closed. After a minute, the host appeared. "Sorry about that. We're short-staffed and Jack, our cook, is in a bad mood. And you know what cooks are when they get in a tizzy." He looked around to see what we were staring at. "Oh, shit."

A tall bald man stood in the doorway, glaring at us. "That's right, Jack the cook is in a bad mood." He took off the little apron he was wearing. "But Jack the *partner*" — he pressed the word hard — "is in the best of tempers. Jack the partner wants to join you for a cup of tea. May he?" He leaned over and jerked the cup and saucer from in front of the host, poured some tea for himself, put in some milk and sugar, crossed his legs and started to sip. He smiled all round.

Fred said, "Is something wrong, sir?"

Jack sighed. "After I've spent all afternoon in the kitchen, I don't take kindly to some twat complaining my Chicken Mandragora tastes of soap."

Ralph was nodding hard, eager to keep his partner on a track towards agreeability.

I said, "What happened today?"

"What *didn't* happen today? At breakfast we had two couples eating together, casting aspersions about the finnan haddie. Then the boiler went, and we had to get the plumber all the way from Southampton because we have a contract with that particular boiler company. And then my mayonnaise wouldn't thicken, and I wanted to make a nice dinner for just the two of us. I was just trying to whisk it once more and the fucking bowl slipped off the counter and smashed on the floor. That's what you heard."

Ralph said, "I told you, Jack, leave it. *I'll* clean it up." He started to stand.

"There," Fred said.

Jack jumped up. "Oh no. No one cleans up my kitchen." He turned to me, "I suppose after what you've witnessed today you won't want to stay here. The manager will give you a full refund." He waved at Ralph.

"We haven't paid anything yet," I said. "Besides, we like it here." I raised an eyebrow at Fred, who nodded and shook his head and sat firmly back in his seat to show his support. "Now, whichever is the manager today, would you show us to our rooms? Can you look after the suitcases, Fred? They're still in the car."

"I'll help him," Jack said. "Do me good to get out." He burst out laughing. "Show me to your car, Fred."

That night, as we were finishing our steak-and-Guinness pie in the pub, Fred said, "I would think the trail would be cold by now, surely."

We had left the two hoteliers to their problems, intending to quiz them when they were calmer, perhaps the next morning. I said, "You're probably right. I'd like to ask, though."

"Ask what?" A shadow hung over the table. Two shadows: Ralph and Jack. "We shamefully abandoned you, so we're here to answer all your questions. What do you want to know, Will? Will. Such a nice *strong* name," Jack said. "Shall we *tête-à-tête*, then, over a spot of after-dinner brandy?"

Ralph said, "We've had dinner. Jack poached the most wonderful salmon for us. And the mayonnaise was perfect. And coffee? On us, please, to say thank you for not taking fright and running away."

I pulled back a chair, and the two sat down. "Four coffees," Ralph called to the barman who was leaning over the counter, expectant. "And brandy all round. All right?" He looked inquiringly at Fred, who nodded, then said. "No. Do you mind if I have a glass of port? I started to drink it last term."

"Separate bill from the dinner, then," the barman said. "This is on you, Ralph, right?"

"What's this in aid of?" I asked.

"He told you, just a gesture to make up for my abominable rudeness, about which he has talked interminably since you left."

"Don't be a twit. A little tantrum? Why should it bother us?"

"We've lost clients for less."

Ralph said, "The point he's trying to make is that whereas the atmosphere could have been fraught, you dipped us all in your extraordinary goodwill and made yourselves special to us."

Jack said. "All right, all right. We've grovelled enough. After you left, we also talked about your story, how you were nearly born in the house and all that. But was that the only reason for visiting?"

"I just wanted to start at the beginning. I really didn't expect to find any trace of my family after this long but if you don't mind, I'll take some pictures of the house before we leave to show my kids."

"Why?"

"It's what you do. Everybody in Canada is doing it, writing family histories, finding out where they all started. I'm going to try to find out where my dad came from, and get in touch with my mother's family. That won't be hard. They're keen to make contact."

Ralph and Jack exchanged gleeful conspiratorial glances. Ralph said, "We *thought* that might be the case. Go get 'im, Jack."

Jack said, "Don't go away," and disappeared into the public bar. Fred started to speak but Ralph put his finger to his lips. "Don't spoil the surprise," he said.

Jack reappeared, pushing in front of him a tiny well-groomed man in his seventies, an elderly midget in a blazer with a scarf at his throat, completely self-possessed, smiling politely, glancing round the group, curious.

"Boots," I said. "You're Boots, aren't you?"

"Well done," the little man responded. "You remember me from seeing me once when you weren't even a year old? That's going it." His voice was deep and rich like a Hollywood father figure.

"I remember the stories about you, and I saw the pictures. But, I'm sorry, Boots ..." I looked appealingly at Ralph.

"Of course. This is Archie Collier; Archie, this is Will Prentice and his nephew Fred."

"I know about Will. Nice to see you again, sir. And pleased to meet you, Fred."

"Here's a chair, Archie, and a cushion. Upsadaisy. Now you're on the same level as the rest of us, more or less. What's all this 'sir' business. You never called me 'sir.'"

"No, well, I started off with your name when you was just a nipper, and stayed with it."

"And what's this Boots, thing? A nickname?" Fred asked.

"That's right. That's what they called me when I went to work for them. It was a joke, and I didn't mind 'cos they shared it with me. Behind the pantry door, you might say, they called me Archie, and I called them Vera and Em and Phyllis. In public it was 'Boots,' and 'Mrs. Prentice' and 'ma'am.' You still don't get it, do you? See 'Boots' was what you called the boy who cleaned the boots in Victorian times, when they left them outside the door at night, and 'Boots' was the general dogsbody the rest of the time. 'Boots!' they would shout, up and down the corridor. 'Boots! Fetch me some 'ot water for my shave.' Well I was Boots'-size, you might say, still am, a genuine case of arrested development, so it tickled Vera to call me 'Boots' until it stuck. But then, when Vera sold up, I asked her not to let on what I was called and after that I was Archie. See, I had two kids by then, and I already foresaw a problem of discipline on account of my size, and them hearing someone shout 'Boots' at me wouldn't help."

"How many have you got now, Archie?"

"Changing the subject, are we? Six. And they're all 'orrible great louts, especially the girls. Now can we get off the interesting question of my fertility? What did you want me for?"

"You've guessed, surely. Will's mother, Vera, passed away recently, and Will is sequestering himself here for a few days, remembering."

"That's nicely put, Ralph," Jack said, consideringly.

I said, "You worked for Mum and Em in the forties?"

"Until 1953, when you were born. My dad wanted to apprentice me for a jockey but I didn't get on with horses. Seemed to me they was always trying to step on me. So your mum took me on, not on account of my size but in spite of it. It was hard to see useful employment for me at any time, so when she made the offer I jumped at it, and stayed with the job for five years. When she moved, I stayed. I was with this lot —" he jerked his thumb at Ralph — "but I had five good years with your mum. Fact is, I loved her, I did." He looked hard at me. "She was an angel to me. So what can I tell you?"

I took out the pictures. "Do you know these people?"

"Certainly. That's David Cullough. He was a prince. I don't know who she is."

"Was he here a lot?"

"He was a traveller, wasn't he? Used to come when he had calls to make in the area, and sometimes on weekends, for a break. Then some time around the Festival of Britain, he didn't come any more. He might have lost his job, or been put on straight commission. I never heard. Then you were born, and right after that they sold up and moved down Devon way. No, I tell a lie. You were born after they moved. That's right, I did see you as a toddler because they came by one day, your mum and dad, but you were born after they left the guesthouse."

"They moved to Coombe Regis."

"That right? I'd forgotten. Too far to walk, anyway. I never saw them again, except just that once. After that my life was in Ralph's mother's hands, and just my luck she was a good boss, too, right outside the law of averages. When she passed on, I stayed with Ralph, and he pensioned me off five years ago. I still help out a bit when they're busy, keep the front tidy, light a little fire on damp days. They don't pay me any extra, though, so I suit myself." He winked at Ralph.

"Then there was my father, Henry Prentice, was it?"

"He was a good 'un, too. The luck I've had!"

"He used to stay in the house before he was my father, didn't he?"

"I'm beginning to get a great big inkling of what you want to know, and it seems to me that this ..." he waved a hand around the bar to include the other curious customers, "... is not the place to find out. I'll come over and have a cup of tea with you at the house after breakfast tomorrow. Tell you all about it."

"Can we hide behind the pantry door and listen?" Jack asked.

"Like you usually do if there's a nice row going on in the dining room?" He pointed an accusing finger at Jack. "You give them the table in the corner by the front window. Then you won't be tempted."

SIXTEEN

"NOW, FIRST OF ALL you have to understand the background," Boots began next morning at breakfast. "Right from the beginning your mum was the power behind the throne, and in front of it. She was always full up because she kept a good table, even with the rationing that was still on after the war. Your mum made people *comfortable*."

"What about Aunt Phyllis?"

He nodded. "She came down alternate weekends from David."

"Why alternate weekends?"

"Well, she bunked in with your mum, see."

"But on every other weekend, Henry Prentice and my mum lived together?"

"Let's just say they were very close. He was a wonderful fella, he was."

"Did he have his own room, too?"

"No need to be sarky, is there? All water under the bridge now.

Don't forget your grandmother was there a lot, and besides, your mum liked to have her secrets. Granny wouldn't have seen anything to object to, your mum would have made sure of that. But I do remember noticing that David and Henry weren't usually around on the same weekends. Henry was best man at my wedding, which, by the way, your mum paid for *and* gave me a week off for a honeymoon. A real week off. We didn't go anywhere, just stayed here, went for walks in the daytime and played cribbage in the evening until it was time to go to bed. No television in those days. But we had a lovely time."

I put Archie down as one of those people who never say anything bad about anyone. Not a reliable witness.

"When did David Cullough disappear?"

"I told you. The same year you was born, as I remember. Or the year after. Or the year before. Right about then, anyway."

"And then she took up with my father permanently?"

"They got married and moved to Coombe Regis."

"Why? Why did they move?"

"Don't take me for a bleeding mug. I don't know for certain they ever *was* married but you can bet your life they wasn't married long enough. This was in the days before everybody started living with each other, wedding or not, remember. Your mum wouldn't have cared about the church side of it but I told you she didn't like anyone to know her business, and I think that's why she moved." Archie seemed to swell a little. "I don't like the turn this conversation is taking," he said. "I'm not saying a word against people who were so good to me. As far as I'm concerned, you're a Prentice."

"What about my father? Did you get on well with him?"

"I get on well with everybody. It's my size. People smile when they see me, and I smile back. I liked your dad, yes. I didn't know him as well as I knew David but I saw no harm in him."

After that, Archie started to reminisce, telling entertaining stories about the past, but he had nothing more to add about my concerns.

Fred picked up the bags and said he would meet me at the car, after I had settled the bill. When I got to the car, the bags were in the back but Fred was nowhere around, and did not appear for ten minutes.

"Sorry, Uncle," he said. "A phone call."

"Your bookie?"

"My what?"

"Your bookmaker. The man you bet with. It's a way of not being bored. I heard a man in a pub, once, when I was your age, bemoan the fact that you couldn't place a bet on a Sunday in England. He waited, bored, all through Sunday, until he could put a bet on again."

"Things aren't that bad."

He didn't say anything more, but his very demeanor, of a man who is again interested in life, said it all. He made two more phone calls on the way to Cambridge, not seeming to be secret about them, but not explaining them either. So now I knew he was no longer cosmically bored and I knew why we were going to Burnham Market via Cambridge, instead of telephoning.

In the car, Fred said, "My tutor in my first year said, 'In the history of ideas we always speak as if we know the father: You know, the Father of Chemistry, or the Father of Geology, whereas in life we always know the mother but quite often not the father.'"

"What are you chuntering on about?"

"Pretty obvious. I'm beginning to get some idea of one of the things you want to find out."

"Yes, well. Why did they move from Bournemouth?"

"Because your mother became pregnant, you suspect?"

"But she was married."

"Yes. Perhaps she thought Bournemouth wasn't the right atmosphere to begin married life. She was right. It's like a Balham by the sea, isn't it?"

"Don't go on about it. But I'll put a cross against it to warn people off. Except sociologists. They'd be interested."

Suddenly Fred said, "And all the local people are from Lancashire."

"On those mini-breaks, you mean?"

"No, I think I was wrong about that, or only partly right. Everywhere we've been I've been hearing accents from up north. I think Bournemouth is where all the people from Blackpool and Leeds come to die, like you people go to Florida."

"Americans won't know the difference, though, will they? I think I'll recommend it, after all. Now, please, to Oxford."

There was no way of avoiding Salisbury but it looked as if the A338 was routed firmly round it. The next attraction to be avoided was Stonehenge, towards which busloads of European and Asians were shoaling. The Salisbury Plain itself was a relief, the first major natural landscape except the coastline we had seen on this trip. Almost a hundred years ago E.M. Forster talked about "the red dust" that was spreading out from London, the roofs of suburbia that were filling in the landscape, still the major impression from the air. A hundred years have increased the size of the stain so that Fred and I, on a trip from London to Bournemouth, and then back up through Oxford to Cambridge, seemed to be driving steadily through suburbia, except, now, for the hour or so it took us to cross the plain.

This is Hardy country, and I tried to tell Fred the story of Tess, which he had heard of but never read, but it was difficult to evoke the spirit of the tragedy with all the world's tourists chattering happily round about. I considered having a look at Woodhenge, then decided that it would be best not to raise the question of henges at all (though I changed my mind about that later), and we made our way up the A343 to Andover, and thence to Newbury and Oxford. It was late in the afternoon, and it made sense to stop in Oxford for the night.

There was no room at the first six inns we tried, and a bad instinct led us out of town to a large village where we found a couple of rooms at a two-star inn for about the same price as we might have paid in New York. The rooms were squalid — dampish sheets, a forty-watt bulb in the single bedside lamp and a notice asking us not to take baths before seven in the morning as the hot water was needed for the kitchen. I asked a travelling salesman who shared our breakfast table the next morning (one sausage, one egg, white toast, instant coffee, and orangeade standing in for juice — the full English breakfast) who awarded the two stars and he told me a number of organisations did, including the AA and the RAC, but in this case the owners had awarded the stars to themselves, by painting them on a bit of wood to hang under the hotel's name. This would be illegal anywhere else in Europe, he said, but the English authorities hadn't yet got around to accepting responsibility for the accommodation available to tourists, and setting standards. You had to keep your wits about you.

Staying in that village had one enormous benefit. We got to have a look at Blenheim Palace, the family home of the Churchills (the great man himself is buried in a village churchyard nearby). It is the only historic building that has ever completely engaged me. The house, in its grounds, is like a small principality. We got into the grounds early, before the tourist coaches from London arrived, and we felt as if we had discovered it ourselves. Thoroughly recommended, I wrote in my atlas, ticking it twice, but arrive by 9 a.m. so as to be first in line when the palace opens, and take the day.

Oxford had to be dealt with. I had a base to touch: *Three Men in a Boat* ends there, so we asked our way to The Trout, and I had a commemorative pint in honour of Jerome. And then we parked by the bus station and set out on foot.

With the aid of a mini-guide I bought in a newspaper shop, we walked about the most celebrated university city in England if not in Europe, and except for one Sunday morning on the Cherry Spit in Toronto harbour, it was the dullest afternoon's walking I have ever had. There are twenty-seven colleges in Oxford, and we saw the outsides of fifteen of them. Every single one had a sign up at the gate, "Closed to Visitors." The Japanese were all sitting on the tops of double-decker buses and so could point their cameras over the walls of the colleges, but Fred and I saw nothing except ancient stone and traffic. I made a note to warn tourists to avoid Oxford, and then decided not to mention the town at all for fear of intriguing the reader.

The travelling salesman in Woodstock had warned us that we would be all right at lunch time, because the pubs served food, but at night we would find nothing to eat. It was hard to believe — the English can turn a very limited experience into a sweeping statement like, "The shops in Norway only open in the morning" because the day they were there it was a half-closing day, like Wednesday, still, in English villages. But the salesman was very experienced. He showed us a review from a London newspaper about a new restaurant in Oxford. The review began, "When I find myself on death row ... and the guard asks after the last meal ... I want the chef (if there is one) from the X restaurant in Oxford flown over to replicate precisely the dinner I ate there recently. After that, death by lethal injection will be comic relief." The rest of the piece, a detailed account of every course, justified the opening paragraph.

We were on our way to accepting the salesman's advice to drive to a restaurant in a village on the fringe, until we stumbled over Brown's, which was exactly what we wanted, good food, reasonable prices and a nice atmosphere not artificially arrived at. I gave it three checks.

After a good dinner, I was inclined to give the city a second chance, but a short stroll showed that although there were some restaurants open and serving, the rest of the city was still off limits. Hotel prices were high, so we drove to another village the salesman had recommended for dinner, and we found the inn where the beds were soft and dry, the water was hot, and the breakfast included finnan haddie. I gave Wytham a tick and a half.

Over a nightcap in the bar, Fred continued to cross-question me about Canada until it seemed time to ask some questions myself. I had accepted his reasons in the beginning for coming on this trip, reasons which amounted to no more than that he had been jilted, and was at a loose end. Canada had presented itself in the form of an "uncle" with a need for a guide, and then gradually turned into a possible next step. Another question occurred to me. Fred and his grandfather seemed very directly connected. I wondered about the missing link. "What do your parents think of what you're doing?" I asked him.

"You mean here, now, or career-wise, as you would say?"

"Fred, my boy, that's the first conventional crack you've made about North American idiom ..."

"Uncle, I was just, you know ..."

"I know, I know. You didn't mean to sound pissy, but you did, to me. So let's push it a bit. Although I will defer to your infinitely superior preparation for life in one of the ten greatest universities in the world — or is it one of the two greatest? — backed up by the daily reading of the *Guardian*, and the further wit-sharpening of playing *Scrabble* with the 'Footlights' crowd, I am not prepared to be instructed by you in grammar and style. I have made my living from words for twenty-five years and I've thought about the language a lot, and read all the usual books from Strunk and White to ..."

"Christ, Uncle ..."

"So, if you like, I could point out the solecisms you hourly commit. So far it is mainly the use of adverbs when adjectives would be correct, but there are lots of others. Or we could amuse ourselves by quizzing each other on figures of speech. What's 'hendiadys' for instance. Your turn."

"Fainites, Uncle. Fainites." He held up crossed fingers. "I give in. All right? I promise never again to make fun of your parts. Jesus!"

I said, "Do you correct the grammar of your relatives? Great-Aunt Olive, for instance?"

"God, no. That's the first thing you learn when you come down."

"You mean rise up? No, no, I know what you mean. I read *Decline and Fall*. Do your parents have the same accent as your grandfather?" As I spoke, I realized that more than grammar was involved. So far Fred had hardly mentioned his parents and I had the distinct impression that his parents were missing, perhaps dead. Surely not. Even given the fence my mother had thrown up to keep them all at a distance, I would have heard something.

Fred did all those things you do when you are about to make a speech, adjusted his shirt and jacket at the collar, pushed back his hair, cleared his throat. Then he said, "I thought you would know, my mother died when I was in high school. My father moved away, but I wanted to stay in the same school so I moved in with my grandparents. They became my substitute parents."

"And still are?"

"I'm a big boy now, as Grandad would say."

"Where did your father go to?"

"A place called Wokingham."

"For Christ's sake, Fred. I lived here for the first twenty years of my life. I've actually heard of Wokingham. A village near Reading, not to be confused with Woking, right? Don't treat me as if I'm from Alabama."

"Sorry. Yes. Not a village, actually, not now. A town where the Reading meritocracy live. A lot of money has wound up there. I knew a couple of people at Cambridge from there."

"And is your father ..." I searched for whatever phrase had replaced 'Something in the City.'

"He's a quantity surveyor. You know, someone who ..."

"I know what a quantity surveyor is. We had one at school."

"His wife has money."

"Your stepmother."

"Yes. My wicked stepmother"

"Better explain that. Or not, and change the subject."

"My mother died of cancer when I was at school and it quickly came out that my father had been involved with another woman for some time. He's now married this woman. Her father made money building houses. After my mother died, they moved to Wokingham and he bought into a local partnership, with her money. She then cut him off from his family."

"Having poor relations can be embarrassing for the nouveau riche. Did she cut you off, too?"

"I cut *her* off, I think. I went down to Wokingham at first, very dutifully, during the vacations, and then I didn't. My grandparents were much more to me than the witch of Wokingham."

"That's silly talk."

"Is it? I dislike her a lot."

"No doubt she feels the same way about you."

"Oh, no. To borrow a phrase, I was her trophy stepson, the one at Cambridge, until I stopped going down to Wokingham."

"And how does Daisy feel about this? Her? I'm assuming this flurry of phone calls betokens a new turn in your life, and Daisy might have an interest in your connections again."

He blushed slightly. "Yes. I did take Daisy down to Wokingham once but the two women didn't get along at all. I'm not a very political animal, but Daisy is — right now she's trying to find a left-wing alternative to the Labour party. And of course my stepmother worshipped Margaret Thatcher."

"Is Daisy interested in Canada?"

"Actually, not much."

"We should turn back then?"

He grinned. "We might as well finish the tour. Daisy is tied up in Cambridge for a couple of weeks."

The next morning we checked that Oxford wasn't swarming with people called Prentice who looked like me; there was only one rumour of Dad's brother. The police said they had an old listing of the name but they couldn't or wouldn't say why he was on their records. From the ironical attitude of the constable, I got an impression of a charge of indecent exposure, probably incurred when Prentice was caught in an alley taking a pee. The entry occurred long enough ago that there was some sort of statute of limitations protecting his privacy. From the sound of it, the less he was aware of my existence, if he was still alive, the better for me. A pity. I'd hoped I was related to someone distinguished, someone who was ashamed of his connection to us. After all, Oxford? A professor? Maybe a bishop? Not a flasher, anyway. One of the risks of researching one's ancestors.

SEVENTEEN

LEAVING OXFORD, FRED ASKED, "Is ice hockey the national sport in Canada?"

"Of course. Why do you ask?"

"Someone in my college claimed the national sport was lacrosse. Why would he think that?"

"Your friend was making a point, a silly, trivial nitpicking point, suitable for airing by undergraduates on quiz-shows to show their learning: 'Lacrosse is played on a field or in an arena by men who use a sort of webbed field hockey stick to throw a little ball about and into a net. It's a very old game invented by Indians.'"

"Uncle, I should have said, I know about lacrosse. I even know that 'crosse' is Canadian French for crook, the stick used in the game."

"Erudite bugger, aren't you? How did you know about it?"

"My girlfriend played it at school. It's got quite a following here, as I assume it has in Canada."

"So I always believed, but I've never seen a game, except on television and I've never met a lacrosse player. It's not like ice hockey, as you call it. I doubt if you'll ever find two garage mechanics arguing over it. But Canada is a big country. Perhaps in Yellowknife ...? And by the way, don't say, 'Canadian French'; it's probably offensive."

"What should I say?"

"French. They may speak with an accent, no, I'm sure they do, but so do Parisians. It isn't a dialect. They do have a dialect — it's called *joual*, derived from the way they pronounced 'cheval', I understand, and though it was once a sign of a low-life, I believe the intellectuals are now rather proud of it. Let's get back to hockey. What's on your mind?"

"Ice hockey's pretty much of a blood sport, isn't it? The way you play it. They showed a few minutes of a Canadian game on television the other night. Brutal. Lethal. It isn't like that here."

"Just among the spectators."

"What?"

"We're talking about violence in sports, I assume. The other day, I read, eight hundred patriots from Britain on their way to a football match destroyed a cross-channel ferry, terrorizing the passengers and rendering helpless the twenty or so policemen hired to keep them in order. And this wasn't a rare event. The article said that it had been going on for half a century: gangs with knives, bicycle chains, rocks, iron bars — carving each other up at soccer matches. Nobody seems able to stop it, and no law-abiding citizens dare go alone to football matches any more. No one else, except possibly the Turkish fans when the British visit, go in for similar brawls. Now, brawls don't happen among the spectators at hockey games, violent as you seem to find them. The violence is all on the ice. There are no brawls at North American football games, either, or at baseball or basketball games, and as for our soccer games, you would think you were at a wedding. The spilling of blood on the terraces is a purely British phenomenon, this article said. I'm just quoting, you understand."

"It may be no more than a ritualization of an atavistic instinct."

"This is Cambridge talking, is it? 'How the British ritualize their what you said?'"

"The theory is that the hooligans go to soccer matches primarily to get into a fight with the other team's hooligans. You see them on television. Two gangs taunting each other."

"So the actual game doesn't matter?"

"No, no. The game is the high point of the weekend for a huge number of folk. Should that be 'folks'? It's just that we have these yobbos. Could we get on to something else? I don't know much about this."

"No. You started this, accusing Canadians of liking hockey for its violence. I've just had a thought: for the spectators the violence is part of the spectacle, as it is in bull fighting or gladiatorial combat. You may be right about their — what's that word? 'atavistic'? — impulses, but the crowds at hockey games release their impulses by projecting them on to the players. The hooligans at a soccer game, on the other hand, come to the game to kill each other personally."

"I've had a thought, too, though," Fred said. "Very rarely, if ever, do the hooligans actually kill each other."

"Really?"

"No. I don't think they want to. They want to knock each other about a bit, cut each other up and get cut themselves, then go home with the scars, like German students in those old duelling clubs. Yes, I think that's a crucial point. When yobbos fight, no one gets killed, and yet when you look at the weapons they use ..."

"Could be the natural British instinct for fair play, do you think?"

"Now you're being sarky, Uncle."

"I'm intrigued. Is it only the English who have soccer hooligans?"

"Italy has its own, I think. They killed a policeman last season. But I don't know! All right, uncle? I don't know! Can we drop it?"

We were on our way to Norfolk via Cambridge. We had gone through the best bit of the route, through Aylesbury and now we seemed to be trudging through the light industry centre of England, miles of little factories, and market gardens and allotments. I have some respect, even admiration, for the coal and steel country north of Birmingham — the people who live in the Black Country look larger than life to me, a former softie from the south — but the bicycle factories and sewing machine works of Luton and Stevenage seem piddling in comparison.

I pointed Fred towards Royston. I knew we would be some time crossing England. Anyone who has driven in England knows that all roads lead to London, and if that's where you're going you will make good time. This kind of trip, though, from Oxford to Cambridge, requires the experience of a furniture mover to choose the best route.

Fred, brooding, said, "You really don't have any violence at sporting events in Canada?"

I said, "You aren't going to win this one, Fred. I've done a lot of thinking about soccer hooliganism. But, yes. There was one famous night when the greatest hockey player in the world at the time was banned for the rest of the season for threatening the referee with his stick. It was in the middle of the playoffs — cup-ties to you — and the crowd reacted by turning over a streetcar. That was the only time when it might have been dangerous to speak English in downtown Montreal."

About now we got lost. I still can't figure out where we left the trail, but I suggested we stop because I wanted to know how to pronounce the name on a signpost (we never learned). Oundle, we found, is a real town that the superstores have left alone so that instead of a high street full of catalogue stores taking over from the former village shops which were bankrupted by the superstore on the edge of town, the shops are still there: the two butchers, the delicatessen, the bakeshops and, best of all, the nicest second-hand bookshop I have come across in England. We bought some smoked salmon sandwiches and coffee and lunched on the public bench in the square to watch the young matrons dash back and forth, hair and Barbours flying. There's money in Oundle country, as there is everywhere in England within weekend distance of London, but it hasn't driven out the natives yet. We spent half an hour in the bookshop, coming out with eight books between us.

"How would you define a good second-hand bookshop, Uncle?" Fred asked.

"It's the place that has the five books that you didn't know you had been looking for until you see them in the shop. Geraldine Waddington's here, is terrific."

"So we're in Quebec already. Tell me about that."

"I don't know anything about Quebec. I can only tell you how the Anglos I know talk about Quebec."

"And Quebecers?"

"Say 'Québécois'. Now, there's just you and me in the car, so I'll tell you exactly what I think if you promise not to quote me, here or if you get to Canada. Okay? First of all, at one time some people created a kind of rallying point for independence, the separatist movement, which did have the objective of an independent or sovereign Quebec. This was a seventies' phenomenon — it had started before I arrived in Canada, but fortunately — remember this is me speaking, not some professional thinker on the op-ed page — we had the ideal man for the job of prime minister, Pierre Trudeau, enormously intelligent, deeply patriotic, independently wealthy, tough and French. Remember what I said about *joual*? Trudeau could speak the language when necessary. 'Eat shit,' he told them, in French, when they demonstrated against him. And when they kidnapped a British diplomat and a French cabinet minister, and murdered the cabinet minister, he brought in the *War Measures Act* to create the authority he felt he needed to restore the state's control. A lot of people, even in his own party, the Liberals, worried about the loss of liberty that was involved and asked him how far he was prepared to go. 'Just watch me,' he replied. A tough bugger.

"But murdering one of their hostages was the peak of the kidnappers' activity, and they had gone too far. The other highlight of that period was the appearance of General de Gaulle, waving from a hotel balcony and shouting, "Vive le Quebec libre," which irritated even some of the people in the independence movement, who didn't feel they needed advice from Paris, any more than from London. Everyone found de Gaulle embarrassing, and the Canadian government told him to shut up and go home. I suppose the political climax of the time came with a referendum which showed that a tiny majority of the Québécois favoured staying within Canada. That small majority has held up since. One lasting result of the movement has been their language laws. In Quebec now, all signs, street signs, names of shops, everything, must be displayed in both languages and the French words must take prominence. In France, I understand, the stop signs say 'STOP'; in Quebec, they say 'ARRÊT', with a circumflex over the 'E.' And I believe they've re-jigged the educational system to preserve the language."

"Like the Irish."

"I don't know anything about the Irish. Yes, I do. It's the only country where old age pensioners get Viagra on the National Health or whatever they call it there. A breathtakingly wide-minded lot, never mind the shirt-lifters in the teaching orders. One free one a week they're allowed.

"Anyway, now that French is no longer the most important language in the world, I would have guessed that the movement to prop it up would fail, even in Quebec, but I hear that it is working. Friends tell me that there's much more French spoken in downtown Montreal than there used to be fifty years ago. Do you speak French?"

"No."

"You should learn some before you come."

"Do you?'

"No, but I didn't have a wise old uncle to advise me. I think every permanent resident of Canada should speak both languages, as well as whatever language they brought with them. It's a truism that if Canada (and England, as I remember) took language teaching as seriously as they do in Norway, say, the country would be bilingual in twenty years. But the current teaching of French in the better schools of Toronto is as pathetic in its results as the instruction I got in Coombe Regis. And like us then, they aren't even ashamed of it."

"I suppose there's a lot of bad feeling between the two, what do you call them?"

"'Cultures' will do. 'Nations,' if you like. 'Two solitudes,' one novelist called them. There's a lot of bad feeling at the top, all right. The Quebec intellectuals can articulate their historical hatred of the Anglos and lay out the injustices they have suffered as a people at the nod of a talk-show host, but still you'll find most people in Montreal a lot more civil than Parisians are supposed to be. And Quebec City is one of my favourite places for a two or three day visit. It's historically interesting, pretty and the food is good. Let's see what your man found when he came." I took the old notebook from the glove compartment, and scanned the first few pages. "Apparently he only spent a few hours in Montreal, and then took the bus to Kingston. He expected it to be like Paris, but everyone seemed to speak English." I flipped the pages. "You're right: a dull list of all the buildings he looked at and an account of a bus tour round the city. No original perceptions. I sympathize with him a bit. I tried keeping a journal when I first emigrated but it takes practice, and a decision to reveal yourself in an interesting way. Listen to this: *'I read before I came that Montreal is the thirdlargest French-speaking city in the world, but today except for one or two workers addressing each other, everybody I came in contact with spoke English — bus drivers, waiters, everyone. And yet I understood from school that French was the lingua franca of the world. You would think it would survive here.'*

"Actually, Montreal is now the *second* largest French-speaking city, but he's right, English is the lingua franca now. I think the big change came when the airlines demanded that air traffic controllers speak English. One pilot I met said that now the only traffic controllers he couldn't understand were the Scotch."

"You mentioned food. As a general rule, Uncle, is all French food good and Anglo food bad? See, I'm getting the vocabulary."

"It's more complicated than that. When we start on Toronto, which should be some time after Burnham Market, I'll tell you about the good food places. There are lots, mainly Italian and French. Oh, yes, we're very proud of our cosmopolitanism. And yet I was in Montreal a few months ago and some friends took me to a little restaurant, a 'Bistro Gourmet,' it called itself, on Rue St. Mathieu where, without any fuss, we had a superb, inexpensive dinner which would have made them famous in Toronto. My hosts that night said they could take me to twenty such places in Montreal. That's the difference. This wasn't a big-night-out place in Montreal, but it would have been in Toronto. But that's enough about Quebec, eh?"

"Not quite. So, apart from the intellectuals, they don't hate the Anglos as much as they used to?"

"That's my guess. See, they can't keep blaming the old Wasp establishment for everything. Most of those villains are dead. Quebec's miseries were caused by an — I was going to say 'unholy,' but one third of it was holy — alliance between the Scottish bankers, a man named Duplessis — the Quebec premier whose name was synonymous with corruption — and the Catholic Church, which until very recently controlled much of the vote of its parishioners through the priests. The Church's interests lay with Duplessis. The bankers had no trouble getting and keeping control of the economy, mainly by paying off the Duplessis gang. Now, knowing it's their own politicians who are to blame makes the French intellectuals hate us more, of course. But the ordinary people are beginning to care less, I think. Now they have made us, the Anglos, suffer, by frightening us with closely contested elections and referendums on independence, and now we have done our penance, they are ready to move on, as long as we try to learn to speak French."

"What was it that made the Catholic Church less important?"

"Here I think Quebec's intellectuals had a lot to do with it, encouraging the people to take less notice, as it were. The Church,

I gather, hasn't been very nimble in maintaining its position and influence, but is involved in a continuous rear-guard action, mainly, but not solely, because of all these priests and lay brothers who've been buggering their choirboys. Not only in Quebec, but in the rest of Canada, and in the States, and in Ireland — and just about everywhere where there are dormitories full of choirboys. I read somewhere that because of the revelation of so much sodomy among the priesthood, the Catholic Church in Ireland has lost much of its power to put the fear of God into its parishioners. And then there was the Pope who threatened to send our prime minister to hell because he voted for same-sex marriages. That's the Vatican's idea of the separation of church and state."

"Do you want Quebec to stay? I mean, do you care, you Anglos?"

"Fred, understand that I am an immigrant, and always will be. From England, to be sure, but still not entitled to be called 'Anglo,' as you used the term. Your question requires a response from a born Canadian, a thoughtful response, of course, but one grounded in emotion. When you ask me a question about separatism, then I think about it and tell you what I think. But if I were born in Winnipeg, say, I would respond out of a different and much more complex set of thoughts and emotions, some of them inherited. The longer I live there the more I feel like an Anglo, but I'll never become the real thing. So in answer to your question, personally I would see the split as a major loss, a disaster, and I think so would most of the Anglos. Certainly my friends would. True, it might be interesting to see what life with an independent Quebec would be like, but it would be sad, too, because Canada would be gone. To say it wouldn't be the same isn't strong enough; Canada wouldn't exist, and might even break up into fragments. For me, the Anglo-French friction *is* Canada or a good part of it. That make sense?"

"How do you think you would feel if you'd been born in Quebec, Uncle?"

"I'd be manning the barricades. *A bas les Anglais*. Bastards. We've suffered long enough. *Je me souviens.*" I sang, "*Mon pays da da da da da da da da da da da* ..."

"I'm looking forward to seeing Quebec. Who's the great man there?"

"René Lévesque. Look him up. It's your chance to find out how it all began."

"How much farther do we have to go?"

"Ten miles, and that suits me fine. Let's find a hotel and get on our feet. I'm tired of this car, and these factories."

I returned to the notebook. "It's all about food. About this wonderful hot beef sandwich he had in a bus station."

"What's a hot beef sandwich?"

"A slice of grey meat between two slices of white bread with gravy over it. I remember my first hot beef sandwich well, eaten at a bus station somewhere in Manitoba at two o'clock in the morning."

"Did *he* like it?"

"He liked everything. Remember, in England the ration was still one egg a week. Shall I go on? He travelled on the bus with a man who illustrated Eaton's catalogues."

"What are they?"

"Mail-order catalogues. The catalogues people in rural areas order from, then put in the outhouse. A great source of rural humour. But Eaton's is gone now. When I came, every community big enough to have traffic lights had its Eaton's, but the chain went belly up a few years ago. Now the rural folk have computers like the rest of us, and they buy their stuff on the Web."

EIGHTEEN

IT WAS A RELIEF to find the world opening out under the wide skies of Cambridgeshire and ourselves driving towards an unbroken horizon. I made a note to recommend to visitors from the Canadian prairies to give themselves a rest stop in Cambridgeshire or Norfolk, just to be able to take a big breath again.

And after Oxford, the city of Cambridge was a treat: I gave it a check immediately. (I think I've decided to reduce the guide to an article in an airline magazine called "The Real England" — "real" is the in-word for this kind of thing — then I can say what I like for about three thousand words.)

I wanted to see Fred's room in college but he said that for the last two years he lived "out." He gave me a very sensible little walking tour of Cambridge: we started in Fulbrooke Road where he had boarded with an Anglo-Indian couple; she was English and he, Indian. Fred was very grateful to them, he said, but they had become a bit of a strain because she had adopted him, instructing him on clothes, diet, sleeping habits, personal cleanliness and every other area where she felt he had not been properly brought up. Her husband, a Sikh who came originally from the Kashmir, was a retired lecturer in history specializing in the British Empire, and enjoyed debating with Fred the questions that occurred in Fred's studies, especially the political questions, since the lecturer was extremely left-wing — but gently so, Fred said — and learned beyond his discipline. The couple was out when we called, which for Fred was a huge disappointment, since he wanted them to meet me, and a great relief. "We'd have spent the morning talking," Fred said.

From Fulbrooke Road, Fred took me along the route of his morning walk to his lectures, past this famous library and that chapel famous for its choir, across a lot of neatly cut grass and through several colleges. I didn't see a single "No Visitors" sign.

That was enough. I had seen that Cambridge was nice and worth even two checks. We ate dinner in what Fred said was the restaurant he and his mates made their parents take them to, a place called the Bar Ha Ha, and found rooms at the Arundel House Hotel, which was nice, too, and no more expensive than everything else in England. After dinner, Fred excused himself, claiming he wanted to look up a pal; I had been on to him for some time so I didn't press him. I went for a walk in the evening under a sky as serene as any in Manitoba; it was all just as Rupert Brooke said it was, except for the Japanese visitors clicking their cameras at every building.

The next morning Fred was nowhere about and I breakfasted alone. Fred returned to the hotel as I was finishing, and we went for a walk. We had a look at the Cam, much more puntable I thought than the Isis at Oxford, and set off to drive across the Fens for the place called Burnham Market where my mother's sometime taxi driver now lived. "All well in Cambridge?" I asked.

"Oh, yes, Uncle," Fred said. "All well in Cambridge."

"You still might come to Canada, though?"

"We might," Fred said. "Have we left Quebec?"

"Not quite. There are whole areas of the province I know nothing about. I've driven the south shore of the St. Lawrence River to Rivière-du-Loup, and I'd like to try the north shore and beyond, one day. That's where the old Quebec is more in evidence, I'm told. By the way, if you ever drive the south shore, you could clear up one mystery for me. In every village you will see kids, urchins, at the crossroads, selling quart bottles of liquid in Life Saver colours, yellow and red and green, and so on. Find out what it is, would you? I always meant to ask the next one we met but I always left it too late.

"No, we haven't left Quebec until we've seen Ottawa, the capital of Canada, technically in Ontario, but which, with its sister-city, Hull, straddles the Quebec-Ontario border, symbolic of the two nations, I suppose. Apart from its importance in the nineteenth century as a lumber town, there is no earthly reason why it should be the capital. It's a quiet little town — provincial is the word that comes to mind. Someone once said that Canada is the only country in the Western world whose capital is a village. Its economy is artificially sustained by the civil service, like that of Brussels, but they say the restaurants aren't as good as those in Brussels. I've visited the place several times because for an advertising agency with the right connections, a government department can be a very bankable client. But we never made it, possibly because we never bribed the right party at the right time."

"Bribed? Like in ..."

"Yes, like in made a contribution to party funds. It's a pretty town, with a nicely landscaped set of government buildings but I'm not into views myself. I'd sooner visit Birmingham than Edinburgh, just to mention two places I've never seen. Still, let's see if I can be fair. Yes, a couple of years ago I was in Ottawa with time on my hands — there's a lot of that in Ottawa — and I got into a conversation on a park bench with an American. He assumed I was a visitor and liking it, and he went into a paean — have I pronounced that right? — of praise for Ottawa. He said he brought his children up from Vermont for a visit every year to show them what a small city could be like — clean, safe, inexpensive, full of agreeable folk, none of whom were allowed to carry guns. He said there was nothing like that in the States any more.

"I didn't believe him; he was obviously a misanthrope but he gave me another view. I asked him if he knew that Ottawa was the second-coldest capital in the world, after Ulan Bator, and that in the winter the civil servants skate to work on the Rideau Canal just to keep warm, but he said he never visited it in winter. Then, without any warning, he got angry. He called me a Limey asshole — I'd told him I was a sometime immigrant — for whom Canada was too good. He said I should go back to England to kiss the asses of all those dukes and earls who owned the place. He grew more and more violent and stood up to hit me but two women came running across the grass and grabbed him and took him away, saying something about his having missed his medicine."

"Uncle, are you making this up?"

"I swear to you that is exactly how it happened. He was mad, of course, but that doesn't invalidate his view of Ottawa as a municipal Eden, in an American's eyes. Nor does it make sense of his hatred of England. It's not only the French who hate you."

Fred let it go. "Where next?" he asked.

I knew what he meant, not Burnham Market. "Ontario proper," I said. "The hinterland, which is what Ottawa is in the middle of. One road out of Ottawa takes you to the Algonquin Park."

"What's that?"

"It's a provincial park. A huge area set aside for the enjoyment of nature, but when it is habitable, i.e. in midsummer, it is also full of people. I went canoeing in it once. That is, an acquaintance of mine bought a canoe and persuaded me to go with him into the park for a weekend to test his canoe. I thought I should give Canadian nature a try. The park is only about three hours from Toronto, but it's a day's drive from Montreal, where he lived.

"The trouble started with the traffic. The backup began about three miles away from the park and steadily intensified all the way in, like the road to Bournemouth from London on a holiday weekend. Then, in the park, we launched the canoe and paddled about looking for a place to camp. There are portages. You know what a portage is? At one time the word meant a place where the Indians and voyageurs picked up their canoes because the rapids were unnavigable. Nature is still the same, but now there's a long lineup at each portage.

"All the regular camp-spots are taken by eleven o'clock in the morning, and if you do find a spot, there is no wood. I'm not exaggerating. There, in the middle of the wilderness, the wolves howling, there is not a scrap of burnable wood to be found, all gleaned back in June by the thousands of campers. Wise campers bring their own firewood, bought in a store in Huntsville, before they enter the park."

"Is there any wildlife?"

"I never saw any on that trip, but there must be. For wildlife, go to northern Alberta or Newfoundland. When I was in Farfell in northern Alberta for the honey festival, we went for a drive one night and counted four deer and several bears, all close to the highway. We never saw any other cars so I suppose they had become somewhat tame."

"Fish? In Algonquin Park?"

"You buy it in the store at the entrance to the park."

"Still, it must have been a change from the city."

"Oh, it was. There are no black flies or mosquitoes in the city. In Toronto, anyway. I can't speak for Winnipeg. In Algonquin Park, as soon as you feel the first mosquito, you pee, then zip yourself into your tent, and spray for insects. And you stay there until dawn, and the need to pee returns."

"Is this the whole Canadian outdoors you are talking about?"

"No, no. Just Algonquin Park. And only for most of the summer. We used to rent a cottage in August about two hundred miles north of Toronto. Up there, in August and September, it's quite habitable."

"What else does Ontario have to offer?"

"Niagara Falls."

"You visit Niagara Falls often?"

"Only when I have to show people like you. The rest of the time I leave it to the tourists, the Germans and the Japanese. I am just trying to give you an impression of what you'll find in Canada."

"Ontario, then. Algonquin Park at one end and Niagara Falls at the other. That it?"

"Not quite. You're forgetting Stratford, and Toronto, and the Mennonite villages."

"Start with those. The *what* villages?"

"Mennonite. The Mennonites, religious communities of sixteenth-century German origin, started settling in Canada, I think, in the eighteenth century, and more arrived in the nineteenth and even the twentieth, some seeking shelter from the US, where they had become unpopular because of their refusal to fight in the war. They do not believe in military service, and they live an agricultural life little changed since the sixteenth century. They won't use internal combustion engines, just horses and buggies. They are completely self-sufficient, I'm told, making their own clothes — that sort of thing. What they are is picturesque, driving their little buggies around the country lanes in their hand-woven garments. Once, on a Sunday, I came across a group of young men at play at a crossroads near Stratford. Two of them were dressed in bright blazers and wearing straw boaters — don't ask me how that consisted with their week-day costumes which are black and grey — but the most interesting thing was they had preserved a marvelous two-person bicycle; not a tandem, the two riders sat side by side on a frame above a single pair of wheels. The machine was painted bright yellow and the riders were having a hysterical time as were the whole group, all of whom were waiting for their turn on the bike. It was like coming across a road-show company of *Paint Your Wagon*, rehearsing a chorus scene. I wondered later if in fact that wasn't the truth of it, that they had unearthed the entire props and costume of a musical comedy that had been left behind by a stranded company."

"Are they a part of the local community?"

"They *are* the local community, but I know what you mean, and I don't know the answer. I haven't stopped long to look at the Mennonites or the Hutterites or the Amish or any of the other agrarian religious communities that dot the country, especially in the West. I'm waiting for the CBC to do a television feature on them."

"The CBC?"

"The national television and radio network."

"You watch it much?"

"Every time someone declares war. I trust it. They get a bit earnest sometimes, but the possibility of not having it to turn to when there is a major emergency and having to rely on the private networks is frightening."

"Tell me about Stratford."

"What is there to say? Someone had an idea to produce Shake-speare and suchlike in this town of the right name and it worked. Some years I've had the chance to compare the productions in England with those in Ontario, and over the years I'd say we've held our own."

"Who is 'we'?"

"Who what?"

"You said we've held our own. Who is we?"

"Got it. Touché, Fred. Yes, we Canadians. Okay? I've seen a terrific *King Lear* in Ontario, a great *Much Ado About Nothing*, and a lovely *A Midsummer Night's Dream*, as well as a lot of plays that sent me straight to sleep. Actually, I've had more fun at Niagara-on-the-Lake where they have the Shaw Festival. It makes up for what Oscar Wilde called the honeymooners' second biggest disap-pointment, The Falls."

"Toronto?"

"Ah. That can wait. We are now approaching Burnham Market and we are looking for what road?"

NINETEEN

"LISTEN, FRED. I'VE BEEN composing: 'First impressions of Burnham Market.'"

We had found the last parking space in Norfolk and Fred had gone to make one of his ever-more-frequent phone calls. I took the opportunity to catch up on the draft of my guidebook. Now he was back, content and ready to humour me.

"Twenty years ago," I read, "they proclaimed an ordinance: All males born and residing within the boundaries of Burnham Market shall be known as Tristram.

"You start hearing it in the parking lot as the mothers load their push-chairs: 'Sit still, Tristram, and I'll give you a piece of celery.' The name echoes hauntingly over the outskirts like that of Tadzio on the beach in Visconti's *Death in Venice*. Closer to the centre of the village, the sound deepens as it becomes the sound of young males seeking their companions, then, deepest of all, the sound of the adult male Tristrams, seeking mates.

"All these mothers and many of the young males drive Mercedes. There were plenty of SUVs and one or two Jeep-type runabouts, but mainly they drive Mercedes. We wanted to ask why, but none of the natives would let us approach close enough.

"A stream runs through the middle of the town called the Goose Beck, a stream that looks as if it is inhabited by a spirit who could swell it into a flood without any difficulty if anything irritated it, but now it was a silver thread unifying the picturesque little scene and leading the eye along."

"A bit poetic, Uncle?"

"Too fancy?"

"Yes."

"I like it, though. Let's go for a walk."

It was almost noon and there was a sound coming through the windows of one of the buildings, a sound I had heard before on the radio, a chorus of voices making a noise like "H'yah, h'yah." That time it turned out to be the Conservative Party in Westminster, applauding its leader. This was the same sound, but coming now from fledglings, as if we had come across a Conservative Party nest, full of the young, crying out with open beaks for beer and game pie.

"Lunch?" Fred said.

The place advertised itself as an inn and restaurant, though it had obviously been several other things in its day, before its current conversion. Today, it seemed no place to expect a quiet lunch, so we looked for a fish and chip shop, but apparently the invaders from Chelsea who had driven out the natives in my dream had also sacked the original eating houses. Because we could not expect to find another parking space within a couple of miles, we decided to continue to explore on foot. We had a bit of luck in finding a delicatessen called The Humble Pie, an excellent shop where we bought a couple of slices of veal-and-ham pie to eat as we walked along, and we decided to make that do for lunch. (In my experience, owners of brightly named food stores and restaurants have used up too much of the imagination they might have spent on the food on the name of the business. In Canada, the worst cafés are usually called The O'Kum Inn. The Humble Pie, though, was an exception.)

Now that the natives have been driven back to the marshes by the Kensington and Chelsea invaders, three classes of the new inhabitants can be distinguished. There are the "h'yah" strata, obviously at the top: mostly Tristrams, and now we heard their Camillas, too, and here and there a Henry, chirping. Two other groups were filtering through the town, both dressed alike and both bearing field glasses, but the members of one group were also carrying little books like missals. I found the space to chat up a native policeman, leaning against his car. I was pretending to ask directions, but actually seeking to identify these two groups. "They're birdwatchers," he said. "Them with the little books are new to it, though. The real birdwatchers don't need books because they know what they're looking at. If you want a proper sight of them, you should go to the Titchley Marsh."

So we did, and a very curious experience it was. A good path crosses the marsh to the sea, and then the sands stretch for miles, and together they create the best space for a long walk I have ever had, a world composed of sky, sea and sand, with a perfect horizon, uninterrupted by gates, stiles, hedges or cow shit, or by other people. There were birdwatchers, singly and in pairs, but they are not like people you meet on ordinary country walks. They never smile, these birdwatchers, or even make eye contact, but look continually into the distance. If I were making a science fiction movie and needed a shot of benevolent aliens moving silently and mysteriously about their business, I would bring a camera crew to Titchley Marsh.

And then we found the West Norfolk Radio, one of the finest hardware stores I've ever been in. I'm not a natural handyman, but I've had to learn because in Canada I've helped more than one friend build a summer cottage, and not knowing, when you are framing a wall, that the risers should be eighteen inches apart marks you as effete. Everybody in Canada seems born with the knowledge of how far you have to dig down to create the pit for an outhouse, and I have learned from them what an asset to a community is a well-stocked and knowledgeable hardware store. The West Norfolk Radio was a gem.

Now we got directions, and made our way along a muddy side road to Kestrel Alley. My mother's old taxi driver, Sid Hayes, was sitting in his front garden on a wooden kitchen chair, reading the racing section of the morning paper. We stopped at the gate and he put down his paper and opened his mouth but I got in first. "I'm Will Prentice, Vera Prentice's son, and this is my nephew, Fred."

"Simpson," Fred added.

Sid Hayes said, "Her son's in Canada."

"No, that's me. Yes, I do live there, but I'm here now."

He made no move to stand up and come forward and open the gate, just watched us as we waited for instructions. Then, "It's not locked," he said.

I opened the gate and we walked in, using as much time as possible to give him the opportunity to meet us halfway.

When I was nearly on him, he folded his paper up into eighths and put it on the chair as he stood up. "A cup of tea, then?"

I nodded and took a look at Fred, who nodded in turn.

"Let's go inside," Hayes said. Now he stepped forward, but only so that his face couldn't be seen from his neighbours' windows as he winked at us, wrinkled his nose, closed and opened wide his eyes, pulled his ear and raised his eyebrows, clear sign language that the neighbours would be interested if we stayed outside.

In the kitchen, he said. "So you're her son," and drank his tea with a giant slurp, watching me over the rim of his mug. "Yes, I can see the resemblance."

"Do I look like my father, too?"

"I don't know that I ever saw him to look at. Just a figure in the doorway, like. I was sorry to hear about your mum, Mr. Prentice. Always treated me right."

I took out the photographs. "Do you remember seeing either of these?" I asked. "The way my mother left them they seemed to be important to her."

He considered them carefully, then put them neatly, one on top of the other, and handed them back. "No," he said. "For a minute there her face looked familiar but I think it's just that lady-of-the-manor look I expect she was born with. You know, class. Either you've got it or you haven't. She's got it. So what can I tell you?"

I said, "I'm trying to put together the story of my mother's life. I'm spending a few days talking to the people who knew her. Did she ever talk to you about herself?"

"Not much. Just, 'I prefer kippers to bloaters,' that sort of thing."

"Her neighbour says you took her to the station about once a fortnight."

He laughed. "She would know. I missed once, early in May, year before last. Did the neighbour make a note of that?" He laughed again. "Nosy old biddy. Yeah, that's about it. Took her to the station every Friday to catch the train to Oxford, then picked her up Sunday evening."

"Oxford? You sure?"

"That was where she changed trains."

"For where?"

"Moreton-in-Marsh."

"You sure?"

"I was with her at the window once or twice, when she bought her ticket. Carried her bag, or her umbrella, when she didn't have much time and might have had to make a run for it."

"And she never said anything about who she was visiting?"

"I assumed a relative, but it was none of my business. I always found it best not to know anything personal about a regular pickup, otherwise you're on the hook for remembering and asking after them. You know, 'How's your sister's lumbago, Mrs. Prentice? Sorry, I meant your aunt's sciatica.'"

We sat there for a while longer, unspeaking, until I made getting-up motions. We had spent a lot of time in the hardware store as I flaunted my familiarity with the stock to Fred's admiration, and it was getting towards time for an early dinner. I said, not hoping for much from Sid Hayes, "Can you recommend a restaurant for dinner, and a place to stay, Mr. Hayes?"

"'Course I can't. I never go to those places, but hang on." A Mercedes was pulling up outside the house next door. Sid went out to meet the driver, a woman. We followed him out.

"Mrs. Paling," he said. "These gentlemen are from Canada. They're looking for a place to eat their dinner and a room for the night. Can you help them?"

"Fishes," she said. "Fishes. The best dinner in town. Don't bother comparing. And people say stay at Le Strange Arms in Old Hunstanton. I expect it's all right. See you later, Sid." She disappeared behind her front door.

"You can trust her," Sid said. "Though she's not a local. She's from London, Epsom, I think, but she don't put on airs."

In the car, I said, "We're getting somewhere. Where's Moreton-in-Marsh?"

"Up near Wales, I think."

"On the other side of the country, then. We won't go back the way we came. I have a call to make in London, and then we can head up. I'm assuming, of course, that you want to come?"

"I'm enjoying this. But how long will you be in London?"

"Better say overnight. How about spending a day along the coast here first? I've never seen it. Have you? I think it might be interesting and something to put in my guide. I don't think I've ever seen Great Yarmouth recommended to tourists, have you? It's where David Copperfield was born. I might try giving my guide a more literary flavour."

"Uncle, it seems to me the focus of this guide is getting a bit ..."

"Fuzzy? That's all right. We'll cobble it together at the end and find the theme then. A lot of books are written like that."

So we ate dinner at Fishes, a good dinner and only twice as

expensive as Toronto's finest and thus in line with all our other eating experiences in England.

Over dinner, Fred said, "Always treated me right."

"What?"

"I was quoting. You know, Uncle, we've heard nothing but good things about your mother except from you. First her boarders obviously liked her; she was very good to Great-Aunt Phyllis; and now the taxi driver attests to her generosity."

"Yes?"

"None of my business, but interesting.

"She cut her own family off."

"You could see that as a gesture of survival."

"And me. She cut me off, too."

"She provided for you. Didn't she?"

"She kept me at a distance."

"Or did you keep your distance from her? Adolescence is a time when people go their own way. Some people secretly carry on the childhood thing of thinking they must have been swapped in the cradle, that their real parents are cleverer, handsomer and richer than the ones they seem to have."

"Fred, is Daisy majoring in psychology, or social work?"

Fred smiled. "Nearly right, Uncle. It is something we've talked about, she and I. She's fascinated by the phenomenon.

"I think it's simpler than that. My mother was the provider, and she was usually too busy to be the nurturer, to make much of a nest for me. That's all. Nowadays, most women are mothering in this way. But you're right, I'll have to be careful not to be too hard on her. And I'll watch that your family isn't, either. I had another idea to tell you about, though. A long time ago, I thought I'd like to try writing a novel."

"Really? What about?"

"I didn't actually get to that point. Thackeray wrote a novel without a hero. I thought I'd try writing one without having a subject. I started by doing the research. I read all the books in the

Toronto Public Library on 'How to Write a Novel.' I was very struck by Forster's book, especially the bit about flat and rounded characters. Do you know the book?"

"No."

"You've *heard* of Forster? I know you didn't do English."

"I've heard of Forster. I read *Room with a View*. I thought the movie was better."

"Read *Aspects of the Novel* and we can talk some more. For the moment, he's the one who invented 'flat' and 'round' characters. Flat characters don't change in the course of the story but round characters are full of surprises. My mother was a round character."

"And your father?"

"He was the nurturer. I think I was a mistake, to tell you the truth. Why don't I have any siblings? Because children would have interfered with her game plan."

"Which was?"

"To have a life that went beyond her parents'. A pretty common ambition, then, I think. Maybe she had me to give Dad something to do. He raised me until I stopped listening to him."

"When was that?"

"When I was about fifteen. Mark Twain was wrong about that."

We found rooms at Le Strange Arms and the next day made our way to Great Yarmouth.

We started with a walk along the Norfolk coast path, which was smashing. The tide was out and the sands were wide and the sea quiet (unlike the sea in *David Copperfield*), and it looked like a birdwatcher's paradise; altogether, it was one of those times when you can almost see the attraction of someone else's passion.

We stopped at Sheringham on our way to Great Yarmouth because I wanted to visit the Norfolk Shire Horse Centre: of all creatures known to me, the shire horse is the most beautiful. But it was Saturday and the centre was closed.

We drove on to Great Yarmouth and on to the Broads. Luckily for us, a storm blew up as we approached the town, so we were able to go down towards the beach and imagine we were waiting for news of Ham.

The Broads looked the way Graham Swift said they looked in *Waterland*, and we made our way back to Le Strange Arms because we were tired after too much walking and driving, having again underestimated the time it takes to get from one place to another in England, once you leave the M-series roads. The journey from Oxford to Cambridge should have taught us.

At dinner I brought out the atlas and started to plot the route from London to Moreton-in-Marsh. Fred listened and said, "Do you have time for a diversion, Uncle?"

I had begun to appreciate what an extraordinarily cheerful and accommodating companion Fred was being, almost as if I was paying him, so I was inclined to agree to anything. "Where to?"

"Durham"

"As in County Durham?"

"Yes."

"Okay. Why?"

"My great-grandfather fought in France in the First World War, so did his brother. I have my great-grandfather's cap badge at home and I know the names of some of the places he fought in, but no one ever talks about his brother except to say he was missing, believed killed. Or they didn't when I was growing up."

"Why Durham?"

"They were in the Durham Light Infantry, and that's another thing I'd like to know. How did a labourer in a brickyard in Camberwell find himself in the Durham Light Infantry?"

"I can tell you that. I learned it in history. How old was your great-grandfather?"

"Probably close to thirty. They had four children when he was conscripted."

"He wasn't in the first wave, then. The first wave was recruited by county and town, so that after a big battle the entire young male population of an area was wiped out. Very bad for civilian morale. After that, they drafted them into different regiments so the slaughter was spread out a bit. Okay, then. I've got the time but I'd like to see to some things in London first. Take me about a day. Then we'll do a lightning tour, York, Durham, maybe Harrogate, Leeds, a quick dash across the country to look at the Lakes, then down to the Cotswolds. A week extra, okay? It might be useful for my guide. Have you ever seen an article in the travel section of the weekend paper headed 'Come to Lovely Durham'? Maybe I'll do a chapter, 'Off the Beaten Track — And Why.'"

The next morning we left early to get to London for lunch. I still didn't want to drive, especially in London, so Fred dropped me at the hotel in Covent Garden and took the car home for the night. We agreed to rendezvous at noon the next day, and head out to the West Country after lunch.

My hotel in Covent Garden was nice, and I was pleased with Grisham for putting me in it but I thought it was time to look for the kind of hotel I would have chosen if I had been paying, something to put in my guidebook.

I hadn't faced this problem in England for a long time; even when I had stayed somewhere other than Lyme Regis, it had not been London. Mostly I had visited my parents alone, because my wife wouldn't come after the first time, and I had never had the urge to become a temporary bachelor. In other words, I knew nothing about being a tourist in London, and it was time to find out. So I left my bag with the hotel porter and went out to find myself a more suitable hotel.

I had a bit of luck when I called in to a bookshop and asked them to recommend a hotel guide for such as me. The woman who served me said she knew *exactly* what I wanted, and sold me *A Select Guide to Select Hotels and Guesthouses in England and Scotland*. She said, "It's a *jokey* title, and that's rather a good sign, don't you think?"

Together we looked up London and found a hotel in Half Moon Street, a street, she said, that was right opposite the Ritz. The price for a single was a hundred and twenty-five pounds which, she said, was not bad. She even called the hotel, established they had a single room left, and reserved it for me. I collected my bag and took a taxi to Half Moon Street.

I was curious: I don't have Grisham's experience; in Canada and North America the hotels I've used just have rooms, booked for the same price no matter if one, two or even three are going to use them. But in England they treat rooms like cabins on a ship priced at so much a square foot and you have to pay a premium if you want one to yourself. Some hotels have genuine single rooms, mostly those hotels that have been renovated or rejigged from an old house or several old houses in a row. An odd-shaped space the size of a closet will occur during the renovation and the new landlord will say, "That's a single." My room in the hotel in Half Moon Street was one of these.

The hotel seemed promising enough, smelling of furniture polish and cleaning agents and Brasso; the youth who signed me in was obsequious, and a porter waited to carry my bag.

Breakfast was included, and the porter said, "Let reception know when you're ready and I'll bring it up in the morning. What newspaper would you like, sir?"

I told him, paid him off and unlocked the door, and I saw what a single room meant. The door would not open fully into the room because it came up against the single bed that took up all but two feet of the width of the room. I pushed my bag in ahead of me and got inside. At the end of the room, at the foot of the bed, a row of hooks held some clothes hangers. Beside the hooks a tiny window gave on to a view of the street. As I approached the window to look out, the head of a window-cleaner swam up and winked at me.

I lifted the bag on to the bed to unpack what I needed, but when I stood facing the open bag, I was too close to the wall behind me, so I sat on the bed beside the bag and unpacked as far as I had to.

There were three shelves in the room, all hinged flaps of lacquered plywood that could be raised and locked in place. The two shelves by the bed blocked off the passage to the end of the room when they were raised, so I left them down for the moment and raised the third shelf, which was under the window. I put my toilet bag on this shelf and decided that was where my wallet and glasses would go when I undressed. There was a telephone in a little hole in the wall and a sink about three inches deep from back to front with two tiny taps, one hot and one cold, in the bottom corner of the room, under the clothes hooks. A piece of soap the size of a throat pastille, wrapped like a gift, sat on a ledge beside the sink. Above the sink was a notice, "Your Private Bath is across the hall. Only your key will open it."

I sat on the bed cross-legged in a way I hadn't for twenty years, poured myself a glass of whiskey, and took stock of my chamber. I could see now that the flaps provided a writing desk and a break-fast table. There was no chair: the bed served as a banquette, and presumably you could adjust your height for writing or eating by sitting on a pillow. At the end of the room high up on the wall beside the bed there was a television set in a cradle, to be swung out when needed. To watch it, you had to be in bed, or resting, at least. Absolutely everything had been thought of, then shoehorned in as if by the interior designer of a space shuttle.

I got ready to go out to eat, but before I left I checked the private bathroom, guessing it would be a porcelain cylinder I would have to lower myself into from the top, but it turned out to be a bathroom left over from a previous age, one they had not been able to convert. A giant tub about twelve feet long with a little step-ladder at one end did not even crowd the room, and to cope with those singles who had spent the day mud wrestling, there were four huge thick towels and half a dozen small ones, a bar of soap weighing about two pounds, a bottle of cologne, a jar of bath salts and a loofah. At the end of the room, a toilet like a throne invited your thoughts while you waited for the bathtub to fill.

TWENTY

IT WAS MID-AFTERNOON and I phoned my aunt to let her know what I was up to and to remind her I was going to take her to Manzi's.

She said, "I'm glad you called, Will. I've come across a lot of photographs of your parents on what looks like their wedding day. They're all the same. I've never seen them before, but there are twelve of them, all the same. I found them when I was sorting out her things ready for the rummage sale, like you asked me."

"Why would she have had so many done?"

"I wondered that myself. If you count them, there's a full dozen, and if you look on the back you'll see there's no date. There's usually a date, isn't there? I think she planned to send them out as announcements but, well, something interrupted her."

"As announcements?"

"P'raps she planned to use them as Christmas cards and forgot she had them." She giggled. "She wanted to let the world know but not too much and not too soon. Something like that."

I couldn't make any sense of this, but yet it sounded like my mother.

"You were with her off and on after I was born, weren't you?"

"Off and on, yes."

"You spent a lot of time in Coombe Regis. As far as you remember, did it do well, as a guesthouse?"

"She was full up all the time. Never had to take anyone in off the street, never put a sign up. And she charged top rent because ... because, well, I told you the travellers understood they were free to bring their wives for the weekend and no one would ask to see their marriage lines. You're not judging her, are you?"

"It's not that. Again, once more, where are all the bills and the books? You can't run a business for forty years without books."

"She did. Everything was cash with her. She didn't write cheques and she didn't accept any."

"Why?"

"The authorities. If the authorities came round and asked me questions, she taught me to say that we very rarely had guests, just the occasional one who used to come in the days when Aunt Em ran a guesthouse, who didn't know that Aunt Em was gone. Sometimes a guest would come back for nostalgic reasons but they were friends by that time; your mum never charged them. That's what she taught me to say."

"But Aunt Em had run it as a proper business?"

"Oh, yes. Proper books, reservations. All that. We had a look at the books after Aunt Em died, before we burned them."

Jesus. "What did the authorities say to that? Burning them."

"They said it was wrong but your mum acted daft, said how was she to know, and in the end I think they settled."

"Where did Mum keep track of reservations and so on?"

"In her head."

"Did you ever see her with another bank book? Apart from the one we found."

"Never. If she had one she kept it under the floorboards. I think I can hear what you're getting at. You think there's a lot of money missing."

"What do you think?"

"Forty years of paying customers adds up. But I've seen no sign of it."

I took it from this that she had thoroughly searched Mum's possessions without finding anything more than the solicitor had accounted for. It was hard to estimate. In the beginning, I guessed, a slightly upmarket guesthouse would not have charged more than a pound (probably a guinea), though I couldn't be sure even of that. I remember Dad's reminiscences included stories of getting a bed and breakfast in Brighton for half a crown, but that must have been a long time before. Again, from looking through today's brochures of associations of superior guesthouses, I guessed that Mum was probably charging forty or fifty pounds at the end. It was impossible to estimate, but if one room, say, would fetch in four thousand pounds a year, then there must be a hoard somewhere. Surely.

Phyllis had told me all she knew. I had just one more question, the real one. "Who did Mum know in Moreton-in-Marsh?"

"Ah, found out, have you? How did you manage that?"

"It wasn't hard. I started with the woman who lived next door to you in Lyme Regis."

"How would she know? Your mum was never pally with her. For that matter, your mum was never pally with anyone outside the house."

"So everyone says. Her neighbour told us about the taxi that took her off about every two weeks, and after that it was easy."

"Us? Who's 'us?'"

"Your nephew Fred is driving me around."

"Does he know about this money you think is missing?"

I could hear what Phyllis was thinking and moved to cut her off. "Of course not."

Before I could add anything, she said, "By the way, the solicitor phoned, wants you to call him."

"Something I have to sign, probably. Did Mum ever tell you where she went?"

"Like you said, Moreton-in-Marsh. She had to tell me, of course. Couldn't just do a flit every couple of weeks without letting me in on some of it, could she? When I asked her she said she had a boyfriend there."

"Did she? Really?"

"I didn't believe a word of it. She'd left all that caper behind, I reckon. But your mum was one of those automatic liars: they get into the habit from being slightly outside the law from the beginning. Our mum, your grandma, was the same. 'Never tell strangers your business' translates into 'Always find out why they want to know before you tell them anything.' Where your grandma came from, as a kid she knew that when there are two blokes in raincoats at the front door asking for your brother, you start lying right away because those two blokes are looking for the gang of kids who knocked over the newsagent last night. So, if your mum said she had a boyfriend in Moreton-in-Marsh, chances were she was covering up for something else. Besides, there was Henry, your father. He knew, or perhaps he thought he knew, and never mind that he played second fiddle to your mum in running the guesthouse, he was too much of a man to put up with nonsense like that. So she must have told him something different but he never talked about it. 'Visiting friends' was his answer if anyone asked where she was. So there it was. A mystery."

"Any guesses?"

"I don't remember her travelling up there from Bournemouth, though by the time I started wondering, I had to think back too far, and I could have missed the signs. But she never let on to me. Even lately, here in Clapham, if Moreton cropped up on the news, say, like when they had that trouble with the gypsy horse fair at Stow, she'd look at the calendar to see if she planned a visit there soon. But no, dear, I don't know any more than I know where the money went."

"Why didn't you tell me about Moreton-in-Marsh?"

"I didn't know you'd be interested, dear."

It was more likely, I thought, that she was continuing instinctively to guard my mother's secrets, even beyond the grave.

I reminded her of our date at Manzi's and hung up.

I ambled around London for the rest of the day, ending up back in Covent Garden, wondering what to do about eating. I wasn't hungry, and a glass of bitter and a ham sandwich in a pub did me perfectly. Sandwiches are the best bargains in food in England. The English put great store on formal eating, even at the lowest level. A so-called salad plate consisting of a slice of ham, a bit of lettuce and a tomato will cost four times as much as the same amount of ham and lettuce in a sandwich. The key to the difference lies in the word "proper." When an Englishman or woman talks about a "proper" lunch or dinner, or anything else — they apply the word to every activity, like a walk, or a holiday, for example — they mean a traditional one, one with a plate and a napkin and a knife and fork with a cruet and a glass of water, the kind they grew up with and are used to. Thus you can hear an English couple in a restaurant in Paris on a Sunday, after a lunch of an omelette, tarte Tatin and a piece of St. Andre, pronounce it "quite nice but not a proper Sunday lunch," meaning of course, that it contains no roasted meat. So no sandwich can ever be a proper meal, and thus is usually bargain-priced. The idea of a lunchtime menu with soup and sandwiches on one side, and pasta and other dishes on the other and not much difference in price between the two sides baffles the English. In England, the right-hand side of the menu is always twice the price of the sandwich side.

It took me three-quarters of an hour to shuffle back to Half Moon Street and my bed. It was still only nine o'clock but I didn't want to drink or go to a movie, so I turned on the television and lay on the bed to watch a group of people turn a garbage dump into a garden, complete with rockery and fountain, all in thirty minutes. Actually they made it clear for the sake of folks in retirement homes who might get confused that it took the whole weekend and they had speeded up the film, but it was still impressive. At the end, I switched to another channel and this time the gardeners were all women and the problem was to make the garden accessible to someone in a wheelchair who was allergic to bees. It took them three days. The next program tackled the problem of inserting a patch of herbs into a flower garden in a decorative way. And so on. In England, someone somewhere is making a television program about gardens, to be shown in prime time on Saturday night, back to back with a program about house renovations. The other alternative is snooker. It's all very soothing, and I had had a longish day, so I watched one more program about a group of nuns recreating a Jacobean garden and went to sleep.

TWENTY-ONE

I WOKE AT SEVEN, called the desk for breakfast, put on my raincoat and crossed the hall for a bath. I poured too much of the complimentary bath oil into the giant tub, so I slipped about a lot; once I went right over on my side and wondered briefly if I was trapped like a mouse in an enamel bucket before I remembered that I could always pull the plug, and I went on to enjoy myself.

Breakfast was waiting for me outside my door, freshly squeezed orange juice, coffee, and a rack of toast, nicely chilled. I ate it searching the paper for a Canadian item but the news was totally parochial, so I switched on the television to catch the weather.

The next bit was the trickiest but I finally figured out how to pull on my pants without impaling myself on the bed post. I shaved in the quarter-pint of water that the sink held, and brushed my teeth with my chin almost in the basin to avoid splashing the room. The illusion of being on board a ship was very strong; I kept expecting the water to slop out on to my feet the next time the ship rolled. The mirror was too low, and I goosed myself again as I crouched down to put straight edges on my sideburns. I packed my bag, pushed it out the door ahead of me, and checked out, leaving the bag at the desk to be picked up later.

I had a call to make on the solicitor. A couple of questions had formed, and before Fred and I went on to the next town, I wanted to find out if the solicitor knew any answers. I found a bus at Victoria station that had Clapham as one of its destinations, and figuring that a bus was more appropriate for a sightseer than the Underground, and that I might get an item for my guidebook, I climbed hopefully to the upper story. We lumbered across London for what seemed like an hour but I learned only that there is very little to see from the top deck of a bus grinding through Kennington and Stockwell that is worth climbing the stairs for. Certainly not worth a check.

I had called the solicitor before I left Victoria and he was waiting for me. First I showed him the photographs. He considered them carefully and handed them back. "No bells struck, I'm afraid," he said.

Now I asked him if he knew of any connection between my mother and Moreton-in-Marsh. None at all, he said. Finally I asked him if he could ascertain exactly when my parents got married.

"Do you suspect they — er — weren't married?"

"No, I don't. It says they were on my birth certificate, and it would have been a criminal offense to tamper with that, surely. I suspect they weren't married for long enough before I was born, though, else why did they move to Coombe Regis?"

"Does it matter?"

"Not much. Just interesting. No big deal, of course. Not even if the other possibility is true."

"Which is?"

"That Henry Prentice wasn't my father. Oh, don't think I'm concerned. As I say, it wouldn't be a big deal, and it would add a bit more to what I know about my mother. It all gives me an excuse to ride around the country with my nephew, as I make up my mind what to do with myself. Did I tell you my wife has left me, and I'm probably going to quit my job? And I'm thinking of coming back to England to live? Well, no. I'm having a look just in case, when I get back to Canada, I want to include England in my plans."

"How far have you got? With your thinking."

"Here's a sign," I said. "I caught myself several times on this trip generalising about the English as if I was a foreigner. You know, 'The English always something or other ...'"

"Well, you are Canadian. You still sound English but you've lived there for thirty years."

"I don't know what I am."

Fred and I had parted at Victoria Station and agreed to meet up there for lunch, choosing a large pub nearby that was advertising all kinds of good old-fashioned "fayre." Fred was waiting for me inside. As I sat down, the waitress brought his order.

"What is it?" I asked.

"Sausage and mash with extra gravy and peas," the waitress said. She had a strong French accent.

We looked at it together, all three of us. A large shallow plate had perhaps a quarter inch of clarified grease covering the bottom. Resting in this were two bright grey cylinders. Fred poked a hole in one with his fork and a stream of hot fat shot up and out, reminding me of an article I'd read in *The New Yorker* about the arc of ejaculation. This sausage had a very strong arc.

"What's that?" I asked, pointing to the scoop of dark orange matter.

"Ze mash," the waitress said. "Dat is ze mash."

"It's got ice crystals in it." I said. "Did they forget to microwave it?"

"Shall I taste it?" Fred took a tiny piece on the end of his fork. "It doesn't have any taste," he said.

The waitress decided it was time for her to leave.

"Try the peas," I said. That is all they could have been, another ice-cream scoop of brilliant green matter, like a ball of pus.

"I don't think I will," Fred said. He lowered his face almost to the plate. "No heat comes off them," he reported.

The waitress reappeared. "Ready to order?" she asked me.

"Another minute," I said. She went away.

"What are we going to do, Uncle?"

"I'll tell you. You go past the bar to the door marked Gents. Go in, count fifty, then go out the other door of the Gents that leads into the outer bar, and carry on into the street. Then walk to the car as rapidly as you can without running. Where's the car?"

He pointed out the window. "Down that street, then two streets along on the left. I found a space with a meter outside a bookmaker."

"I'll meet you there."

"What are you going to do? The same thing?"

"I'm going to make a phone call. The phone is beside the outside door of the second bar. I'll ask the barman to point me to it so that he'll know where I'm going and won't watch me. Ready? Off you go."

Fred stood up and looked around like a man needing a washroom, saw the sign and disappeared behind it. I waited for him to come out the other door and head for the street, and I strolled over to the barman with my request. He directed me to the telephone, and I walked over and fiddled about with coins until he returned to his newspaper. I waved through the window to someone outside, replaced the receiver and ran out to catch the imaginary friend. No one shouted from the pub, and I set off for Fred and freedom.

He was waiting for me already with the engine running, and we drove to Half Moon Street where I collected my bag from the hotel, then Fred started to pick his way north.

He said, "Have you ever done that before, Uncle?"

"What?"

"What we just did, done a bunk, leave without paying."

"Stiff someone? Once. In North Carolina. See, Toronto is a bit of a village ..."

"Like Ottawa?"

"No, not like Ottawa. A very sophisticated village. I mean that in any downtown restaurant I am liable to know someone, so I wouldn't risk a fuss."

"Why didn't we just complain?"

"First of all the waitress was French, and totally unsurprised by what she was serving. She was a student probably, new to the country and for her, this was English food. So it might have taken a long time to tell her what was wrong. Then, before we knew it, she might have whisked it all away, put it in the microwave and brought it back, hot. Then what would we have said? 'It's not just that it was cold; it's disgusting in every way.' Something like that? Did you see the barman? He was Irish. What we used to call a navvy. He might have had something to say if he thought the waitress was getting a hard time. Then again, they might have offered us anything else on the menu. Did you want anything else from their kitchen? For all I could see it was run by a student, too, perhaps from Galicia, and iced peas might be a delicacy where he came from, to say nothing of goat sausages. We'd have been there for an hour, explaining. Besides ..."

"Besides what?"

"I've never done a bunk here before."

We made our way across London, coming eventually to signs pointing to the MI, and then, after a long and stressful time, to the MI itself. After that it was easy, and two and a half hours later we were in Leeds.

London is a nightmare if you are fool enough to be a non-native in charge of a car. I, at least, had some background in the place — I knew, for instance that from where we were I shouldn't cross any bridges if I wanted to go north, and that Ealing, a frequent sign post, was west and Stratford was east. And then I saw a sign marking the beginning of the MI trail, but it wasn't easy. Compared to this, driving in New York City is child's play: you just turn north on Broadway and you are on the road to Canada. But we emerged successful, or rather, Fred did. I simply watched for the signs of the MI, and stopped a policeman occasionally to ask the way.

Behind our cabin in northern Ontario there is a trail blazed by deer hunters. Every fifty yards or so there is a bit of cloth tied to the branch of a tree to mark the trail. Early in the season the path underfoot is not evident to the urban eye, and if you miss one of the markers you need a compass to settle the arguments among your companions, especially if one of your guests is an American, panicking at finding himself swallowed up by the Canadian bush.

London is like that. But Fred was a good driver; he ignored his better judgement several times, letting me direct us, waiting patiently while I asked a policeman.

We found a place to park in the market square, and went to look for something to eat. The pity was it was pouring with rain, and though Leeds looked interesting, even in the rain, with some wonderful nineteenth-century glass and iron arcades, altogether a city to walk about in, we were getting wet, so we found a place to eat a sandwich in and pushed on, promising ourselves that we would return some day, maybe on the way back. The rain was coming down so hard that we also skipped York and headed straight for Durham, and there we were blessed with the return of the sun on a city that deserved it.

Durham doesn't feature much in the travel section of *The Globe and Mail*, so I had no preconceptions about it. Fred was as ignorant as I was. "It's a coal-mining town," he said. "That's all I know. But I think it must have a good university because a man I knew at Cambridge chose it as his first choice and couldn't get in. He's interested in Anglo-Saxon, Old Norse, things like that, and he said he felt that Durham would have the right atmosphere."

We found rooms almost immediately in a pub near the centre of the city. The first impression of the rooms was that they were normally used by the pub-owner's nephews, layabouts sleeping four to a bed, but the place had three AA stars and for all we knew these were the last vacant beds in town, so we took them. It turned out to be a good billet. Everything worked, the beds were clean and comfortable, the breakfast was as good as bacon and eggs get (producing a plate of perfectly cooked bacon and eggs is a much better test of a cook's natural ability than knowing how to serve poached duck breasts with a raspberry reduction on top), the television in both rooms worked, and there were small fridges and microwave ovens, and bags sufficient for making a hundred cups of that brick-coloured tea they like up north, all spread about on shelves and (the fridge) in a cupboard. The towels were a bit thin, but otherwise it was faultless, unless you expected flowers in your room for thirty-five pounds a night.

I remarked to Fred, as we walked into the city, how the place was so much better than it looked at first. He said, "We're oop north now. We don't fart-arse about, sticking folderols on owt like you southern folk," enjoying himself creating a poor imitation of northern speech. In his normal voice, he added that a man he knew from Lancashire had let him in on the northern view of southerners. If you wanted to make money, go south, the man had said. They're all softies down there. They don't like to get their hands dirty, and where there's muck, there's money.

We crossed over the River Wear into a shopping area, and from there into the market square, dominated by a large pointless statue of a man on a horse, erected by his descendants. And then, over the top of the buildings lining the street we saw the cathedral, and decided to do that first, and walked through the cobblestoned streets to the cathedral close. Everything in Durham is cobblestoned. The streets look as though they were paved a thousand years ago and will last for ever. I hope so, for already I liked this city very much. It seemed to have evolved without the endless building and rebuilding and organ-transplanting that other cities have suffered. The young may have trouble finding work in Durham but the old must take comfort from a world that looks the same as it did when they were growing up. I was enchanted with the place.

The cathedral continued the spell the city was laying on us. Growing up on the south coast, I'd gone on the usual school outings to Winchester and Salisbury cathedrals, and I believe once we were taken to Wells cathedral — I have a distinct memory of the Cheddar caves nearby. All of these had been interesting in a school-outing sort of way. But Durham cathedral was more than interesting, though it was that: it was *impressive*. It was a northern cathedral, massive, grey, rained-on. The accents of many of those helping to show you round the cathedrals in Winchester and Salisbury are 'county' — rounded, smooth, unglottalised — but the beadsmen of Durham cathedral are one generation away from the miners, and they are still incomprehensible to southerners and foreigners. Anyone with half an ear can put together a sentence of Yorkshire speech that would sound all right to an outsider ("Istha' coomin' down t'road, lad"), but I worked with one of the Durham beadsmen for ten minutes without getting enough sounds transcribed into my notes to make any sense. It's a soft (but firm) accent, like the Geordie accent of Newcastle (but not to the natives). When I was comfortable with my beadsman (not everyone is pleased to be asked, by foreigners, "Why do you speak funny?"), I gently raised the question of his accent, and he told me then about his father, who spoke the miner's dialect. He warned me I would have trouble understanding his imitation of his dad — I was having enough trouble understanding *him* — and then let me have a couple of the sentences his father might have spoken to his mates. It sounded just like Anglo-Saxon, if you didn't know Anglo-Saxon, an agreeable rhythmic but totally private language. "That," the beadsman said, "is ..." and then he told me the name of the dialect but after several requests to repeat the word I still couldn't understand it, and we were then in a tangle of misunderstandings so I let it go.

Meanwhile Fred, the historian, was being equally delighted with the discovery that here lay the tomb of the Venerable Bede, whom

I'd heard of, but Fred knew all about. Then we looked at Saint Cuthbert's tomb and began to absorb some idea of the power of the belief of those early Christians that enabled them to survive the assaults of the Danes and the other savages from across the North Sea. Fred said, "Hell was up north for everybody, then."

At six o'clock, they chucked us out because they wanted to worship, but we'd had our fill. If you are lucky enough to have one real experience of what it must have been like back then, you should quit while you're ahead. Fred still had to find out about his great-great-uncle, and I wanted to walk around the town for a bit, but we were hungry, so we allocated the following morning for a further look round Durham and drank a pint of bitter and ate some sausages in the Market Tavern, surrounded by German students (how did they hear about Durham?) and went back to our digs to watch some *Dalziel and Pascoe*.

The next morning we walked in to town, where we separated for no better reason than that two people, travelling together, occasionally need to separate.

I spent some time in the covered market, which was better than most, though I like all markets. I drank some coffee and walked round to the library, where I inquired if any of the librarians were brought up in Durham, still hoping to find out what the miner's dialect was called, and was introduced to Sheila Forster, the in-house expert who was making a study of the speech of Durham County, exactly the person I was looking for. She said, "The word he was trying to give you is 'Pitmatic,' the dialect the miners used that originated down the mine," and gave me a sentence that her father used to send her to bed with, when she was a child: "You're ower the kaps," which meant that she was tired past the point of no return. To help me understand, she drew a diagram of a miner's cage at the bottom of a pitshaft, past the "kaps" or "keeps," the name for the device on the bottom of the rail that kept the cage from descending further (I think), and that gave me a general idea, which is all I could manage, even from Sheila, as she led me through a translation. She added that in her father's day every village in Durham county had a slightly different dialect so that, though to an outsider they all sounded alike, they could tell when people were from another village.

And then as a bonus, she told me that a supporter of Sunderland Football Club is known as a "Mekam," and the term is sometimes more widely used to distinguish the local people from "Geordies," the natives of Newcastle. I felt full of information.

Fred and I met back at the pub and then drove to the Durham Light Infantry headquarters to begin Fred's quest for his great-great-uncle's story. The regiment has now been disbanded and the old records are kept in the county records office so I let Fred continue on his own while I talked to the attendant in charge of the museum. Pinned to the wall, for sale, was a green sweatshirt with the DLI regiment's emblem. Fred hadn't noticed it so I thought it would be nice to buy him one as a memento of the trip. But they only had the one sweatshirt and it was size "Small." The attendant looked sheepishly through a few drawers but that was the only one, so I let it go. Every other museum or place of historical interest I've ever visited has a shop full of overpriced souvenirs, but Durham just has one small sweatshirt, and, on the counter, some packs of playing cards commemorating the 1914–1918 war. That was it. It was just right. I bought a pack of cards and went to look for Fred, eager to leave Durham before I found something wrong.

Fred met me at the car, looking bemused. "So," I said. "What happened to Great-Great-Uncle Jack?"

"I don't know," he said. "They don't know. They've never heard of him. There's no record of a Jack Ludlow."

TWENTY-TWO

THERE WAS A LONG silence while Fred picked his way through the Durham suburb and on to the A181. We had agreed that having scuttled north in the rain we should at least drive across the North Yorkshire moors, which we did, and they are worth any amount of trouble. The sun was shining and all things were so bright and beautiful that I kept expecting to bump into Siegfried himself; James, anyway. We may have passed one of them on our way to Hulton Rudby. We had been recommended by one of the beadsmen to have lunch at The Bay Horse Inn in the village, which we did, a roast pork with apple stuffing sandwich for me and smoked salmon for Fred, for a total bill, including a half of Guinness for me and a cup of coffee for Fred, of thirteen pounds. Even translated into dollars it didn't seem bad, because the sandwiches were big and came with a lot of salad, but by now I had done the trick of judging prices as if they were in dollars, so thirteen dollars for that lunch was dirt cheap.

I said, "I can understand someone getting homesick for this, and for Durham."

Fred said, "Did you ever get homesick?"

"Sometimes on Sunday nights at first I missed the sea a bit. Otherwise not. You never had any twinges of it, I suppose?"

"I don't think one *could* be homesick for Worcester Park."

"Maybe for Lambeth, though. Newington Butts on a Saturday night, all the stalls selling jellied eels, pie and mash, stuff like that. Then, when the market closed, off to the Elephant and Castle for a mild-and-bitter."

"What are you talking about?"

"Great-Great-Uncle Jack. I think he got homesick and took off. Became a deserter. In those days you could get shot for that. So he disappeared, and whenever he tried to surface, the police were waiting for him. They never saw him again. You could write a novel about it."

"Surely the police would have told the family what they were looking for."

"Of course, so now they were ashamed. Better to leave him 'missing in action' than run away. So they don't talk about him. Turned his picture to the wall."

"Do you think that's a possibility?"

"It's the best I can do at the moment. You have a go."

Now the skies were beginning to threaten again but we set out to have a second try at seeing York, and to call in to see Castle Howard on the way.

We missed Castle Howard for the same reason we might have missed Siegfried or James. I was the map reader, and I was too busy understanding the map to watch the signs. Fred, of course, like all drivers in these situations, took no responsibility for the route, or the scenery — that was my job — so we had the odd tense moment. You really need three people to tour properly in a car, one to drive, one to read the map, and one to exclaim at the scenery and act as the go-between for the other two, translating the map instructions into the real world. It is this one, the third one, who should be in charge, the cox, as it were.

In the event, we were sorry to miss the road to Castle Howard but we knew what the house looked like from *Brideshead Revisited*. And now it was pouring again. We drove past the racecourse in the middle of York's rush hour and continued on to Harrogate, and started to look for a bed for the night. We found a motel on the edge of Harrogate, and in the rain were grateful for it as we might not have been if the sun was shining.

I had been looking forward to crossing England, but the next morning it was still coming down hard so I gave up any thought of having an aesthetic experience and concentrated on guiding Fred through West Yorkshire until we reached Kirkby Lonsdale. Here we found rooms at The Snooty Fox, a hokey, unpromising name, but it turned out to be as good an inn as the one we had found in Durham. It was dinnertime, so we had a drink at the bar, and, the rain having lifted, we did a walkabout, looking for a restaurant that might cook local food (Yorkshire hotpot?) without pretending to ape some international cuisine. We found it, we thought, in a small place that was a tea room by day, and stayed open to serve "home-cooked" meals in the evening.

It was mistake, of course. In North America, no one who has a choice would risk eating at a place called "Ma's Kitchen," or even "Mom's." What North Americans need to be wary of in England is "Home Cooking." Afterwards, we agreed that, though we had both grown up in England, where neither of us had experienced eating anything memorable at home, we were still taken in by the associations of "home cooking."

We were the only customers for some kind of meat pie, five sodden vegetables, and suet pudding covered in Bird's custard, all washed down with a third of a bottle of screw-cap wine that the owner found at the back of the serving table, among the HP and

Worcester sauces. Walking back to the inn, we passed half a dozen restaurants with menus posted outside, full of happy-looking diners eating French and Italian food. As the older and more experienced traveller, I should have known better, and I apologized to Fred. My excuse lay in a true story I told him about a time when, a little younger than he is now, I went cycling on my own through Dorset, and "overdid it" as my mother used to say, landing exhausted near closing time — about two o'clock — at a pub in a quiet village, where I asked if I could get something to eat. The landlady said she didn't do meals, and then at my look of despair, thought she could manage something in the back room as long as I wasn't too fussy: a couple of lamb chops, potatoes, peas, that sort of thing. I envisioned a plate of food that had been kept warm for the gardener, all dried-out gravy around the edge, but I was hungry.

It was unbelievable. True, I was hungry, but at any time it would have been extraordinary, three exquisitely cooked lamb chops with mint sauce, new potatoes, and peas which she shelled for the meal, followed by a jam tart still warm from the oven, all of which she apologized for as "nothing fancy." It won't happen again but the suppressed memory of that dinner must have fuelled my suggestion of trying a "home-cooked" meal that night.

The sun came out next morning and Kirkby Lonsdale redeemed itself. After a "full English breakfast" which, at The Snooty Fox, included black pudding and fried tomatoes as well as all the usual stuff, we had a very nice walkabout, which included a stop at the open-air market where I confirmed one suspicion I had been forming about England.

Every visitor must notice that it is difficult to walk around the towns in England because of the enormous number of handicapped people scooting about in electric vehicles of various kinds. It seemed to me that there were many more motorized wheelchairs per square mile in England than there are in Toronto, and in the market I got some confirmation of this. There were only half a dozen stalls, selling the usual farmers' produce and marked-down clothing, but one of the stalls had a big selection of wheelchairs and electric carts, somewhat confirming my impression. I discarded the theory that there are more handicapped people in England, and the theory that the lack of snow means that they can get about in their carts all year round (though there may be something to this), and the possibility that it's the Dunkirk spirit, a refusal to give into old age, and I wound up putting my money on the fact that the English health care system provides these vehicles free.

At lunchtime, it started to rain again. We had had enough of a walkabout to be able to recommend Kirkby Lonsdale as a good place to visit for a few hours or overnight (I gave it a check and a half). We thought to have a look at the Lake District but a man in a pub told us the roads were clogged with tourists, and we should come back in February. It was a pity, but it seemed like good advice, so we bought a lemon drizzle cake from the Women's Institute, made by S. Barber, which was delicious, and ate it, standing in the rain, while we looked at the view from the end of the churchyard, a view which Ruskin said was the most beautiful view in England, and therefore in the world, an assumption which must irritate visitors from, say, the Italian Lakes. Then we looked for the M6, the road south.

We decided to stop at Birmingham because no one ever does. Fred said, "But a man at college is from Birmingham, and he never invites anyone home."

"Let's find out why."

More countryside, but in the distance the factory chimneys of nineteenth-century England. It continued to rain.

I said, "'When that Aprille with her showers soote.' A bit out of season, but that's the only poem I know with 'rain' in it."

Fred said, "Do you read much poetry, Uncle?"

I heard his diffidence. Poetry is not spoken, or spoken of a great deal these days in the ordinary world outside of literary festivals. I could hear from Fred's voice that the same situation prevailed in his world, but I had quoted a few favourite bits along the way and now it was as if he was asking me to confess to a fetish. Show me a man who still reads poetry after he's come of age and I'll show you a what? A cross-writer? A trans-literate?

I said, "Nobody reads much poetry, Fred, not in my circle anyway, although, oddly, I know a couple of copywriters who *write* it."

"Is theirs any good?"

"I don't know. They won't show me, and I wouldn't know, anyway. Poetry is too difficult to read, nowadays, let alone judge and respond to. Very hard on old people. The only modern poets I can say I read and understand are Edwin Brock and Al Purdy."

"Canadian?"

"Purdy is; Brock is English. No, I don't read poetry. I remember some, though, and what I remember is very important to me. I can still remember the way my ears tingled when I was thirteen and first read "The Lotus-Eaters." We took "The Lady of Shalott" about the same time. Didn't you? Tennyson's still respectable, isn't he?"

"We didn't take him. We didn't take any of those people."

"Who are those people?"

"Tennyson, Browning, all that lot. We took John Donne, and Phillip Larkin, people like that."

"Any Americans?"

"No."

"There you are, then. We don't have a thing in common."

"One of my teachers asked us to define the difference between poetry and prose. Apparently it was his standard opening with a new sixth form. After we'd tried, he said it couldn't be done."

"I know that discussion, all about the poetic qualities of the King James Bible. And whether if you set it out differently on the page, blank verse isn't just broken up bits of prose. But it isn't that difficult. Of course it can be done. Poetry is metaphor; prose isn't. 'Poetic,' though, has come to mean pretty and artificial. When I read that a novel is poetic, I make a note to avoid it."

"Didn't you ever aspire to write poetry?"

"Never. Poetry is written by poets and you don't become a poet by aspiring to be one. Let's get back to Toronto, or have I said enough about it?"

"A good place to live is what I heard you saying, but nothing to see. Just good eating and good shopping."

"An hour on a tour bus will do it all, and then a run up the CN tower to look at it from above. No, there's nothing of any interest for tourists. There's a shoe museum. No? There's not much street crime, though that's picking up lately; still, it's quite hard to get mugged. Here, people in Hampstead are mugged and stabbed on their doorsteps daily. Not in Toronto. Come and see.

"Birmingham is a must stop on any tourist's agenda. Parking is adequate, so drive in to the centre and begin with a walk round Victoria Square. Then pick up a brochure at the tourist information kiosk and make your choice of the day's events, of which an energetic and imaginative city council will have provided plenty. Leave time for a visit to the museum and art gallery, not for the Pre-Raphaelite paintings it contains, all familiar enough from reproductions, but for the building itself, an exquisite iron and glass structure.

"There," I said. "That sound like guidebook prose?"

"I'm afraid it does."

"Yes. Crap, eh? Won't do, I hear you cry. Why? Because it doesn't sound like someone spoke it, just sort of assembled it out of a guidebook word kit. And I'm supposed to know how. Words have provided me with a good living. But I do like Birmingham. I've just drifted into a bit of lazy writing. I'll get better."

"What is it you like about Birmingham? It doesn't make many lists of good places to choose to live in," Fred said.

"Didn't I say? All right. You see those two small buildings over there, joined together." We were sitting drinking coffee beside the canal in the reconstructed area of downtown. "My guess, or maybe my fancy, is that they once belonged to two prosperous nineteenth-century merchants, either their residences or their counting houses, you know, their offices. Let's say a ships' chandler and a dealer in hides."

"We're a fair way from the sea here, Uncle."

"Don't interrupt. The thing that strikes me about Birmingham, that's been striking me all day, if you know what I mean, is that although Birmingham may be the second largest city in the country, as with Durham you can get the whole of it in your head at once, I mean you can know the past — the history — and experience the present, all from where you are sitting. This place where we are now is nice but looking across at those two houses, you can imagine not only the nineteenth-century prosperity, but the squalor, too, the back-to-back housing, the windowless factories — all that. I imagine this area is built over the ruins of the bombing in the last war — London got all the press but Birmingham was heavily bombed, too — and some slum clearance projects. Anyway, the result is a pedestrian's town. You realize how much walking we did today without being forced off the road by cars? We must have strolled the town for a couple of hours before we wound up at the museum and art gallery for lunch. By the way ..."

"I know, another good museum to eat in?"

"Right. Where did you go afterwards? Or am I intruding?"

"I went into the library?"

"To read up on Birmingham?

"To check my email."

"Did the mailman come?"

"What? Oh, yes. There was a letter."

"Good. Don't fret, we'll soon be home. As I was saying, or rather trying to put into words, you can get control of Birmingham. You can't do that for London: it's too big, too much history, too much space and time — in short, so you have to pick a bit to fall in love with. But you can absorb the whole of Birmingham and think about it all together. Like this. Three hundred years ago it was a small market town like, say, Stratford. Now I haven't seen any castles or nunneries or minster-type buildings so we could probably see the beginnings of the modern town, call it the 'workshop' town, emerge about 1750, with pottery, I think. Then someone discovered how to blast iron in a furnace and Stephenson invented the steam engine and Birmingham became industrial. About 1850. That's the Birmingham that most people have in their heads: iron, steel coal, *Hard Times*, Bounderby, child labour, muck."

"Aren't you drifting north a bit? Manchester?"

"I'm trying to get the essence. Don't interrupt. Then they moved on to munitions and bicycles, and made enough money to build an art gallery and a museum. Should I go on or save some for the car?"

He waved me on.

"They got everything right. First, in their museum they've got a gallery, the Industrial Gallery — just the right size to walk around in — where a space is devoted to pottery of various kinds, where I learned all about *faience*. I've always wanted to know about *faience*. You know about *faience*?"

"No, but you do, now."

"I do. It's the French name for glazing. Making a glaze with tin oxide." I consulted the notes I'd made on the gallery's brochure. "You may know it as lusterware. Sometimes it's called majolica, and, by the Germans, *fayonce*. The English call it Delftware."

"That about covers it, does it?"

"There was one dish I was very taken with, Spanish, about 1600, a large shallow bowl — more of a plate, actually, with a space on one side to fit your neck into, because it's really what they called a barber's bowl. It struck me, though, that when the time came that I was drooling, I mean *really* drooling, it would be a great dish to serve me my lunch in. Fit it on me, fill it with clam chowder, and give me a big spoon made of something that wouldn't hurt if I jabbed it into my face, wood or horn, perhaps. What do you think?"

"You've made a discovery."

"Yes, I have. I'm about to retire, you see, and I've been thinking what I'll do with myself."

"A hobby?"

"I hate that bloody word. No, yes, no, I want a passion, something to get lost in. I plan to write — did I tell you? — but writing's very hard work and I may not have the stamina for long. I need something else, something that doesn't take five years of study but something I can get on top of, be an expert in. Today I understood every word of the chat I read around the gallery about lusterware, and I wasn't in the least intimidated by the size of the subject.

"In an analogous way, I like Birmingham. You could know enough about Birmingham very quickly to go on one of those quiz shows, competing with the experts on Marlene Dietrich, and Icelandic sagas, and famous dwarfs, and so on. As for lusterware, there's a ceramics museum in Toronto. I thought I would start there, see if there is a Lusterware Society."

"Does it have a good restaurant, this ceramics museum?"

"What? Oh, yes. Toronto is like this place, all the galleries and the museums are good places to eat if you are in the neighbourhood. But I wasn't finished. There's another gallery they all wanted me to see, the attendants, I mean ..."

"The Pre-Raphaelites?"

"How did you know?"

"Birmingham is famous for its collection. Even I know that."

"I remember there was that gang that Tennyson used to hang out with, The Sodomites, or some such. They liked the Pre-Raphaelites, didn't they?"

"You mean the Disciples, I think. I don't know. I didn't read English."

"Anyway, I went to have a look at them and as soon as I saw them I recognized them, of course, and they left me as cold as they always have, but something happened. Can you stand one more whatshisname?"

"Epiphany?"

"What's that? Something that happens in a church?"

"That's where it comes from. It's what James Joyce called the flash of insight, the moment of vision which is what a work of art shows. He made it central to his short stories."

"I thought this wasn't your game?"

"I had a roommate who was reading English."

"I see. Yes, well, that'll do, then. I had an epiphany in front of one of the pictures. Shall I go on?"

"My guess is that this is the rush hour and Birmingham is tied in knots so we might as well wait it out. I think I'll risk a glass of beer. I've just had coffee so far."

I signalled the waiter to bring a pint for me and a half for Fred, since he was driving.

I continued. "I was standing in front of a picture, painted in 1882, called *Men must work and women must weep*. Now, let me go back a bit. I had been looking at the postcards in the shop and come across a painting of the same period, an emigrant group, and it was called something like *The Last Look at Home*. I'd seen this picture before and smiled at it like everyone else, but this time there was a sort of resemblance to, or it reminded me of, my uncle, your grandfather, and then I wondered if I actually showed it to your grandfather if he might have a memory of some real people in the same scene, or remember someone else's memory, if you like. He might feel connected to it. And so, therefore, might I. Not the art, but the people."

"You were an emigrant, too, of course." He was striving to tolerate my fancy.

"Yes. I'm connected once removed, so to speak. But I didn't have any experience you could make a picture of, no *The Emigrant's Farewell*. Actually, though, I've known several old people in Canada who left England by boat — steerage it was called — in the thirties, before the age of flight, and then travelled west in carriages labelled 'Colonist Class.' They took their own food and used a little stove at the end of the carriage to heat it up. These people were all pretty old when I knew them. Some of them never did see England again."

"So, what was the epiphany? Your feeling for them, the fellow emigrants in the painting?"

"What I really felt was something else. Of course I bonded with them a bit but I was really struck with the falseness, the sentimentality of the thing, and the way the art critics make the painting the important thing and not what the painting is about. They talk about something that should be a footnote. About this one, someone had written, 'This work shows Langley's mastery of subtle techniques and colour harmonies.' Something like that. So a middle-class painter has created a fine wall-hanging out of a lower-class tragedy, giving this aesthete something to be an authority on? I think such commentary is a piece of shit. Real widows and orphans never looked like those in the picture, not when they were waiting for news of their men, in this case drowned at sea. If you want to know what lower-class grief looks like, watch the ten o'clock news any night. When the West Virginia mining disaster happened ..."

"Uncle, Uncle ..."

'I know, I'm raving, but I am on to something, something about bad art making pretty pictures out of other people's misery. The painter here wanted to paint a sad picture, so he found some lower-class people in misery, but instead of trying to capture their misery, he uses it as a subject for a composition."

"I'm a bit lost. You seem to have become political."

"I'll tell you something, Fred. In the end, *everything* becomes political, I've found that out. Now let's pay our respects to Stratford."

Fred said, "How about *The Emigrant's Return?*"

I caught the reference. "You mean a picture of me, hanging over the rail of the Queen Mary as we come into Southampton?"

"Yes, one showing all the conflicting emotions on your face as you see England for the first time in thirty years."

"I've been back and forth a few times by air, of course, so I'd have to fake it."

"You and Ford Maddox Brown."

TWENTY-THREE

WE GOT LOST LEAVING Birmingham.

I said, "Stop by that betting shop. I'll ask someone."

The bookmaker's shop was full of small, retired ironworkers, happy to help me out between races. After a lot of discussion among themselves they worked out my route and one of them traced it on the back of a betting slip. What I really learned was something much more astonishing.

I said to Fred, as we started off, "How far are we from London?"

"A hundred miles," he said promptly. "Two theology students in college brag about doing it in an hour early in the morning. Why?"

"I read an article not long ago which decried the loss of regional English. The writer said everyone now spoke what he called estuary English, a kind of universal, characterless, BBC-driven, dialectless tongue, like you. We know that's not true, don't we, from the venerable beadsman of Durham cathedral. And in that betting shop, an hour from London, were four men talking a completely incomprehensible argot which they had to translate for me. Did you know there were pockets of dialect-speakers here, like Gaelic-speakers in Ireland, preserving the patois of their forefathers?"

"Only in betting shops?"

"And showing tourists round cathedrals up north. It's something for my guidebook, don't you think? And now, I suppose we *have* to go to bloody Stratford."

"Why?"

"You being roguish? All right, just to make sure there's nothing of interest there. There's the tomb, of course, and the house he was born in, if we're on a pilgrimage, and if we're lucky, one of the more accessible plays will be playing. Please, God, not *Pericles*."

Fred said, "Where are we going after Stratford?"

I said, "Ultimately to Moreton-in-Marsh, but I don't want to get there too soon. This is like a book that I don't want to end, because the end might be a disappointment."

"We can't just drive round and round. Can we?"

"I'm making notes for a travel book, remember." I looked at the map. "Let's go to Cheltenham, first. I've always liked the sound of Cheltenham, the word, I mean. I'm told they've voted Conservative since Disraeli, so I know what the natives are like. Still, I'd like to see it."

"Stay on this road?"

"To Junction 10."

I was fiddling with the car radio. I find the BBC talk programs a constant source of surprise and delight. Once, visiting my mother and trapped in her living room on a rainy afternoon, I tuned in to a couple of women with accents like the Queen's discussing God knows what general topic. What I got was a bit of dialogue, thus:

"When did you first start to pee involuntarily?"

"It was when I began trampolining."

Then I lost the station.

On another occasion, an announcer found himself with several minutes left to fill, so he read us a poem, "Ode to the Country Gentlemen of England," some sort of call to arms, I gathered.

Now, I like the Canadian Broadcasting Corporation, and I'd be desolated if the country were reduced to country and western and news flashes, but I've never heard a CBC announcer read a poem by, say, Charles Bruce, just to fill in the time. They ought to try it. Visitors from Europe would appreciate it.

"That it for Ontario?" Fred asked. "Traffic jams in Algonquin Park, Niagara Falls and Mennonites on tandems?"

"I was just exaggerating the defects of the famous sights, to clear the palate, as it were, though I meant what I said. You have to see Niagara Falls, of course, the way you have to see the Tower of London, but avoid the *town* of Niagara Falls, which is on a par with Southend."

"Sort of Brighton?"

"Not in the least like Brighton. I read somewhere that Brighton has lately gotten fashionable and horrible but it used to have its own integrity, like Durham, given it during the Regency, and then it was a classic cockney resort until about 1950, and you can still feel both of these influences if you dig deep enough. Now, though, it's trendy, the preferred weekend destination of currency traders. No, I meant the town of Niagara Falls is one huge amusement arcade, and what visitor doesn't have that at home?"

"Why do you keep calling it 'the town of Niagara Falls'?"

"To distinguish it from The Falls themselves, and from the town of Niagara-on-the-Lake, which is a different place entirely, though nearby. Niagara-on-the-Lake bills itself as *historic* Niagara, a sort of miraculously preserved bit of nineteenth-century Ontario, though it's slightly hokey. There's just one street in which some of the buildings are a hundred and fifty years old and sell our equivalent of Olde Englishe schlock. You know, Olde Canadienne Maple Syrup Candy, and Original Horehound Candy, and butter tarts — they all sell butter tarts — Hudson's Bay blankets, check shirts for cutting down trees in, and toy toboggans for the kiddies. And moccasins.

Everywhere you go someone is selling you moccasins, a few of them made in Canada.

"But never mind all that; as I said, what they do have is just maybe the best summer theatre in Canada, including Stratford. I'm making a fine distinction here. You know what summer theatre is, don't you? The straw hat circuit? I don't think you go in for it in the same way, maybe the variety shows on the piers, those that are left. Now, the theatre at Stratford, Ontario, takes place mainly in the summer but it is rather grander than summer stock. The Shaw Festival, on the other hand, is called that because it began by specializing in Shaw, avoiding Shakespeare but cleverly reminding you that it's on a parallel course with Stratford. Look, try this: the Shaw Festival is summer stock but the best possible summer stock: Stratford aspires to greatness but sometimes trips over itself. So when the Shaw Festival does Victorian melodrama or an old musical, and the orchestra consists of two pianos and a banjo and drums, it's fun, but when Stratford, Ontario, stoops to Gilbert and Sullivan and it doesn't come up to scratch, as happens, you feel let down, especially after driving for two and a half hours and then staying the night. After a bad play at Stratford you feel slightly swindled, but after a poor afternoon at the Shaw, you can always go and have another look at The Falls. Am I making sense?"

"Yes, you like this Shaw Festival, but Stratford not so much."

"It's just that you expect more from Stratford, maybe even that they will make Shakespeare's jokes funny. The food at Stratford is better, though, much better. If you want a nice lunch at the Shaw you'd be well advised to get to the Oban Inn early, or take your own. I don't know why Stratford should be more sophisticated in this area, but it is. Just as many Americans go to Niagara."

"And so we come to Toronto, right, Uncle?"

"I guess so. Toronto is trickier. I live there so I can't give you an objective assessment."

"Where are we now?"

"Taking a nice little drive along the Niagara River, soon to get back to the Queen Elizabeth Way, and Toronto."

"I meant here. Now."

"*That* sign said 'To the Inner Ring.' The Inner Ring of Cheltenham proper, I would imagine. Shall we stay here?"

"I'm yours to command, Uncle."

"I know, but I wonder where. There doesn't seem to be any downtown. Find the road to Broadway. I've heard of that. We won't necessarily go there but it's in the right direction."

There is one spot on the road to Broadway from Cheltenham where you have to manage two roundabouts in succession, about six feet from each other. These are not proper roundabouts, but painted rings at the junction of three roads. Thus you have to remind yourself twice in a quarter of a second that traffic on the right has the right of way. And then, just after the roundabouts, you have to notice that your lane ends in the middle of the road until a traffic light orders you to proceed to the right, and then immediately to the left. All this comes to stop you from feeling pleased with yourself just because you have successfully escaped Cheltenham's Inner Ring and found the sign for your road in brackets underneath a more important road.

"Stop here," I said. "Here" was a large white hotel on the top of Cleeve Hill, with the most magnificent view I have encountered outside of Banff in the Rockies (I've never been to Europe). They agreed to rent us a couple of rooms, and offered us dinner, but Fred wanted to stretch his legs, so we drove back to Cheltenham for a walk round before we ate.

I liked what I saw of Cheltenham. Where I grew up, "old" meant Elizabethan and Jacobean, timbers and red brick, mostly owner-built, and I never liked it much. It was just old. "Fine half-timbered inn," some advertisement would say, and you were supposed to fall about in admiration, but to me it just meant that the windows would be too small and the doors wouldn't fit. But Cheltenham is an

eighteenth-century town, or Regency, anyway, and many of the buildings were designed by architects and built by professional builders.
And beyond the looks of the buildings, which I like more the more
I look at them, it's a nice town to walk about in, and I'd like to try
living there.

We found a place to park on The Parade, a big street with shops
on one side and municipal offices on the other with flower gardens
setting them well back from the road, so the word Parade was appropriate: it was easy to imagine the carriages of another age because
there was room for them. We walked uphill and found ourselves on
Montpelier Street, in an area of shops selling up-market second-hand
goods, things they were getting ready to label "antique," interesting
and affordable stuff, none of it cleverly lit. I thought how much my
daughter, who loves junk shops and doesn't care how authentic the
stuff is as long as she likes it, would like the Montpelier district. I saw
a stone gnome in one shop: it had lost most of its paint and looked
as though an ogre had condemned it to stay outside in all weathers
for a hundred years until a stranger from a far country came along to
rescue it. It was marked fifteen pounds, so I wouldn't be losing much
if my daughter didn't like it, but I knew that this was one of those
rare occasions when her taste and mine might intersect. The shops
were all closed, but I noted the street address to come back to the next
morning, and we found a Greek restaurant for a pleasant dinner.

The next morning, when we returned to pick up the treasure, Fred
said, "How are you going to smuggle it on to the plane, Uncle?"

I had been wondering that myself. Not in my checked luggage,
certainly. The excess baggage charges would be more than it was
worth. I said, "I think it will just fit into my carry-on bag."

"Don't put it in the overhead bin."

As I said, I liked Cheltenham.

One index of a place to visit is to find out if they hate Americans
(a generic term which includes Canadians and sometimes South

Africans and Antipodeans), because Americans are the goats, focus of all local hatred of tourists. They hate Americans in London, of course, and in Stratford, York and Harrogate. They hate them in Oxford, where I heard a woman in a bookshop actually declare in bell-like tones how much she hated Americans. (It was a moment for rushing out and buying a Stars-and-Stripes flag and pinning it on my hat and I've always been ashamed I didn't do it.) But they don't hate Americans in Cambridge, and in Durham they seem to like them. They don't hate them in Cheltenham, either, which I was glad to find because I was about to construct a specious theory about the attitude of the different classes to Americans, along the lines of "The upper classes don't like them, but the lower classes do." Not true. It's something to do with having a bit of space so they aren't always being jostled by tourists, and, in Cheltenham, feeling so secure that they have room to be tolerant. The Americans will go away eventually, just as the Romans did.

Cheltenham, then, is a real place, not a place making its living out of the tourist trade while at the same time hating the tourists.

"Where to now, Uncle? I notice Moreton-in-Marsh is only about an hour away."

We had eaten a good breakfast and the sun was shining. "Are you in a hurry?" I asked.

"Oh, not really. I might be in a couple of days. Besides, we haven't reached Toronto, yet."

"No. Right. We'll think about Moreton after Toronto. Let's go to Bath. It's just down the road."

One reason for driving from Cheltenham to Bath is that the scenery, even to my eye, is about as attractive as any in England — green, woodsy, hilly and full of vistas in the gaps between the trees. Another reason had caught my eye as I looked at the map. Along the way we could pass through Slad, and as long as it wasn't too much trouble, I could satisfy an old desire for one of the very few literary pilgrimages I have ever felt a pull towards. For Slad is where Laurie Lee started from, armed with a violin and a tin of treacle biscuits, to busk his way round Spain, and his book *As I Walked Out One Midsummer Morning* was the first actual work of non-fiction that captured me, when, as a sixteen year old, I was devouring all the novels I could borrow from the library, leaving the non-fiction for the old ladies and the retired army officers. After that, I was open to a whole new (for me) category of reading. For Laurie Lee's book taught me at a good age to find out that prose could have qualities other than storytelling, that some of it, at least, was worth reading for its own sake.

We never stopped at Slad — there was no need. We had intended to try for a pub lunch at Lee's local, but there was no sign declaring that food was served so we just passed on, reverentially, and found a good sandwich at the Egypt Mill Hotel, in Nailsworth, in a building that still has traces of its fourteenth-century origins, and of the several changes of function and rebuilding that have taken place in the last six centuries, and well worth a note in any future guidebook.

"Once upon a time a young shepherd was discovered to be afflicted with leprosy and he was banished, along with his flock. One day he brought his flock to drink at a spring and afterwards he and his flock were cured. That shepherd was the founder of Bath.

"How's that?" I asked Fred.

"It's a start," he conceded.

"Crap, still? Okay. I'll work on it. The next so-called founder was a Roman officer who discovered the hot water and built the present splendid bathing facility. But the real founders of the Bath we see before us are the Woods, father and son, the eighteenth-century builders responsible for the Circus and the Royal Crescent. After that you have to give credit to Beau Nash, and Jane Austen for the Bath of our imagination. Sorry about that. I'll change it to 'For what happens in our heads when someone says Bath.'"

For I was stunned into platitude. I knew, of course, about the feast of my favourite architecture that was waiting for me but I wasn't prepared for the view of the town from above, like a huge amphitheatre, or for the impact that the Royal Crescent has the first time you see it, or for the actual presence of the Roman *baths* themselves.

"Let me try again," I said.

"The best introduction to Bath is an hour in The Museum of the Building of Bath, housed in the Countess of Huntingdon's Chapel, where the staff of two who seem delighted to have the job will show you models of the city, and give you a free book which will enable you to leave the building with an educated eye, no longer beholden to Masterpiece Theatre.

"How's that? If I do something about 'enable', I mean."

"It'll do," Fred conceded. "You really liked that one, didn't you."

"It's the nicest museum I've ever been in."

"Including Birmingham? What else are you going to say about Bath?"

"Something about the parking?"

Everyone had warned us not to take the car into Bath. All heads shook to the mantra, "There's nowhere to park in Bath." In fact, if you want to park in Bath and not drive around it, it is the most accommodating city you will come across, because there, right in the area you want it, set in a green park, surrounded by trees, with toilets and a café handy, is a car park where you can stay for a day for ten pounds. Signs should say "Park and Walk," and that is what we did, although you have to be nimble because in the city proper the sidewalks sometimes disappear and often climb the walls. When the automobile arrived the road engineers tore down as few buildings as possible to accommodate the through traffic, and didn't have enough energy left to worry about the pedestrians. They know this, the works people, and as a sop to pedestrians they have set aside a little street with a sign "Pedestrian Priority," but it is hard to figure out what this means. Priority of what kind?

We stayed overnight on Brock Street, and had a look at Wood's buildings but then I suggested we leave it. I was feeling like a tourist: I wanted to spend a couple of weeks in Bath, not drive through it on top of a sightseeing bus, so I made myself a promise, and we left for Moreton-in-Marsh.

We drove back by a different route in order to have a look at Cirencester. My instinct to put Cirencester on my historical tour had been a good one. The town turned out to be a very pleasant surprise, a place most tours from abroad don't embrace. I liked most the church with its flying buttresses, and the park behind, where I had a short nap while Fred indulged himself by having a look at the inn King Charles escaped from during the Civil War by jumping out the window. I liked the very upmarket butcher's shop, which sold me a container of Gentleman's Relish that I had always been curious about but never tasted. It claims to be delicious on toast; I found it okay, but only just. I liked the huntin'-shootin'-fishin' shop where I bought a pair of moleskin trousers because they were in the window, and I'd always wondered what moleskin was: not, sadly, made from dozens of little rodent skins neatly sewn together, but a cloth with a nap like the small animal's fur. I knew from a line in *Juno and the Paycock* that once upon a time moleskin was used to make navvies' trousers but these days the gentry use moleskin trousers for riding practice whenever they don't have to wear the proper jodhpurs. The trousers fitted snugly but without groping the parts the way jeans can.

Cirencester is a very well-endowed town, to be compared, as one fat city to another, with Burnham Market. The difference is that the folks with money in Cirencester — most of them by the look of it — derive their income from arable land, which they inherited, so they don't have to flaunt it. Everyone knows where it came from. The town swarms with Land Rovers, and I was told that on a clear day you might see The Prince, but I found out later that that was Tewskbury, or Tetbury. I liked the bookshops in Cirencester, I liked the church, and I liked the fact that the town had a lot of green space, like Cheltenham. I put a tick beside Cirencester. "Let's go to Broadway," I said. "It's in all the picture books about the *lovely Cotswolds*."

TWENTY-FOUR

ON THE ROAD TO Broadway we ran over a pheasant, a beautiful bird wearing a gold and red necklace. They are thick on the ground in that part of the country. We had seen several lying in ditches, gorgeous creatures decked out as if for a party, and we had avoided several more as they strutted along the road holding up traffic. They are unbelievably stupid and vulnerable. They look artificial, as if, hidden inside the hedge, they have a gilded cage concealed, and a silver key to wind themselves up.

This one fluttered in the road, wounded but not dead. Fred got out of the car, gathered the bird up in his fingers and snapped its neck. He dropped the bird beside the road, wiped off his hands on a bit of grass, and got back in the car.

I said, "Well done, Fred. Where'd you learn that?"

He grinned. "In my previous incarnation, I think. I've never done it before."

I said, "Atavistic?"

"Probably."

We bowled along for a while in silence. Then he said, "Why *are* you avoiding Moreton?" No *Uncle* now. We were practically on equal terms now that he had killed his pheasant.

I said, "Don't get psychological. This is all just an excuse to have a look round the old country, as we call England back home."

"Are you making much headway in this ... journey of discovery?"

"I'm starting to have a new idea."

"Which is?"

"I thought I'd just write up the trip we're on now, see how it comes out."

Frederick was quiet for a mile or two. "Is that how books get written?"

"Some of them, you can be sure."

"This one, though. Do you think anyone will read it?"

"I don't know. I think that's one reason among many why I'm postponing the last chapter. But what I'm really afraid of is finding nothing in Moreton. I'm afraid that the clues I've been following will lead nowhere. We know that my mother used to visit Moreton regularly after I was born but no one knows why. No one knew anything about her except the taxi driver we visited in Burnham Market. The next-door neighbour we met in Lyme knew that she often went off in a taxi on the weekend but that's all she knew. There's no reference to Moreton in the papers my mother left behind but the two photos are interesting. The woman is totally mysterious but the man was possibly a salesman who used to stay at our guesthouse in Bournemouth, with Mum. And the other thing I picked up in Bournemouth was that Mum and Dad were probably lovers for some time before they got married and moved. Unusual for the times. And then there's the money. I think Mum deposited a pot of gold somewhere, and Moreton is likely. I think it is possible that she was also keeping someone else, maybe David Cullough. *They* were lovers, I'm sure of that, but he never reappeared once my parents moved to Coombe Regis. Somewhere around then, the pattern of going away for the odd weekend to Moreton started. And, brooding again, I'm remembering other little things, little mysteries. Periodically Mum claimed to need a break and would go up to London to look round the shops, always alone. She never bought much, something for us, usually, hardly ever for herself. Then she used to 'dodge off,' as she called it, in the afternoons to the pictures in Bournemouth but she could never remember much of what she'd seen. Then one day I saw her coming out of another bed and breakfast in the middle of the afternoon on a day when she said she'd gone for a bus ride along the front. All this has been waiting for me to dig it up on this trip. What do you make of it?"

"She was having liaisons."

"That's delicately put, Fred. Yes, she was *a loose woman*."

"And Moreton? Did she have a lover in Moreton, then?"

"I think she might have had a man in Moreton, and that's where the money went."

"He could still be here, couldn't he?'

"That's what I have to find out."

A little later, Fred said, "Did your parents marry to avoid gossip, you think?"

"That's something else I'd like to know."

"You think the answer is in Moreton?"

"I'm afraid it isn't. That's one of the things I mean when I say we may find nothing."

We stopped at a "Farm Shop," a name that used to connote fresh bread and homemade jam and pickles sold by a wench in a mob cap but all the farm shops we had seen were in fact gourmet groceries. One, near Stow-on-the-Wold, is called by the locals the Harrods of the Cotswolds.

"Now then, Toronto," Fred began. "It's this chap's first extended bit of writing. Still dull, as you said, but listen to this:

I arrived last night in Toronto. I took the bus from Montreal and was joined in a place called Peterborough by a nice fellow, a student in accounts he called himself, who was planning to spend the next day, Sunday, in Toronto. He said he was doing an audit in Peterborough and whenever he found himself facing Sunday away from Montreal, he took a bus out of town to fill in the time. We established that it might make an outing for us to visit Toronto together. He seemed a decent sort. He planned to stay the night in the YMCA and he suggested I do the same. So that is what we did, walking down from the bus station to the hostel.

The next morning we ate breakfast at a coffee shop on the corner of Yonge (pronounced 'Young') and College, and set off to walk to the harbour, which was surely more interesting than that part of Toronto. Yonge Street is supposed to be the longest street in the Commonwealth; it is certainly the least interesting. At first it was all two storey shops selling shoddy goods and army surplus clothes, a bit like Tooting Broadway, then you come to two department stores, Eaton's and Simpson's, and that is about all except for some banks and so forth. We walked on and eventually came to the harbour, where we caught a ferry to Centre Island, because that's what everybody else was doing. Then we walked round Centre Island and caught the ferry back. I fancied a glass of beer but Duncan (my companion) said the beer parlours were closed in Ontario on Sundays. All we had, he said, was a choice of churches.

We took a bus up to Bloor Street, and found it was a bit livelier than Yonge Street. There were more people about, window shopping. We had a meal of shepherd's pie — very good and very large portions — sitting up at the counter of a restaurant called Palmer's, and then walked about among some university buildings, mostly empty in the summer. Eventually it was late enough to go to bed.

What struck me about our day was not how different it was in Toronto, Canada, from Clapham, England, but how Sunday in the city is just as depressing in both, except that in Clapham you can go to the pictures at four o'clock. Next stop Winnipeg.

Duncan went back to his audit and I decided to continue my travels by train. Duncan had pointed out that I could continue

through the northern United States, but I had come to see Canada,
not America. When I told Duncan he said in that case I had about
a thousand miles of trees to look at, but he didn't put me off.

Fred said, "I'm reading you the lively bits, Uncle. What do you
think?"

"What are the dull bits?"

"Mostly lists. You know, *Eleven people got on, and four departed,*
as if he's not sure what you put in a diary. What about Toronto
today? Is it still as dull as Clapham?"

"You ready for this?" We were coming in to Broadway. "Look
for a place to eat, then. Here goes. Toronto is the most hated city
in Canada."

"Why? Isn't it the biggest Anglican city? Is it the French who
hate it?"

"The word is 'Anglo', not Anglican. First of all, a few assumptions
to upset. Okay? Number one, in case you really meant Anglican,
Toronto's major religion is Catholic, not Anglican. Second, the last
I heard, 40 per cent of the population claim some other language
than English or French as their first. Italian would be very big.
Third, different groups hate Toronto for different reasons. Newfies
hate it because it's not Newfoundland, but it's the place they have
to go to get a job. Quebecers are born hating it for all the reasons
we've already talked about, plus the fact that Toronto still has a
major league baseball team and Montreal has lost theirs."

"You mean hockey, don't you, Uncle?"

"Don't mention hockey to a Canadian over fifty. Hockey has
moved to Disneyland, last I heard, and a team called The Mouse-
keteers or some such has won the Stanley Cup. Let me get on.
Manitoba hates Toronto because all the bright young Manitobans
have to go there to make their fortunes. Saskatchewans are the
exception; they don't hate anybody or anything, but if they did it
would be Toronto for giving politicians a bad name. People in
Saskatchewan like their politicians. They disliked Conservatives for

a while but they put some of them in jail and now they like politicians again. Now Alberta, which is populated entirely by oil men, cattle ranchers and rednecks ..."

"Rednecks?"

"People of simple religious and political beliefs, and faith in nineteenth-century economic theory. Folks in Alberta regard Toronto as a hotbed of sodomy, if I can coin a phrase, and believe Alberta should be allowed to secede from Canada and set up an independent state, as rich as Saudi Arabia, and just as pious, where a man would be allowed to shoot his neighbour if he finds him in bed with one of his ranch hands. They want to make vegetarianism illegal, and refuse funds to any university doing research in fuel-economy engines."

Fred said, "The last one: British Columbia? Why do they hate Toronto?"

"People in British Columbia hate Toronto because Europeans think Toronto is the centre of Canada, literally and metaphorically, and British Columbia is two thousand miles away. When people in BC begin a sentence, 'In the East ...' they don't mean the Orient, they mean Toronto."

"So tell me why I should visit Toronto."

"Let me finish. People from other provinces who are mounting arguments against Toronto point out that apart from the new city hall, now about fifty years old, Toronto is no more architecturally distinguished than ... than Birmingham. Out-of-towners say Toronto's climate is horrible, hot and humid in summer, cold and humid in winter; that its politicians are clowns — they were, but that changed a bit with the last election — that it has managed to destroy its only natural advantage, the waterfront, by first building an expressway to cut the lake off from the city, then allowing developers to build high-rise condominiums for the well-to-do along the lake. And now it plans to complete the sacrifice by building an airport on Toronto Island that will be suitable for jets so the people in the lakefront condos won't have to trudge all the way across the city to catch a plane to New York."

"What do you say in response, Uncle? You Torontonians."

"We start by admitting, agreeing to, all of the criticisms, especially the ones about the island airport. But then we rise above them. First, we point out that though Toronto doesn't have any pretty walking streets, like the little one in Ottawa, or picturesque quarters, like Old Montreal, it doesn't need them. Bloor Street and the Danforth don't need tarting up; nor do Queen Street or King, and there are lots more. Little Italy, Chinatown, the Sri Lankan restaurants on Gerrard, Cabbagetown, and more. It's hard to go wrong, unless you go into Yorkville, a district that started Toronto's renaissance back in the sixties but is now chi-chi, and full of people from Buffalo. There's nothing to see in Toronto if you look up; it's a walker's town, with everything at eye level. Everyone has their favourite districts; mine are the markets, St. Lawrence and Kensington."

"Now it's starting to sound like a guidebook."

"Isn't it, though? And another thing: people from Detroit come to Toronto to go to the movies. People never stopped going to the movies in Toronto the way everyone else did in the sixties. We get all the new movies, and we keep showing them."

"Finally?"

"Finally?"

"One last thing, please, Uncle. I'm starting to hate Toronto myself."

"Okay. The food. The food is total. I mean you can eat Italian, Hungarian, Indian, French, Kosher and Greek and all the others besides. Lots of Middle Eastern. Yes, there must be fifty Greek restaurants along Danforth Avenue, and you know something, none of them deafen you with Nana Mouskouri-type music. That is the major flaw of the others, ethnic and Canadian, and a lot of English restaurants, come to that: the music, played at fairground volume. I don't know why the Greeks don't do it but in my experience they don't. And our so-called restaurant critics are capable of giving a fucking four-star rating to a place where you can't even hear the waiter offer you fresh pepper.

"Apart from the noise, you can enjoy eating whatever you want in Toronto at a price you can afford. There are not just cheap and expensive Italian restaurants, as you would expect in a city of three-quarters of a million Italians, but cheap and expensive Portuguese and Russian and Spanish places, and most other kinds."

Fred cut me off. "There's an underground, too, isn't there?"

"There's a very fine subway, even if, in some of the stations, the elevators only seem to go down so going up means climbing the stairs, but it's getting expensive because lately our governments have spent their money on roads to bring in cars to choke up the city instead of subsidizing the public transit system. We seem to be luckier with the current bunch, but before they came along the municipally-elected clowns spent all their time promising to lower taxes, as did the no-brainers in the last provincial government, who hated Toronto like everyone else."

"I think you're using 'no-brainers' wrongly, there. But I gather you like Toronto."

"I love it, and every time I've been away I go home to realize how much I do. Trawna, Trawna, it's a wonderful place."

"But this time you might not go back, right?"

"It's one of the things this trip is about. I'm trying to find out where I belong."

"I'd say with you, Toronto has the edge right now."

"I got carried away. There's more to be said. For instance, there are no public lavatories in Toronto. This is very hard on senior citizens — I have a slightly enlarged prostate myself — and, too ..." I pointed out the car window. "We don't have anything like this. I quoted: 'On either side the river lie/ Long fields of barley and of rye.'"

"River?" Fred asked. "I don't see any river. And that all looks like wheat to me."

"I was speaking Tennyson. He was saying how beautiful the world is and then, in the poem, it starts to rain, and she, the lady, dies. The point I was making is that the English countryside at its best, like now, can stop your heart, even if, like me, you're not a nature lover. It reminds me of a story that a man I know in Toronto tells, an architect, about how a very successful Scottish immigrant who had made a potful mining nickel or some such had hired him to build a retirement house on the banks of Loch Lomond, or somewhere like that. A Canadian house. This was around 1960, before Scotland had heard of central heating. This chap wanted all the things he was used to in the house, especially central heating and the kind of bathroom his wife had at home, with a big picture window in the living room so he could sit there in a comfortable Canadian house, but when he looked out, there was Scotland."

I looked out the window at the manicured scene. "Here's Broadway now. Look for a place to eat. There." I pointed to a small bar attached to or part of The Lygon Arms. Sandwiches were advertised, and game pie. "Bring the notebook."

TWENTY-FIVE

WE TOOK OUR SANDWICHES (smoked salmon for Fred, ham for me) and drink, (bitter for me, ginger ale for Fred) to a table by the window.

"This is pretty," Fred said.

"A bit chocolate-boxy?" I suggested. "Too well-groomed? Looks like an old-fashioned stage set? I remember when I was a kid, the curtain would go up and we'd all clap because there, in front of us, was the most real-looking street or house or room. If it was a house, someone would then lean out of an upstairs window and shake a mat, and an uncle would explain to us that she was standing on a ledge, inside. 'Clever!' we thought. Nowadays a set like that would be a send-up, and halfway through the first act two actors pretending to be scene-shifters will stage a fight and bring the whole thing down on top of themselves, revealing the real set underneath. You know what I mean? It would be a play about playmaking. That's what this looks like to me, a fake village put up for tourists, to be taken down and put in storage after Labour Day."

"Labour Day?"

"Sorry. The first weekend in September. Now let's get bloody Stratford done."

We got as far as his birthplace, shuffling along with the muttering crowd, reading their guidebooks, telling their beads. I had the pleasure of hearing an aged Teuton read a few lines from *Hamlet* out of a collected works he was carrying, then turn to his wife and say "Goethe ist betther."

The evening performance was sold out, so we ate by the river at a restaurant that catered to the pre-theatre crowd, and we were late enough to have the place entirely to ourselves except for a couple of minor players from the theatre company. The specialty was the usual steak-and-mushroom pie, with chips, and it wasn't bad, though the crust was a bit slimy. The English like meat pies and they can be wonderful, but they're risky. You need a recommendation. Afterwards, we walked around the town for a bit, but the English close up their towns at 5:30, even in summer. There are no outdoor gathering places, no piazzas in a town like Stratford, so we had a drink in the oldest pub in the world and went to bed early.

The night before, I had phoned my secretary at the agency, just to touch base, and she said that Jack Masters, my colleague, had been trying to reach me urgently. Otherwise, everything was fine, she said, and I should call my daughter. There was nothing wrong there, either, she added; Zoe had just wanted to find out when I was due back. And Scott, my son, had called twice to find out what they had heard of me.

I said, "Did he say if there was anything wrong?"

"I don't think so. I think he just thought he should have heard from you."

"I'll call him."

I telephoned Jack right away. He was waiting impatiently for the call. He wanted me to come back as soon as possible because of what he said Grisham was up to. Talk of a link with a German company had escalated into talk of a merger, and a straw vote had been taken among the partners, and they wanted to know how I would vote. Grisham needed one more vote to go ahead with the merger, so I was crucial. Jack was getting to me first to let me know how he felt. He was in favour of the merger but he had registered a "Don't know."

"Why?"

"Tell me what's in your mind first," Jack said.

"No, you first. Why are you a 'don't know'?"

"It's what you and I have been talking about lately. I'm an ideas man, or I was, and I want to get back to the creative side, but if we merge you can bet I'll be in charge of the office, and someone else will be in charge of the ideas. There, I've said it. Go ahead and laugh."

"The merger will probably mean a lot of money for you."

"I've got enough money. Haven't you?"

"I think so. It's one of the things I've been working out."

"What else have you been working out?"

"Whether I want to stay here, in England, or come back. Where do I want to die?"

"For Christ's sake. You're fifty-four, and all you've got is a slightly enlarged prostate. You don't even have high blood pressure, so what's with this 'dying' stuff? And this either/or Canadian/English stuff. It's bullshit. You're taking yourself too seriously. We're not talking about deciding whether to stay on the rubber plantation, with a trip home once every seven years. Whatever you decide, make it temporary. You can fly back and forth once a week if you want. So come back where you belong, where your life works. You aren't thinking of retiring are you? That'll finish you off. Anyway, I need you here."

Now I told him somewhat shyly of my other agenda, the rebirth of my yen to write for myself, now that I could afford it.

"I thought you'd given that up."

"I haven't done any for ten years but that just means I'm not a driven man. I can manage without it, like soldiers and sex in wartime.

But now I don't have to manage without it and I don't want to. I'm a gentleman now, see, and I can afford to dabble ..."

"Crap. You don't mean that. Actually, you really think you can still get it up, don't you?"

"Yes."

"You're probably right. Join the club."

"And I want to know if it will help me to return to my roots."

"Is it happening?"

"Not yet. I'm getting slightly homesick. For Canada."

"I'll try not to get too intrusive but is the kind of thing you are thinking about related to a period of your life? I mean are you going to write a memoir?"

"God. No. No."

"What, then?"

"I've had a lot of ideas over the years for, er, short things, and I haven't had time to work on them." I added in a rush. "And I want to try a play."

"A memory play? Like that Irish one we all saw together in New York?"

"Christ, no. Nothing lyrical."

"Then surely the right vibes are *here*, where you've lived for most of your life."

"It's not that, it's a question of speech rhythms, stuff like that."

"What the fuck are you talking about? Don't keep asking yourself if you're English or Canadian. That's bullshit. Or where you *belong*, in quotes, or what is *home*, also in quotes. Ask something smaller, where do you feel comfortable? Where are your friends? Where is your family, for Christ's sake? Where do they laugh at your jokes? Your kids know where they belong. If you stay in England, you'll feel like that rubber planter come home to a land he doesn't know. You can write a fucking play about *that*. Copy out one of Somerset Maugham's."

"Why are you so angry?"

"I'm not angry."

"Concerned, then." We had never been very close, Jack and I. I like him and he likes me, and we usually got together with our families a couple of times a year, at Christmas and for a weekend at the cottage, his cottage. Our friendship is probably one of those that will bloom when we both retire. But until then, he was coming too close.

"Because I've got a proposition," he said, and told me, finally, what it was all about.

"First of all, this merger: now there's an Australian agency that wants in, and the Germans are talking to what they call 'some other EU countries.'"

"Big stuff, eh, Jack? You don't sound as if you're bragging about it, though."

"It is, and I'm not. I want out."

"I thought you said you wanted the merger to go ahead."

"I do. Without me."

I waited.

"I want them to buy me out. And you, too. See, they need one of us to vote for the merger, or it doesn't go. But Grisham and the rest want it badly, so what I'd like to propose is that they buy us out first, then they can do what they like."

"Us? Why me?"

"Where did I get the idea that you've been thinking? You reminded me of a man I know who was once a novice in a monastic order. When it came time for his final vows, he told them he'd been thinking. Apparently that's a classic announcement of doubt. Am I right?

"More or less. I told you already, there are some other things I'd like to try before I get too old."

"You could do that, too. In fact, I think what I am proposing would be just the right context. My idea is that we leave Grisham and the rest to get on with it; we take our money and use a bit of it to start up our own little agency, just the two of us. Have some fun, and if it doesn't work, we'll just clip our coupons and watch Grisham take over the world."

"How would this work in with my little dream?"

"I think we could work half-time, both of us. Wouldn't that leave you enough time to write a play?"

"Probably. As you say, I've got enough money to live on now. And the alternative to leaving the partnership is working for the Germans and the Australians et al. No, I want out, and this'll do as something to tell the world. But you don't need me, do you? If you could get Grisham to buy you out, he would have the votes he needs, so he could go ahead and leave me twisting in the wind. Probably give me an office and a salary and nothing to do, wait a year and boot me out. That's why he was so keen that I take lots of time on this trip. So he could work this out."

"Be fair, Will. Grisham doesn't play by those rules. He's ambitious and greedy, but he's not a prick. You just probably wouldn't get a seat on the new board. You'd feel it, all right. But you're right. Either one of us will do. We're talking now so that you will know where I stand when they come looking for your John Henry. I'm not going to do a deal except with you, if you want."

"You're really keen on this idea, aren't you?"

"Yes, I am."

"All right, then. I'll vote against the merger until I hear from you, too. They have to buy us both out. At the same time. Right?"

"When are you coming back?"

"A few days. Does it matter?"

"A week?"

"Maybe a bit more. We'll get together the day after I get in."

Jack giggled. "I feel like Ulysses. Not Homer's, the other guy's."

"'Courage,' he said, and pointed towards the land," I quoted. "'The Lotus-Eaters.' You feeling tired, Jack?"

"No, no, the one that goes 'Tis not too late to seek a newer world'. The one about the old men getting it up one more time."

"Right. *That* Ulysses. Myself I feel more like Mickey Rooney. You know, 'We'll use my uncle's barn; you bring the curtain and I'll get some candles. Who will we get to play the girl?'"

"Right. By the way, your son called. Give him a call. Tell him not to worry about you."

TWENTY-SIX

"HOW'S THE RAILWAY TRIP coming?"

"Uncle, it's awful. He had a lot of time on his hands on that train, and he spent his time writing every detail of the journey, what he saw through the window, what he ate — a great thick slab of roast beef for dinner on the train, and apple pie with cheese — is that standard in Canada? — what the other passengers ate — it's like Kinsey with food instead of sex. And periodically he tries to rhapsodize about the woods and stuff, but there isn't enough variety in the woods or in him."

"*Over Prairie Trails.*"

"What's that?"

"The first book a librarian in Portage la Prairie offered me when I said I wanted to read some Canadian literature. I'll find you a copy. So where is he now?"

"Winnipeg is next. He's looking forward to Winnipeg. I'm not. Do you know it?"

"Yes, I do. I'll tell you about it when he gets there."

"Moreton, then, Uncle, finally?"

"Don't be in such a hurry. I have a couple of things to see and do before Moreton. One is at Blockley, where I want to experience what someone has called the best bed and breakfast in England. And just along from there, in a place called Paxford, is the best pub/restaurant in Gloucestershire."

"Who says?"

"A colleague of mine. And he is a man who would know. Grisham is an insider; he likes to be the man who knows about restaurants, where to buy striped shirts, shit like that."

Grisham, it was immediately clear, was right about the B&B as he usually was about such things. I gave it two checks and we proceeded on to Paxford.

The Churchill Arms is furnished with an assortment of furniture — pews, wooden armchairs, stools — that look as if they were assembled by an impoverished eighteenth-century landlord who had lost all his money at White's, hoping desperately to make a go of the place with his last few guineas as he tried to replace what had been removed by the bum-bailiffs. Now, of course, the furniture had been exquisitely aged by the tens of thousands of moleskin-covered arses and leather-patched elbows, then, more recently, as the real estate values soared, by the softest of tweeds and stone-washed chinos as worn by the newest well-stocked and bonded gentry. I tried my hand at a bit of travel writing:

"The food is superb. The menu is written in chalk on three sides of the main pillar supporting the roof. We started with venison terrine with damson chutney. Then I had roast salmon with Jerusalem artichokes. Fred had a steak, on Grisham's recommendation; both of us had the French fries, which were fried twice, the first time in Paris, that afternoon, and then flown over for a second frying in Paxford. That's what the bartender told us. Afterwards, I had summer pudding made with blackberries and Devonshire cholesterol and Fred had a triple chocolate torte which for him, he said, was an introduction to the way chocolate cake could taste. I was

glad, finally, that an English meal had confronted the memory of those sausages in the pub by Victoria station. There isn't much about food in this record because food wasn't the reason I was riding around England. But these two experiences, in Paxford and in Victoria, stand for England's cuisine, like England, full of surprises."

"That should work into your guide nicely," Fred said, admiringly, as we sat over our coffee. "Now, Westward Ho?"

"I still have a couple of places I want to visit in this area," I said. "Don't rush me."

"I meant, what comes west of Toronto?"

"Had enough about Hogtown? I suppose you're right. So we come to Winnipeg. About now you will meet your first Elmer, then gradually, as you move through Saskatchewan into Alberta, you will come across lots more. I used to think that Red Deer, Alberta, for instance, was entirely populated by people called Elmer. But first, Winnipeg is in Manitoba: as you say, it's a thousand miles from Toronto, two good days driving, three if you have a child in the car, all along the north shore of Lake Superior. Very rugged, I understand. I've never been on that road."

"But you've been to Winnipeg. My chap quite liked what he saw of it in a walk along Portage Street."

"Avenue. Portage Avenue. He wasn't there on Sunday, then. I worked there for a while, not long after I first emigrated and began to feel pretty sure that I could always find work, and therefore I should see as much of the country as I could. I'm glad I did, because if I'd stayed in Toronto, I would not have had to confront Canada. I suppose nowadays you'd call Toronto cosmopolitan, meaning that strangers feel at home there. Hardly anybody I know in Toronto actually comes from Toronto. They're mostly from away, as the Newfies say. But most Winnipeggers are from Winnipeg, or at worst Portage la Prairie or Dauphin. The people you meet in Winnipeg are the real thing and can tell you what it was like growing up there. I like them and I like Winnipeg, but the natives boast that the intersection of the two main streets, Portage Avenue and Main Street, is the coldest spot in Canada south of the Arctic, so you can't live there in winter. And the summer isn't much fun, either, because of the flies. If you go, go in early May, or late September.

"I'm glad I went there early because I got rid of my assumptions about the mix of races in Canada. I arrived in the country thinking it was 60 per cent Anglo and 40 per cent Franco. No one had told me that the Prairies, from Winnipeg to Edmonton, had been settled mainly by Ukrainians brought in by the railroad to populate the country. You should find out things like that before you go, find out about the Ukrainians, and the Italians, and the Greeks, and all the other migrations that have occurred in the last fifty years, including the most recent from India and the Orient.

"I went up to the Arctic while I was in Winnipeg. Well, not the real Arctic — it just felt like it. A place called Churchill. At one time it was called Fort Prince of Wales, built to fight the French in the fur wars of the eighteenth century. You should find out about the fur trade, find out how the French River in Ontario got its name. Churchill was rebuilt in the 1950s to keep out the Russians, and renamed Fort Churchill. Now it's just Churchill again, a tiny port that is open about six weeks a year for the shipment of grain across the Atlantic. I don't think it's commercially viable but the Manitoba government keeps it going as a living monument to the endurance of Canadians. Just the existence of a grain elevator at that latitude says something about the human spirit, the Canadian human spirit. What's the matter?"

"Don't make any sudden moves, Uncle, but shift yourself so that you can see the floor behind you."

"Is there a scorpion heading my way?"

"Turn round slowly. See her?"

You couldn't miss her. Most people were eating now, but in a space in front of the bar a woman stood, holding a pint of beer, slowly surveying the room. She was over six feet tall and broad in proportion, with a large white face and short black hair. Her spectacles rested on top of her head. She was dressed from head to toe in plaid — jacket, skirt and tie — wearing knee socks, and smoking a cigarette in a long bamboo holder. Now, her feet wide apart, taking the cigarette holder from her mouth, she spoke. "Landlord," she said, in the heartiest of voices, like a captain of a rugby team, "My compliments. This is about the best hostelry in the West Country. You know that, of course."

"Thank you, ma'am," he said, ducking his head shyly. "We do our best."

"And your best is good enough," she boomed, finished her beer, ejected her cigarette end into the empty fireplace, nodded here and there, and walked out.

No one attempted to comment publicly; a few shared smiles, that was all, but gradually the level of the talk rose as they asked each other about her.

"She was like someone in one of those old Ealing comedies," Fred said. Neither one of us could remember the name of the actress but I knew which one he meant. "You think she was for real? I mean, *hostelry*, for God's sake," he said.

I had an answer now, and I tried it out. "No. I think she is hired by the brewery to go round their pubs being English, a certain type of Englishwoman, who would give the Americans something to take home, a story about us, about you. It might have been that the British Council hired her for the same reason, to represent the English at home for the tourists."

"I think that's a load of codswallop."

"You have a better theory?"

"I think she was doing it for a bet."

"I like my idea more. I have to confess that it's not actually my idea. I remembered it from Jerome's other book, *Three Men on the Bummel*. While they are cycling in Germany they come across an Englishman and his lady being gawped at by the natives as they ponced about doing and saying all the things that were supposed to be said and done by the silliest kind of Englishman abroad at that time. You know, the 'I say, I say, I say' noise. Jerome believed these two had been hired by the English government to act like this because there was talk of war. No one, seeing these two, could take them seriously, thus international tensions would ease. Let's have another pint and look at the map. What's next?"

"That it for Manitoba?"

"No. Find St. Boniface. It used to be next to Winnipeg. It's the former French city across the river from Winnipeg. I had a girlfriend there for a while, which bears on what we were talking about. This girl had been touched by the separatist movement, and it had an odd effect on her. She worked as a typist in our Winnipeg office, and when I started to get restless and began looking around, I was told not to waste my time on Louise, for she only went out with Frenchmen. But I'd had some luck with a New Brunswick girl, you will remember, so I asked her out anyway. She said sure, and I dated her all winter. The time came to say goodbye, and we were about to part friends — I think that's how I would put it — and I finally asked her about this reputation she had for not dating Anglos. 'It's true,' she said. 'I never do.'"

"'But what about me?' I asked."

"'You're not Anglo. You're English. That's different.'"

"'How? Why?'"

"'It is a great belief among the Anglos here that the girls from St. Boniface are easy meat, as one of them said to me. That's their mythology, so if you go out with an Anglo you have to tell him right away that you're not. Do I have to go on? It's impossible to have a normal first date. Either he's only interested in getting into your pants right away, or he has to show you he's not. Either way you get to talk about it too soon.'"

Fred said, "I can see I shall have to tread carefully."

I said, "No, no. Rush in. This is probably all ancient sociology. And with that accent you'll get away with murder, for a while. The point of my story is that St. Boniface is a symbol of what you ought to find out about the French in Canada. They don't stop at the Quebec-Ontario border. Much of northern Ontario is French speaking and there are pockets of French speakers right across the country. I should tell you about another mystery in this connection I came across in Alberta. I was passing through a town called Bonneville and I asked someone about the name, and whether it meant that the inhabitants were French originally. I got into a discussion of the French presence in Alberta from which all I remember is that one French Albertan was very concerned to make me understand that though she and her family were French — her name was Ghislane — and proud of it, and they lived in a town that was 90 per cent French, in Alberta, and she herself could trace her ancestry back to a seventeenth-century prostitute, one of those transported to Canada to become the mothers of the future generations, she was not Québécoise, but from quite a different kind of people. I never understood why or how — I was too afraid of breaking the eggs I was treading on to ask the right questions — but I guessed that the root of her anxiety was that I might confuse her with the French people whom all other Albertans hate, the Québécois. It was a Frenchman, remember, who went after their oil revenues. I should remind you here, before we get to Alberta, that I have also spent time in a place called Felhar, north of Edmonton, which is known, to itself at least, as the honey capital of the world. There I saw a man with a beard made of bees. It was the sweetest smelling town I've ever been in. It was French and Mennonite, mixed. What's next?"

"Saskatchewan. Are there any cities in Saskatchewan?"

"Hang on, I've just thought of two loosely related experiences. The first is the night I drank moonshine in Flin Flon. Flin Flon is a mining town that straddles the borders of northern Manitoba and Saskatchewan. A man in the office was from there — Flin Flon is the kind of place a lot of people are from — and he was getting married in his hometown, and four of us were driving up from Winnipeg in an old Volkswagen. It was my first Canadian wedding and I enjoyed it a lot, and then, late at night, the bride's father brought out this jar, the kind of jar you preserve peaches in, full of a colourless liquid. We all drank some to be polite, mixed with pineapple juice, and I woke up next morning under the bed feeling as if someone had trepanned me with an axe. I've been careful of homemade liquor ever since, but who would have expected moonshine in Flin Flon? I thought it was something hillbillies in Arkansas drank."

"Did he make it himself?"

"Apparently not. He was a teetotaller, just trying to be a good host to his daughter's friends from the big city. He didn't know it was about a hundred and ninety proof. He got it from some Norwegian friends."

"Norwegian? Who flew in from Oslo, like? Do they have moonshine in Norway?"

"Canadian-Norwegian. The prefix is usually dropped, so when you want to indicate real Norwegians you say so, as in Norwegians from Norway. It's the same with Italians, Greeks — all of them, and us."

"Anyway, I thought all Canadians drank rye whiskey."

"So did I at your age. Which is a good example of that thing you said, extrapolating from too small a sample, your own experience. See, when I settled into advertising, I saw that all Canadians in fact drink Scotch, and I asked an old advertising man about it. He said when he was in college, in Manitoba in the fifties, everyone drank rye, mixed with ginger ale, except the girls, who drank rum and Coke. When you went to a nightclub, you took your own rye and rum in a paper sack, and they sold you the mix and the ice. Then after you graduated and moved to Toronto, you tried Scotch, and then everyone drank Scotch. He thought perhaps it was a general shift in taste, like everyone in Toronto starting around 1990 suddenly drinking Amaretto. I accepted that; certainly I never saw any rye until I stayed in a summer cottage north of Parry Sound, in Ontario, and one day I went to the local liquor store in Alban and noticed that there was five times as much rye on sale as there was Scotch, the reverse of what you might find in Toronto. The cashier confirmed the ratio and I dared to ask if maybe the French liked rye more. That part of the province is largely French. She said, no, the Anglos drank it, too. As for the recent fashions, she didn't have a bottle of Irish, or malt whiskey on the shelves. There was no demand for it. But she was always being asked for rare brands of rye. At the time, I didn't know there was any rye more than ninety days old. Where were we?"

"Saskatchewan. But you said there were two experiences ..."

"Right. The other one concerned driving. It happened on the same trip. I had never driven before we got into that Volkswagen, but the highway was deserted that evening and the others asked me if I would like to try. I got behind the wheel, did all the clutch and gear-shifting stuff as instructed, and away we went. Soon we were doing eighty miles an hour and I was thinking there was nothing to it, then someone saw a gas station up ahead with a sign saying it was the last place to buy gas before Flin Flon. I was doing so well they forgot I couldn't drive, so when they told me to pull in to the gas station, they didn't tell me to slow down first and it was my good luck that behind the gas station and beyond for a couple of hundred miles it was muskeg, sort of dry swamp with bushes. We must have gone a quarter of a mile into the bush before I had the great presence of mind to take my foot off the gas. As I say, it was an old car, and all I did was scratch it some more; it only took a couple of hours to pull and push it back on to the highway. That was my first driving lesson. What's next?"

"What about a great man from Ontario?"

"Time we left the politicians out of it. Besides, there isn't one anyway who can compete in significance with Stephen Leacock."

"I've heard of him, I think. What's he famous for?"

"Look it up."

"And Manitoba? The great man?"

"Woman. Nellie McClung. I have to vote for her."

"Okay. Saskatchewan, now. Are there any cities there?"

"Hang on; I've just thought of something else you ought to know about Manitoba. When you are travelling west, religious belief, like christening the eldest son 'Elmer,' begins in Manitoba, church-going that is, and gets stronger and simpler until you get to the mountains. I never met anyone in Ontario who went to church, not the evening service, anyway — I'm not talking about Catholics now because they have to go, I understand, but all the others. Us. But in Manitoba you often see people in twos or threes about six o'clock heading for the church. In Saskatchewan, they not only go to church, sometimes twice a day, but they also teach Sunday school, some of them. When you get to Alberta, they're clapping along with the hymns. It's like moving back as well as West: from Ontario to Alberta you travel a century and a half to where people leave their guns in the vestry before they go in to pray, and the hymns are like nothing you ever sang in Worcester Park, or Cambridge. You've heard some of them in old Gary Cooper movies. I'm telling you all this in case you get invited home to Sunday supper in a Western home. Don't eat until you are sure they don't plan to say grace, because they almost certainly will. One family home I was invited to in Winnipeg set an extra place at the table in case a stranger came by, hungry. An old prairie custom, they said. I think it was symbolic by the time I got there but I wasn't absolutely sure. It wasn't symbolic at Christmas, when I was invited everywhere so I could be that stranger. I like the Prairies.

"But you were asking about Saskatchewan cities. There are two, neither one held me for more than an overnight. There's the capital, Regina, certainly not a place you need to worry about, because you will never see an ad for a job in Regina in a Toronto paper. Then there's Saskatoon. Bob Hope could always get a laugh just by saying he was off to Saskatoon, Saskatchewan. Americans find the two words funny when spoken together like that; makes them feel superior even if they are from Oshkosh, or Intercourse, Pennsylvania. But the reality is not funny at all: an unthriving old downtown attempting to stay alive by selling hand-thrown pottery, and a prosperous and nasty shopping mall several miles away which has sucked all the commercial life out of the city. It's a common pattern, not just in Saskatchewan."

"So I don't bother with Saskatchewan?"

"Not at all. I was just clearing the ground, eliminating the obvious. The cities aren't much, but the place to go is Moose Jaw."

"You pulling my leg, Uncle?"

"Moose Jaw, which is accessible only by road, is one of those places of which people say, 'This is the real Canada.' Such places arise out of a conjunction of people, activities, the landscape and the evening light with a result that seems so right that when you get there you feel you have been there before. I remember being in a car that had broken down in a village called Whitewood in Saskatchewan. It was a Saturday night and the people from the farms around had come to town to do their weekly shopping, and to meet. It was like a Thornton Wilder play, only real. Being there in that scene for a couple of hours, I felt privileged to be part of Saturday Night in Saskatchewan.

"Moose Jaw does that to you. It's really only a one street town. I was there for a few days in midsummer once. The climate was flawless — hot, bright, dry and smogless, and cool at night. And the food in Moose Jaw is magnificent. I'm not talking about the kind they sell here, not *haut cuisine*. I mean the best possible club sandwiches made with whole-wheat bread and real mayonnaise, served with good Canadian fries. And they still make their own soup and bake their own pies."

"Which restaurant in Moose Jaw you are talking about? Is there just one?"

"As I remember, there are five or six along the main street, none of them with pretensions, though one of them is also a shoe repair shop, but they compete in little ways. This one will give you their own homemade corn relish with the hamburger; that one makes a specialty of the coleslaw they serve with the club sandwich."

"Are you making fun, Uncle?"

"God forbid. I'm simply trying to describe the nicest town in Canada."

"But you can't live on club sandwiches, can you?"

"No, and anyway those restaurants are closed at night. At night you switch to Chinese. Every Canadian village west of the Maritime provinces has a Chinese restaurant, run by the people left behind when the railroad was finished. The railroad company imported thousands of Chinese labourers to build the railroad, then abandoned them to the government who mistreated them in the various ways that governments do. The result was a diaspora, as the Chinese spread across the land, trying not to be deported, trying to earn the money to bring their wives and families over and pay something called a head tax, finding opportunities to open coffee shops in places like South Porcupine and Loon Lake, Saskatchewan. Chinatowns appeared in every city west of Fredericton, and every small town, including Flin Flon, has its Chinese restaurant. A lot settled in Moose Jaw and the town has made a kind of museum out of the under-ground caves the workers lived in. (They say that Al Capone used these caves — known as The Tunnels — to store his liquor during prohibition.) And finally, Moose Jaw is a spa. The mineral springs for which the town of Watrous is famous can also be experienced in the main hotel in Moose Jaw. Some people vacation in the hotel pool, even honeymooners. But I'm still concerned about that question of yours: am I being funny? Let me reiterate: Moose Jaw is the nicest town to be from in Canada. And before you ask, the great man from Saskatchewan is Tommy Douglas. In his case, don't just look him up: buy the book."

TWENTY-SEVEN

"WHERE ARE WE NOW?" Fred asked.

"Here or there?"

"Here."

"We're on our way to Chipping Campden tomorrow."

"Why?"

"Graham Greene lived there. I have always thought *The Human Factor* is the best spy novel of its kind I've ever read."

"What do you think of his literary novels?"

"I've never made much of the Catholic novels. To an outsider, he seemed to be inventing spiritual problems so he could agonize over them for three hundred pages. But I liked *The Comedians*."

I liked Chipping Campden, too. Unlike Broadway, it seemed a place where people really lived, if they could afford it. There were two greengrocers, several cake shops, and even a French delicatessen, selling genuine *boudins*, cheese and bread. There were six or seven pubs, an impressive silversmith, a real bookshop and very little, if any, tourist schlock, that I could see. And the whole town is made of that yellow Cotswold stone. I gave it a tick and a half. And mention of *boudins* gives me the opportunity to balance off the experience of those grey sausages in London with the very different experiences we've had on the road.

Because real sausages are back. I remembered, growing up, quite liking them, especially chipolatas, but there lingered a suspicion of them, left over from the war when they were made of the butcher's leftover scraps ground up with a lot of herbs and spices; tasty but suspect. No longer, or perhaps the scraps come from more expensive cuts of meat. Tentatively at first, then with real enthusiasm, I tried, one after the other, a succession of the most succulent sausages known to man. Eating in England can be full of surprises, but stick to sausages, especially if they are labelled; it is difficult not to be satisfied. The straight pork sausages are good enough, and there are local variations: Lincolnshire, Cumberland, Gloucester Old Spot, Newmarket, Worcestershire — there are regional sausages everywhere that will turn you into a connoisseur as discriminating as any oenophile. Then there are wild boar sausages (Fred's favourite) and, of course, lamb sausages, beef sausages, turkey sausages, and so on, though one school of thought (mine) would claim that only pork sausages are the real thing. We ate them hot for dinner, and cold, as part of a pub lunch; we ate them in some form almost every day; we never got tired of them. If I were to stay here, I would open a small restaurant that served only sausages, sausages with mash, with fries, baked in a toad-in-the-hole — every which way. I'd make a fortune. I told Fred my idea. He said it's been done already.

Before we left Chipping Campden, we had half a pint of beer in The Volunteer, and I asked a man in ploughman's costume if he knew the road to Hidcote Manor, a famous garden I had heard of. "Ah," he said. "Ah. Go be way of Yubberton."

Fortunately the barman was listening, and when the ploughman left he told me what he had said. "Take the Ebrington road," it turned out to be.

In the car I circled Ebrington on the map and wrote Yubberton alongside. "See?" I said to Fred. "Another surviving dialect."

On our way back to Moreton, we detoured to have a look at Chastleton House on the recommendation of a woman in a tea shop whom I had been telling how little interest I had in country houses. She said this was the exception. She was right. I gave it a tick immediately. It's unlike any other country or stately home I've plodded through.

Early in the seventeenth century, a local lawyer named Walter Jones, having made a lot of money at conveyancing or some such, decided he wanted to become, not merely respectable beyond his fellow lawyers, but a proper gentleman, rather like a Canadian newspaper owner of today deciding to become a lord. He bought a house belonging to Robert Catesby, the mastermind of the Gunpowder Plot, tore it down (the parallels between Jones and our own self-made men are endless), and built Chastleton House. Unfortunately, unlike our newspaper owners, he didn't have enough money and went broke refurbishing it. The result is that this really is a seventeenth-century country house with very few changes or improvements, a wonderful no-nonsense manor in its furnishings and fittings — the kitchen, little modernized since the seventeenth century was still being used by Walter's impoverished descendants in 1952. I could imagine living in Chastleton House, eating lumps of charred flesh from the spit and drinking the homemade beer for breakfast.

TWENTY-EIGHT

THE NEXT MORNING, FRED said, "Maybe he was gay."

"Who? Robert Catesby?"

"No, Great-Great-Uncle Jack. You could get shot for that, too, in 1916, in the army."

"Try that on your grandfather."

"I don't think so. Now what, Uncle? We're here, in Moreton-in-Marsh. Question is, why?"

"What's going on out there?" Men were bustling about the town square; a truck painted with the words "Spook Erections" was parked right opposite the window of the inn. Spook Erections? A truckload of Viagra for spies?

"Market, innit?" the waitress offered. "Every Tuesday."

Not Viagra, then; scaffolding to put up the market stalls. This was Monday. "Let's stay another night. Market day might be the ideal time to find people who could answer my questions."

Fred watched me narrowly. "I'm on to you, Uncle. Now that you're here you're *really afraid* of what you'll find. Right?"

"I told you. Nothing so melodramatic. What I'm afraid of is that the wisp of smoke we've been chasing will turn out to be just that. I know my mother used to take the train to here regularly, and I wonder why. That's all."

"Is it connected to the Mystery of the Hero's Birth?"

"Of course it is. One more reason I'm here. But let's finish our journey, shall we?"

"Where to, first?" Fred inquired in the car.

I consulted the map. "Go along the A44 towards Bourton-on-the-Hill. Just after Bourton, on the left, there's a little side road running parallel with the main road to Stow-on-the-Wold that'll go in the right direction. Take that."

We climbed the hill to the village, and turned off before the Stow road. "Stop for a minute," I said. "There. I thought it might be like this. See, now, there's my entry in the 'This is England' poster competition."

Immediately to our left was a well-kept paddock with four or five beautiful little foals, and their equally handsome parents. Beyond the paddock was the model farm, and beyond the farm was the rest of the view all the way to Moreton-in-Marsh. All it required was five naked members of the Women's Institute, pretending to be getting in the hay, to make a calendar that would sell millions (or five ploughmen artfully shielding their naked members with their coulters — there are lots of variations on this theme).

"Very pretty," said Fred. "As pretty as Moose Jaw?"

"For Christ's sake, Moose Jaw isn't *pretty*. Nothing in Canada is *pretty*. That's England. You can't compare them. Moose Jaw is only a hundred years old. I imagine people have been growing stuff around here since Boadicea. What am I trying to say? Try this: drinking beer in a pub garden in Chipping Campden on a warm summer evening is very pleasant. But driving across the Prairies at sunset is not pleasant: it's stunning. I'd say awesome, except that that word has had all the juice drained out of it. But it isn't *pretty*. Drive on."

We passed Stow and came next to Bourton-on-the-Water, a toy-shop of a town resigned to its role as the destination for elderly day trippers seeking tea and a lavatory. The old folks shuffle from window to window, comparing the goods with those they can buy at home in Birmingham or Swindon, buying nothing, having a day out.

An hour in Bourton-on-the-Water was enough. We moved on to Guiting and got lost, thereby striking gold as we puttered around the Guitings and the Slaughters and the Swells, relaxed in the knowledge that every second signpost pointed to Stow, and we knew it was a straight road from Stow to Moreton. This was England, all right: Albion, the green and golden land. We ate lunch in Ford in a pub that specialized in asparagus in season, although we were too late for that.

After lunch we had a look at the Cotswold Farm Park, decided the shire horses were worth a tick, and drove down to Chedworth so that Fred could get a look at a Roman villa. This was a lot more interesting than most antique sites and we had brought no expectations to it, so it was a nice surprise. I know nothing about Roman England — Hadrian's Wall? Julius Caesar? What else? And I know very little about the sixteen hundred years between the arrival of Julius and the departure of William from Stratford. How long did the Dark Ages last? What does the term "medieval" cover?

I began a little fantasy of putting together a tour for people like me, a tour based in tracing a time period. I said, "What do you know about early English history?"

"Before 1066, you mean?"

"I mean starting with Stonehenge."

"I think that's pre-history, Uncle. About 2000 years BC."

"The Druids, like?"

"I think the Druids were Celtic priests, just predating the Romans. Stonehenge came before them."

"Yes?" I told him my new idea of a tour through the ages. "The tour would start at Stonehenge staying the night at Salisbury, but ignoring the cathedral, which would be on a later tour, then moving on to Wales where the Celts were driven by the Anglo-Saxons. Now a look at an Anglo-Saxon barrow, and maybe, if it fits, a trip to Sutton Hoo where that ship was dug up. Now the group would proceed to Chedworth, with a night at Cirencester, which, you can tell by its name, was once a very big Roman town. Then down to Bath for the baths, ignoring Jane Austen. A quick look at Hastings, where the Normans landed, a look around Norman England, which I shall have to swot up, a ruin or two from medieval England, a Gothic cathedral perhaps, Salisbury, and finish at Stratford. Thirty-five hundred years properly placed in a row."

"I think a couple of centuries are in the wrong place, Uncle, and you've missed out the Vikings."

"Have I? When did they come?"

"The Romans left about 400 AD, so it must have been in the next six hundred years."

"I'll look them up. After the first one, more tours could be constructed, covering shorter periods because from now on there is more history, including more political history. What do you think?"

"It sounds very promising. It could be ten tours before all their dollars are spent."

TWENTY-NINE

"WHERE TO, UNCLE?" CAME the now familiar cry.

We were walking towards the car. I was still daydreaming about the tourist business. I looked at the map "What's the time? 3:30. Let's go back to Moreton. What's your man talking about now?"

"He had a corned beef on rye before the train left Winnipeg. Raves about it. What is it, Uncle? It can't be tinned corned beef, can it? Even with rationing he must have had that before."

"It's a Jewish food, and he's right to rave about it. The nearest thing to it is salt beef, as sold in the East End. Where is he now?"

"He's crossed the Prairies," Fred said. "There's a long dull bit about the Rockies. I've never seen them, but how could anyone make the Rockies dull?"

"Does he start in the foothills, in Alberta?"

"Yes. Redneck country?"

"Not so loud."

"It's *your* term."

"Then let me expand on it a little. You have the Alberta politicians and the Eastern journalists to thank for the term. The journalists usually put the word in quotes to show they are dissociating themselves from it but they still use it all the time. The politicians deserve it. They were born to the sound of bibles being thumped and they still derive their political philosophy from the more vengeful parts of the Old Testament. When they discovered oil back in the forties, they acted as if they had invented it and tried to patent it. They have stashed away a lot of money since. Trudeau stopped some of the worst excesses, which is why they dance, cursing ..."

"This is Alberta? I thought Alberta was all cowboys and cattle."

"So it was, before oil. They are close to Texans, having inherited the same myth of self-sufficiency, and a hatred of what they call socialism. The cattlemen see themselves as part of a tradition of individual rights and responsibilities; the oil men are just greedy. They both regard income tax as a plot to take their money and give it to the drug addicts on the streets in Toronto and Vancouver."

"I should avoid Alberta, then?"

"If you do you'll miss out on one of the loveliest experiences the country offers; I mean arriving in Calgary at night and waking up in a hotel bedroom — choose the western side of the hotel and the sixteenth floor — and seeing through the window your first view of the Rockies. That's the way I like to experience nature — through the window. It's extraordinary that the thousands of pictures you've seen of those mountains still do not prepare you for your first sight of the real thing. Maybe it's the light. Well-travelled friends tell me that the light in Calgary is as pure as that in Greece. I can believe it; it's even purer than the light in Moose Jaw. Yes, stop off in Calgary. I should backtrack a bit. The other reason for spending time in Calgary is to experience the huge difference between Alberta politicians and their constituents. The people I met in Calgary all seemed descended from characters in a Hollywood movie about pioneers and homesteaders and such, you know, good folk who sing "Bringing in the Sheaves" a lot. It comes out in many ways: cowboy boots, of course; all the stockbrokers wear cowboy boots but it's the little signs, like in a sci-fi movie when hairy ears and fangs start to grow on the normal looking visitors; in Calgary, it's a bootlace tie here, the sudden appearance on the bank clerk on Friday of a white Stetson, the wide leather belt holding up the lawyer's trousers.

"They still believe that a man can do anything if he works hard enough and is allowed by the government to keep all he earns, and their clothes show it. It's an enormously attractive scene, which again has something to do with the light, making it a bright world to start with, and something to do with their temperamental need to be agreeable. They smile a lot. I'm talking about Calgarians — I can't speak for Edmonton. I think people who call their hockey team the Oilers have defined themselves.

"But down East, in Toronto, all we hear are the voices of their politicians braying for independence in good times and for subsidies when times are hard, and setting up new political parties because the traditional parties are not right-wing enough for them."

"Next stop British Columbia?"

"I've just had a thought. When you are doing your research, spare some time for this question: Why is it that the most socialist province and the most right-wing province lie next to each other, without, apparently, affecting each other's view of the world as it is, and as it should be. I mean Saskatchewan, justly proud of inventing Medicare, and making Canada, in the area of health care, currently the most progressive in the Western world (and from what I've been reading in the papers, not yet in the state of decay that this country's health system seems to be in), and Alberta. It's got something to do with the fact that Saskatchewan was colonized from Europe, and in Alberta, the new settlers came up from the USA. That's what people tell me. A name to remind you of here. Tommy Douglas, sometime premier of Saskatchewan, the hero of Medicare, and the finest public speaker I've ever heard. I'm wary of hero-worship: I start looking for the feet of clay right away, but it's a waste of time with Douglas. Look him up."

"You already mentioned him. Saskatchewan's great man."

"And a candidate for the federal one, too."

"I'll look him up. Next stop British Columbia?"

"I've been thinking about who is the great man in Alberta. I think I'd have to say Bill Aberhart. Look him up. He might be listed as 'Bible' Bill Aberhart. That's a start to understanding Alberta. And just when you think you've got Alberta pegged, ask yourself why, nevertheless, it has the best secondary school system in Canada, maybe on the continent. At any rate, all the brilliant math students come from there.

"Now I'm not very reliable on British Columbia because I've only visited two places in the province. One was Radium Hot Springs, where I spent a night lolling under the stars in warm mineral water. Try it. Half an hour in the waters gives you the same physical sense of absolute fulfillment that writers of romances give their heroes and heroines after sex. And then there's Vancouver. But you can't trust me on British Columbia. As I said, I don't get off on nature, and that's all BC is, really, rocks and stones and trees, and the sea, which, I hear, is colder than the English Channel. People who like scenery, and don't mind rain, rave about the province, especially old people from Winnipeg, fed up with shovelling snow in winter.

"But Vancouver?"

"Vancouver's got a complex. It thinks it's too far away from the action, and in thinking so, it is. It's odd that there's no equivalent uneasiness in the States. Los Angeles, for instance, may be, no, is, the nastiest metropolis in the Western hemisphere but it's also, for its inhabitants and for a lot of other Americans, the centre of the world. San Francisco, too, has its own reasons for being — better ones than Los Angeles. People move to San Francisco from New York in search of a richer and more interesting life. Even Seattle has Starbucks and Frasier. But Vancouver. Once, a few years ago,

I was out there working on finding locations for a commercial — Vancouver's got great locations — and I was having dinner with a former Torontonian, a man I worked with previously. He spent most of the evening bragging about Vancouver, the wonderful sailing, the skiing, the scenery, the seafood, and then, late in the evening, when he'd run out of things to boast about, he said, 'So what's happening?'

"It wasn't a casual query. Vancouver had everything, except Toronto's advertising gossip, and he missed it like a Kalahari bushman too long away from the tribal storyteller. I imagine it's the same in all the creative industries. Live in Vancouver for six months and you want to know what's happening."

"So tell me, what's *your* idea of a good place to live?"

"Somewhere where you can walk into a café and see people you know and like at three different tables."

"That happens in Toronto?"

"It's always possible. Two is common, on Bloor Street, west of Spadina Avenue."

Fred pointed to the map, squinting sideways as he drove. "What's that down there?"

"That's Victoria, a mass of cranky bylaws thought up by old folks who have nothing much else to do. The only provincial capital that is habitable both in winter and in summer, but without the action of say, Quebec City. Okay? Now all we have left is the territories, about which I know nothing."

"We need a great man for British Columbia."

"We have one of those, all right. A man named Bennett, 'Wacky,' from his initials, W.A.C. Look him up. Where is your man now?"

"On his way to Vancouver, I would think. I was going to tell you, the journal ends there, just like that."

"He forgot it. Left it on the train. Some charitable soul found it and mailed it back to England. How it got to your grandfather's lost property office I don't know. What are you going to do with it now?"

"Throw it away?"

"No way. Don't you recognize it? A valuable historical document, that's what that is. Belongs in an archive where it can be available to students of Canadian history like you who are putting together books and theses and so forth on 'The Immigrant Experience in Canada after World War Two.'"

"I should take it home? Give it to the British Library?"

"I'm not sure they'd be interested. Here, leave it with me. I know a man in Toronto who runs an archive; he'll gobble this up. Mid-Century Life-Writing, he'll call it. His library has shelves full of it."

It was late enough, about six o'clock, to miss the rush hour in Gloucestershire, but Fred was feeling peckish so we found a tea shop open and had tea and crumpets, then drove home, taking in Stow-on-the-Wold on the way.

Stow-on-the-Wold was all right but somewhat on the Broadway side, full of people on a day out from Birmingham. But still, unlike Broadway, you could see the old town underneath, the shops, the inns, the public lavatories, though a new supermarket nearby has drained some of the life out of the town, and too many of the shops have switched from their original purposes to selling souvenirs, and to fronting for catalogue companies. They have to survive The Age of Tesco, of course, but it's a pity.

Fred said, "I think they have an agreement, Broadway is for American, Japanese and Continental tourists, Stow is for English weekenders, and Bourton is for day trippers, especially pensioners. Chipping Campden is for people who like to eat out."

Coach-loads of very old people from the neighbouring villages appeared the next morning and the stallholders started selling everything that market stallholders sell, mostly clothes, but books and plants and food, too. A man with a truckload of meat offered it in job lots: "Ere, a fiver the lot!" the lot being an extended arm covered in pork chops and pot roasts. A crowd had gathered to watch an

Asian demonstrate his car polish. I did my homework before Fred was up. "I'm going to have a look round the stalls," I said to him, when he appeared. "When you've finished breakfast, we'll start our inquiries."

He blinked at me, still young enough to need a long time to surface.

"In an hour," I added.

He nodded, happy that he had time for the cereal and figs that were included in the breakfast, as well as bacon and eggs and black pudding and toast and marmalade. Fred isn't greedy, and on this trip he never seems to yearn for more, like Oliver Twist, but there was still something of the rugby-playing adolescent in him. When it was there, he ate it.

"Where to, first, Uncle?"

"I've been looking at the map again. The railway is marked and Moreton is the only station in the area. It seems likely that she came to Moreton for that reason, just because that was the nearest train station to her destination. See there's no railway station in Stow or in Broadway or Chipping Campden — all well-known, highly inhabited and visited places. She could have been on her way to almost anywhere around here."

"So what are you going to do?"

"Ask around. Finish your breakfast."

I walked south along the main road as far as the library, where I found a woman to tell me that the local senior citizens got free coffee and biscuits on market days in the back room of the Woolpack, a pub on Sheep Street. I walked back along the main street as far as a bridge by a supermarket then came back and explored a bit behind each side of the main street. I was confident then that I could follow any directions in the town.

The stalls ran from just outside the hotel all the way along the village green, two long rows laddered by smaller rows set sideways to the street. The shoppers, mainly pensioners, old people pushing their elders around in wheelchairs, filled the spaces between and around the stalls, shuffling and squeezing past each other, retreating a step when the space in front of them filled up from the other direction, occasionally standing their ground, waiting for the other to give way. Fred and I joined the flow, energized by the scene, but me slightly put off by the shoving.

We were standing on the corner of the main road near the public library, waiting for a gap in the stream of traffic, when, just as a gap occurred, a car came up the side road and nearly took my toes off as it turned in front of me. As I've already pointed out, in England pedestrians have no rights whatsoever. They still call the road the "carriageway" when they are repairing it, and that should tell you something about their mindset, that people in carriages (cars) own the road, and pedestrians (peasants) had better watch themselves. There are signs painted in the road, telling them so: "LOOK LEFT" or "LOOK RIGHT" they say, to the pedestrians, not to the motorists.

An old bent couple waited for their own gap. Beside them stood one of the town gossips, an enormously fat woman with a bright red face carrying a shopping bag, who shouted out to her acquaintances as they appeared from between the stalls, making herself at home in the street. Then, without warning, the old man left the curb and scuttled through a gap in the stream of cars, landing safely and triumphantly on the other side.

"Hoo-hoo," the gossip cackled to the old man's companion, left fluttering on the sidewalk like a frightened pigeon. "Hoo-hoo. 'Im didn't look to see if you'm were follerin' 'im, did'im?"

I offered this to Fred as another sample of a speech pattern that had survived Estuary English.

Inside the hall, women volunteers were making ready the coffee and biscuits.

"This is for oldies, dear," one of them said, as we came in.

I thanked her for noticing we didn't belong, and explained our mission. The woman said, "You don't sound American, does he, Beryl?"

I said, "I was born here, in England. But it's my father's family we're searching out. I lost track of them, but I remember the name, Moreton-in-Marsh, and I think there might be uncles and aunts in the district."

"What's their name?"

"Cullough."

The woman held her bottom lip. "No, dear. You heard of a Cullough round here, Beryl? Open the door, love, let the old dears in."

Cups and saucers had been set out on the tables, with plates of biscuits. The seniors entered, mostly in pairs, a man and a woman, or two women, and took their places as Beryl took round a giant jug of coffee. One couple told another that they hadn't been on holiday for more than twenty years. "Ah," said the other man, "We found that, too. There's no doubt about it, tropical fish *are* a tie."

When every cup was filled, Beryl announced that they had visitors from Canada, inquiring about possible relations that might be in the area. Would they please look at the pictures that they were passing round and speak up if they recognized the people.

There were seven tables of coffee drinkers. Fred and I gave the first table the pictures then went to the back of the hall beside the coffee urn, accepted cups ourselves, and waited.

The scene became animated, as the question turned into a quiz, then a competition for who could recognize the people first. Warm debates ensued. "That's Elsie Cornwell who died of food poisoning!"

"Never! Elsie Cornwell never had hair like that and it wasn't food poisoning. She swallowed some liniment, on purpose."

All round the room the guesses rose and were shot down. Slowly the chat died as each time the pictures were reluctantly returned to the end of the table for collection, until they reached a table where they stayed as the group got excited. An old lady put up her hand, as if in school. I hurried over.

"This is David Cullough, isn't it?" the woman said.

"You know him?"

"If it's David, I did. He's dead but his widow, Bessie Cullough, lives in Wellborough, off the Stow Road. Is that her?"

"Are you sure about him?" It had to be right; no one had said the name aloud to this woman."

"No, I'm not sure, but I think so. I suppose this is Bessie Cullough, but she's changed a gradle."

"A what?"

"A great deal," an old man with elegantly coiffured white hair interpreted.

"Did you know them?"

"I didn't know him well, if you know what I mean. Old Doris Bloomingdale did. She used to live in Wellborough. Here, I'll take you to her. She can't see very well but her mind is as clear as yours or mine."

She led us down the room to an old lady who sat still at a table near the end of the room, moving her head slowly at the shapes that appeared and disappeared.

"Doris. These people want to know about David Cullough. You remember him?"

"'Course I remember him. David Cullough his name was. Saucy young bugger. Naughty, too. He used to come home to Bessie every other weekend. They wouldn't even answer the door some days when he was home. Every other weekend. Then it stopped. They said he was killed in a car accident."

"Here?"

"On the Fosse Way. Up near Shipston. Not long after the war."

"You sure?"

"It's the sort of thing that stays in your mind."

"Were there any children?"

"No."

"Did she have any other visitors?" I asked.

"You know about *her*, eh? After David was killed, there was a woman come every other weekend, or did until this summer."

"Who was that?"

"I was never introduced. Someone from London, I should think. Not the Welfare people, I shouldn't think. Well-dressed."

I pointed to the woman in the picture. "This woman?"

"I can't see faces any more, dear, not even yours. Why do you want to know all this?"

"I think I may be related."

"Why don't you go and see her yourself. You got a car? Then drive it down towards Stow. The road to Wellborough is on the right, unless they've changed it."

"Can you describe the house?"

"Ask them in the village shop. The Post Office. They'll point you. It's a guesthouse. Big place. I'd come with you but I still haven't finished my coffee and Mr. Carberry's daughter drives me home on market days. I have to be waiting by the roundabout at twelve. Mr. Carberry's daughter is very strict."

"Thank you."

I went round the tables, thanking everybody for their help. I wasn't impatient; the prospect of finding an answer to my question was starting to alarm me.

I said to Fred, "He's dead."

Fred said, "I'm sorry, Uncle. Disappointing."

"Yes, it is." I felt the stuffing start to ooze out. Ever since I had heard the name I had been building myself up for the meeting. But the real man was gone; and I just had the parts of a story to fill in.

Fred said, "You're sure he's the one you were looking for? What about the woman?"

"Whoever she is, it's him I would expect to be recognized. I've been guessing he was the one my mother was visiting."

"They were lovers, do you think? And your father didn't mind?"

"It happens."

"But that old lady said that she used to, er, visit this Bessie Cullough."

"None of it makes sense, yet. At least, I'm not going to meet an old David Cullough, who may or may not have been my father. He's dead."

THIRTY

WE FOUND WELLBOROUGH, AND the village shop, and from there the house of Bessie Cullough, a substantial nineteenth-century brick building by the village hall.

Fred had the car door half-opened when he saw that I hadn't moved. He withdrew his leg and closed the door. "Frightened?" he asked.

"Something weird is about to happen," I said. I showed him the picture I had been carrying around of the woman standing outside the house.

Fred said, "That's the house!"

The front door of the house opened and an elderly woman in the doorway smiled a greeting as if we were expected. She was dressed in a sand-coloured caftan that covered her feet. Her hair came down her back in a thick grey plait. "I don't think I have a booking," she said. "Did you call?"

"We got the address in Moreton," I said.

The woman was tall and solid, and about eighty years old. In spite of the caftan, she looked very human, friendly and sort of amused to see us. I've found that most women over fifty when they go in for caftans take on an expression with it, a sort of wistful calmness to show they are in touch with the wellsprings of the universe, and they swan about, tolerant of us earthier mortals. You get three caftaned women in a room and you are in a temple of the spirit. Bessie Cullough, though, was wearing a caftan to avoid having to get washed and dressed.

"To tell you the truth, I'd pretty well decided to have the day off. I haven't even put my hair up." She pointed to her head. "This is how I sleep, not how I usually meet people, but I'm not going out until much later. I expect I can accommodate you if you don't mind not being fussed over. I can't provide dinner on such short notice but everything else is yours for the asking. Your car will be all right there. Some of the new gentry are trying to get parking banned on the village roads but they haven't won yet. Bring your bags in. I'll show you your room."

"There's a bit of confusion here," Fred said. "We weren't looking ..."

I put a hand on his arm to shut him up. "You're Bessie Cullough, aren't you?" I said, to the woman. "Your house looks terrific but we've taken a room at the big pub in Moreton and told everybody that's where they'll find us, so we'll have to come back to you again, some other time. And we will."

"He doesn't seem quite so sure," the woman said, pointing to Fred. "But come in. My name, as you say, is Bessie Cullough. Who am I talking to?"

"Will Prentice and Fred Simpson, my nephew."

"Just say that name again. Yours."

I did so.

"Then I am expecting you. I thought you would be here before this. Come in, come in. Make yourself at home."

We followed her through to a kitchen, a huge brick-floored room that had been recently added to the back of the house, a room big enough to serve as a dining room.

"Let's have some coffee round the table," Mrs. Cullough said. "Excuse me a moment." She picked up the telephone from the windowsill, dialled a number, and said, into the phone, "I'm going to be busy all day, I'm afraid. Let's have a bite in the Coach and Horses — no, not the one in the village; they just have potato crisps and nuts — the one on the main road — pick me up about seven. Sorry to give up our little outing but I'm about to have the most important conversation in my life." She put down the phone and began to assemble the coffee.

I said, "If this is inconvenient ..."

"No, dear. Now we'll drink our coffee and see how it goes, and if it's getting on I'll make a sandwich and heat up yesterday's soup. Then we can have all afternoon, which ought to be enough. If not we can start again tomorrow morning." She put cups and saucers on the table, milk, sugar and a cafetière of coffee, and sat down with them. "Now," she said. "Ask me a question. That might work."

"Who are you?" I said, promptly.

"Bessie Cullough." She was practically twinkling, turning the conversation into a game.

"Your husband was David Cullough, right?"

She smiled and reached back for the end of her braid and held it up to give it a look. The gesture made her seem about seventeen. "I'll tell you a story, shall I, see if we're all still alive when I'm done. More coffee?"

Fred pushed his cup across the table. I shook my head.

"Take yourself back to 1951, The Festival of Britain," Bessie Cullough said.

"I wasn't born then."

"You can imagine, though, can't you? All right, I'll tell you a story."

She organized herself, swishing her caftan around to fold it under her legs as she settled into her chair. "People live a long time round here. Old Doris Sillings is ninety and still driving a car, though she can't get on a horse any more." She giggled at the picture of old Doris Sillings, climbing on a horse. "But the memory's not what it was, so I can never be sure what I saw then, and what I saw at the pictures or even on the telly, later. It all gets stewed up together. Still, 1949 it is, more than half a century ago. I was a city girl in love with the country and I had managed to get myself sort of apprenticed to a local farmer, someone my father was connected with. I had been to agricultural college, got a diploma, and with a bit of experience I hoped to get a position on one of the estates around here. Then I met David."

We waited while she looked out the window, remembering. "I used to cycle into Chipping on Saturdays to go to the dances they put on there. They weren't the sort of dances I would have gone to at home in London but in the country it seemed different, and besides, no one from my family would know. They had quite a good little band and it was just far enough away so that you didn't know everyone. I caught David's eye the first time he came — or he caught mine — who knows? — and he bought me a cup of tea and a rock cake in the intermission. We clicked right away. That's what we used to call it — 'clicked.' He couldn't dance, he was all over my feet, and normally that would have barred him for me, but not David. He had a car, a little Austin Seven, it was, and I'd never had a boy with a car before, and we put my bike in the back and he drove me home to Wellborough, where I had a room in a cottage near the war memorial.

"We arranged to look out for each other at the next dance. He wanted to pick me up at my digs but I thought it was too soon for that. Even after a couple more dances, I still insisted on meeting inside the hall so that he didn't spend any money on me; I didn't want to feel obligated, not just yet. After the band had played a couple of dances, we would slip out and go for a walk along the lane towards Broad Campden, across the meadow into the clump of trees in the corner. Those trees are still there. They always will be as far as I'm concerned. Your first love always stays bright in your memory, doesn't it?"

I wondered if it might be courteous to comment at this point but she held up her hand as I opened my mouth. "But don't misunderstand me. This went on for a few weeks. He was very ardent by nature but he never took advantage of me. This isn't going to be a story of seductions and illegitimate children. Mine is a lovely story. I was a nice girl from Mill Hill, in North London. I'd always wanted to work with my hands, in the outdoors. I was a big girl, and was soon accepted.

"But I met David, and I didn't give in to him right away, the way they do now, I understand — no, that's not fair, I didn't give in to *myself*, what *I* wanted, just as much as him. It wasn't my precious virtue so much as my upbringing. Mother had never told me what I should not do, like going with a man before I was married, nor did she talk about the disgrace if I got caught. She just assumed that there was no question of my straying from the straight and narrow, and all her teaching was about the joys of marriage as the conclusion to a romantic engagement. She was quite explicit, but in a positive way."

Fred said, "Should I go for a walk round the village?"

Bessie said, "Not unless you're feeling faint. This story is just getting interesting. Where was I, as they say? Oh, yes, David and I were nearly catching fire, and David wanted us to be real lovers. So did I, but Mill Hill and Mother were very strong. In the end, we drove into Stratford one Saturday, bought a special licence and I came back to my digs in Wellborough as Mrs. Cullough.

"Mrs. Flowerdale, my landlady, was a real treasure. She wasn't even surprised; exactly the same thing had happened to her and Mr. Flowerdale in the first war when they got married to have a few days before he went to the trenches. In the event, Mr. Flowerdale came back in one piece but she said she was still glad they had done it because it all happened so quickly she had no time for bridal nerves, there was too much else to think about and do. She remembered thinking she didn't want him to be killed in the trenches without at least one good memory to go with.

"So Mrs. Flowerdale gave us her bedroom, and she made her husband sleep on the floor in the little room while she took my bed. It was only right, she said, but when David came back, two weekends later — he was a travelling salesman for Crosse and Blackwell, did you know? — Mr. Flowerdale had made a bed-sitting room for us in the front room. They had found a divan with a pullout spring underneath to convert it into a sort of double bed, and there we slept when David was home.

"He came home every other weekend until one day I got a phone call that he had been killed on the Fosse Way. So there you have it. I never married anyone else. I opened a little bed and breakfast place to support myself, not this one, Mrs. Flowerdale's old cottage actually, where I used to live. Her husband had died and she'd gone to live with her sister in Stow, so I rented it from her. I think I paid half a crown a week. I could have bought it for fifty pounds, then, probably less; the one next door to it sold for two hundred thousand last year. Everyone has a story like that these days, don't they?

"Then not long afterwards I moved into this place. It was very run down but the local builder fixed it up, and in a couple of months I started taking in guests — we called this place a guesthouse because by then I had done a cooking course in Cirencester and I wanted a richer class of customer than I used to get in the cottage. I listed the house with a superior agency and offered dinner by arrangement. It worked well from the start. Now I'm about ready to retire."

"Then wasn't Cullough two-timing you with my mother?" I said, when it was clear Bessie had finished her story.

She frowned. "It's after two already. Help me make a bit of lunch, dear. Cut the bread. Cheese and pickle sandwiches all right?"

Over the sandwiches, Bessie resumed. "When David was killed, a man from Crosse and Blackwell came to me to discuss his entitlement to benefits. David hadn't worked there long but they paid out enough to bury him properly, and I thought that was that, except that I knew that one day she would turn up, and so she did, two weeks later. You see when he didn't appear at Bournemouth when he was expected, she phoned Crosse and Blackwell, who told her what had happened and how his widow — they meant me — lived here in Wellborough, so then she came to see me."

Fred said, "God, this is interesting. Did he tell you that the reason you couldn't get married was because he was already married?"

I couldn't believe what he was saying, but Bessie spoke before I could get a squawk out.

"Quite right, dear. You're *very* quick. When did you realize that?"

"It's the only answer. You wanted to become lovers but the times wouldn't allow it, and you would have got married except that he already was married, he told you."

I said, "But David Cullough married her, she just said so, in Stratford!"

Fred giggled and said to Bessie, "Shall I explain?"

Bessie put her hands between her knees (through the caftan) and looked shyly at her own feet: eighty years old, going on seventeen, hugely enjoying herself. "If you would, dear."

Fred turned to me. "She said they went to Stratford and got a special licence and she came back as Mrs. Cullough but they didn't hang their marriage lines on the wall, because they didn't have any. They never actually got married in Stratford. Did you?"

"That's right. But married we were in a pagan sort of way, once we made up our minds. We should have gone back to that clump of trees to celebrate." She laughed.

"Why?" I wanted to know. "Why didn't you marry him?"

Fred said, "Because he was already married, Uncle."

"But he *wasn't*. There's no record. Oh, for Christ's sake. He was conning you both, you and my mother."

Bessie said, "At the time, I thought it was very candid of him, and brave. He didn't have to tell me about the first Mrs. Cullough, and telling me might have meant the end of me and him, because we'd never discussed how important religion was to me; not very, as it happened. And if we ever did decide we wanted to be regularized, he would have had to get his wife to agree to divorce him. Collusion they called it, then. So the prospect of me becoming a respectable married lady was very slim indeed, and in the meantime having one of those passionate affairs you read about in books was too tricky. Where would we go? We couldn't afford the sort of hotel where we wouldn't be known so it would have to be a bed and breakfast in an out-of-the-way place. In those days suspicious landladies sometimes asked to see the marriage lines, especially in Wales."

"So he suggested you fake a wedding?"

"Not a wedding. A Gretna Green type thing. Stratford registry office. *He* didn't; *I* did. I wanted him, very badly — did I say that? — and I wanted him to have me. *He* wanted to find a safe nest somewhere. Actually we did try it once, the memory's still fresh, but, well, I won't go into details, but I got so nervous we never went through with it. My, it's such a relief to be telling someone all this."

"So how did my mother react to meeting you, suddenly, after how many years?"

"Of course she knew all about me before she arrived. She'd known about me from day one. She thought I was his wife. She thought she was the mistress."

"And you thought *you* were."

Fred said, "I think we need another cup of tea. I'll make it. I watched you doing it at lunch."

I sat back in my chair and looked steadily at Cullough's Wellborough lady. "It's a comedy," I said. "One husband, two wives and the husband is a sea captain played by Alec Guinness."

"There's more than one example, I should think. A plot like this can stand a lot of repetition. This is the one with the travelling salesman," Bessie said.

"And instead of two wives, there were two women who wanted to be wives but thought they couldn't be. He told my mother all about you, I suppose?"

"Oh yes. Right at the start."

"And after you 'got married,' he spent alternate weekends with you?"

"That's right, dear."

"And neither of you minded."

"We each thought we were his true love. What was there to mind? Your mother and I counted ourselves lucky. And we were. Once the first passion has subsided a bit, it isn't all bad to have your husband only for alternate weekends. That side of life stays exciting for much longer, I think. Your mother agreed."

"He could have married one of you, though, couldn't he? Then one of you would have got a widow's pension."

"We did compare notes about that and decided that David must have reasoned that if anything happened to him it would have been unfair to choose one of us over the other, as well as making one of us unhappy. It was just a fib, and this way, if he'd been caught — well, it wasn't illegal."

"But Crosse and Blackwell had you listed as his wife."

"That's right. He wanted any benefits to come to me because he said your mother was well taken care of."

"And this went on until David Cullough was killed? Was that when you first realized about my mother?"

"Realized what? I told you, I knew about her from the start, all about her and the guesthouse in Bournemouth."

"And when he died, mother found out about you?"

"Uncle! Listen!" Fred banged the teapot down in front of him. "Use your loaf, can't you? Your mum knew all about Bessie here from the start, too."

"So he didn't deceive either of them at all?"

Bessie said, "Well, it wasn't quite like that. You have to realize a woman's feelings in this. What kept it going was that David made it clear to each of us separately that we — that is, the one he was with — were his real choice, and he would have liked to marry us but unfortunately he was already married. And he managed it without ever running down his other lady. For me, I felt as if I was living in a novel and I liked that. Very few women get to have the experience I had without going on to some kind of tragedy, do they? Of course, David's death was terrible but it didn't end my life, or take away the wonderful years we had had together. The romance was still true. Your mother felt the same way."

"When did she appear?"

"Right after the funeral. A week or so after. That was a day, that was. The day she appeared, I mean. You can imagine. A knock at the door and there's your mother, saying, 'I would like to speak to Mrs. Cullough, please. Mrs. David Cullough.' 'Speaking,' I said, as if I was on the phone. 'I was a friend of David's' she said, and I saw how it must be, immediately. 'Come in,' I said. I'd sort of been waiting for her, you see, his legal wife, who therefore owned the cottage I lived in, which David had bought for us. I didn't dispute it, or rather, I wasn't going to. I'd had some good years, and I knew I could manage, and I wasn't going to sour the rest of my life with a row over a grave.

"Well, she came in and then before she said anything she put out her hand to shake. 'Let me introduce myself,' she said.

"'You don't have to,' I interrupted her. I was very frightened. I could tell something was up, and yet her manner was very friendly and open. Actually, she seemed on the verge of giggles, which I thought was a touch of hysteria, but it was just that she had been thinking about us, her and me, I mean, all the way from Oxford.

"I said to her, 'You're the real Mrs. David Cullough, aren't you.'

"She said, 'Not quite. It all came to me on the train, coming in from Oxford. I'm not Mrs. Cullough, nor are you. There is no Mrs. David Cullough.'

"Well. I won't bother you with all my 'buts' and 'there must be's' and 'surely to God's.' Suffice it to say that when the smoke cleared

I realized what your mother realized on the train and what I see you have, too, now. What's the matter?"

I patted my pockets, said, "Shit, I left the pictures in the car. Stay there. Don't say a word. Just stay there," and I dashed off out to the street to the car.

I came back with the pictures in my hand. She nodded as she took the pictures from me. "That's us," she said. "And I have something for you." She crossed the room to her desk and took out a document and handed it to me, putting her finger to her lips to silence me until I had read it. It was the deed to the house we were sitting in, showing the owner was Will Prentice. Me.

Fred, looking over my shoulder, said, "The treasure, Uncle!"

Bessie said, "I thought that's what you had come for, to take possession, at last. The sooner the better."

"What do you mean?"

"I mean I want to move back to my little cottage and concentrate on growing wallflowers. I've just been waiting to give you the keys. To tell the truth, I never thought Vera would be that secretive, not that it mattered. I think being secretive was a habit with her. She should have known I would never have claimed the house after all she'd done for me. I'm all right, and it's because of her I am.

"When she turned up, the week after David's funeral, she had already realized how both of us had been deceived, but as I told her, no deceiver was ever so gay, if you can still use that word in the old sense. 'I love you both,' he said. 'And that's a fact.' And when I met Vera I could see why. She said the same about me, bless her. 'Naturally bigamous,' she called him. I suppose I could claim his preference because he told Crosse and Blackwell he was married to me but that was just so I would get the benefits, the few pounds I buried him with. As I said, I wasn't as well off as Vera so he directed the money to where it was most needed.

"Vera was well fixed by then. She said so. 'I can raise the wind for ten thousand,' she said, to reassure me, and that was then, when it would take ordinary people two lifetimes to save that much. Now you know where it went." She pointed at the ceiling. "Here. It took her two visits to realize that with David gone I was going to have to go out to work, and she made her proposal.

"Remember I was in the cottage when she came. She'd seen this house was on the market and she proposed installing me as manager of an upscale guesthouse, which she would own. That suited me perfectly, so she bought it and over the next six months we had it done up. With her money, of course. All in cash, by the way. No documents, other than the deed, no bills, no receipts, nothing. The arrangements were simple: it was her house to maintain the fabric of, as she put it, and mine to look after and make a living from. She explained how I was to do that. All the income was mine, out of which I paid the rates, and electricity and small repairs, while she paid for any major renovations, like a new roof. She said it was an investment but I don't think she ever expected to cash in while I was alive. See, we became friends, bosom friends. We had David in common; I still kept his name. More than that, it was the attraction of opposites. My mother would have completely disapproved of her, well, casual attitude to all the rules of a proper moral life. She would have thought her common, too, but I found her exhilarating.

"She used to come here for alternate weekends for a long time, then, lately, perhaps once a month. For her it was an outing, she said, her weekend in the country. It soon became a treat for me. I used to buy us tickets for the theatre at Stratford, or sometimes we'd go to the pictures, and then on Sundays we'd go out for lunch to a pub, and she'd take the afternoon train back.

"I never found a replacement for David, as she did with Will's father, another difference between us. I had plenty to keep me busy with this house, and I never got lonely — you don't in this business — and, well, I found that David was the love of my life, and after him it suited me to be a widow. Vera, though, took up more or less immediately with Will's father; at least I assume she did. I think he was no grand passion, but she found herself comfortable with him and they got married. For Vera, even David was only one of, well, several, although the way she spoke, he came first. For me, as I've said, he was the only one, then or later. I'm sorry dear, I'm forgetting. I've no business talking about your mother like this."

"I guessed most of this before we got here. Don't worry about me; go on with the story."

"When David was killed, Vera was pregnant and soon would have had to do something about it. In the event, she married Henry Prentice, then moved far enough away so that no one knew her story except her family, and she cut them off, all except Phyllis, her sister, to construct a new story when the baby arrived, a story with all the wrong dates, of course."

For two weeks, ever since I started to think about dates and who David Cullough was, I had been looking for this answer, and now the suspense was hard to bear. I said, "It doesn't fit. I wasn't born until more than a year after David Cullough was killed."

"She had a miscarriage, dear; she didn't need a story, after all. That's something only I knew until now."

Eventually I said, "So Henry Prentice was my father."

"Well, David Cullough certainly wasn't." She looked out the window over the hills towards Moreton. "We had some lovely weekends together, Vera and I, and I've become part of the village, so I've had a good life. David's death threatened to lay me low, leave me stranded, but Vera propped me up and then we were all right. She was wonderful.

"I'm too old to run a guesthouse now. I haven't advertised for three or four years, and months go by without any bookings, although I'm always full up for Gold Cup week. But I want to hand it over, and the sooner the better. It's time for me to go. I shall move back up to Mrs. Flowerdale's old cottage. I might take the odd guest still: Vera taught me that it is always good to have some cash you don't have to account for but I've earned and saved enough from this place so I'm comfortable whatever happens. You don't have to worry about me, Will. Your mother did that. By the way, dear, what shall I tell the income tax man when he calls?" She took a card from the mantelpiece. "Mr. Merton," she added.

"When did he call?"

"Last Friday."

"What did he want to know?"

"A lot of things about this house, when it was bought, how much income it earned, that sort of thing."

"What did you tell him?"

"Nothing. I told him I couldn't answer any questions because the house didn't belong to me and therefore I was not at liberty to divulge anything."

"I think that's what he wanted to know."

"I put him off, then. I told him I would consult with my solicitor, and he would hear from him. Did I do right?"

"Absolutely."

"What shall I do if he comes back?"

"Here." I scribbled on the back of Merton's card Purrott's name and phone number. "Tell him to call this solicitor, and deal with him. Tell him you are being turned out." I kissed her on the cheek.

THIRTY-ONE

IN THE CAR, FRED burst out, "Treasure or not, Uncle, it's her house. You can't turn her out."

"Didn't you hear? She wants to retire. We'll have to sell the house, or find someone to manage it. But I know what you mean. It all adds up to a complicated message from my dead mother that I should look after Bessie. And I will. I suppose I'll sell the house and give her the income until she dies. Something like that."

That shut him up until we were passing Moreton library. Then he said, "Rounded. She's really become rounded now."

"What? Who?"

"Your mother. Remember. In the beginning, the opening chapters of your story, when we only had your version, she was hard-headed, casual, even neglectful, and secretive. Now you have to add in what we've been told about her generosity to Great-Aunt Phyllis, to Bessie and to you, in the end. She's become a fully rounded character. That right?"

Back in the hotel there was a message for me from my son, Scott. He had arrived, registered at the hotel, gone for a walk and would find me later. I should stay there until he returned. I showed the note to Fred.

"What's he doing here?" I wondered aloud.

"Checking up on you? Here he is now, I think."

Scott stood in front of us, smiling. "Dr. Livingstone, I presume," he said. Scott has never been able to pass up a cliché.

After the introductions, Fred stood up. "I'm going up to my room for a bit," he said. "If you two would like some time, I can look after myself for dinner."

They have good manners, these Cambridge boys.

"No way," Scott said, bless him. "Let's all eat together."

"I'll come and find you," I said to Fred.

When we were on our own, gin and tonics in hand, Scott said, "My second cousin? Seems a nice guy."

"He is. It's good to see you, son, as always; but why are you here?" I was pleased to see him, but I was slightly irritated, too. I was too young to need looking after, and he was, too, to be a nanny.

"We thought you might be dead. We haven't heard from you since you left. I was in London for a meeting, so I took a couple of days to run down and say hello."

"Fuck off," I said, making him laugh, because this was starting a new vocabulary between him and me. "You're checking up on me. Right?"

"Oh, sure, that too. But I'm mainly here about Mum."

Now he had me. Was she dead? Was she making threats or promises? Were the lawyers right, that it always turned nasty? Or did she want me back? Was this after all going to mark the beginning of the next phase, the period of bitterness and wrangling I had seen so often at home? I hoped not. I hadn't thought about the breakdown of my marriage much while I was driving around England, looking for my father, but time had passed and I wanted to move on. I waited for him to continue.

"She asked me to come and find you if I could."

He wasn't just fussing, then. "First of all, how *did* you find me?"

"Your Aunt Phyllis. It took three phone calls to find the hotel you were staying in, and then a rented car to get me here. I think I must have got to Mrs. Cullough's in Wellborough just after you left. She did the phoning to find your hotel."

"What does your mother want?"

Scott settled himself, leaning forward slightly in his chair, the body language of deep seriousness, showing that he was taking charge. Scott scraped through university, switching from courses as they made greater and greater demands, into other, more manageable ones, finally getting a degree in Commerce. There was no question of his going on, even for something as workmanlike as an MBA, but his B.Com. was enough to get him this job with the oil company, and there he looked set for life, already making as much money as I did. He enjoyed his work and I suspected he was exactly right for the job. He was obviously a great employee, loyal, hardworking — all those things — and it would take a major depression for him to lose his job. He was a bit hearty, and he went in for rules a lot, rules of life, I mean. He began a lot of sentences with phrases like, "I think a son ought to remember the duty he owes to the one who brought him into the world," which made me feel shy if anyone else was listening.

He had, then, for some time taken himself very seriously. He thought carefully about what he should do, then did it, especially in his role as the first son (there were no others). Sometimes I had the feeling that he couldn't wait for the day I had a stroke to demonstrate how responsible he was and ready to step in. For that was what he prided himself on being — responsible. (As Scott himself said, Zoe was the bright one.) Friends told me that he was the salt of the earth. I don't know about that but he may be the glue that holds the family together. From high school he had always given the family an identity, talking of us as if we shared a history and a consciousness like one of the great English shire families.

("The family has never holidayed in Florida, have we.") It struck
me now that his continual emphasis on the family unit suggested
that our separation and the break up of that unit had probably hit
him much harder than it did his sister, and, too, perhaps there was
an implication that he envied his friends, the children of third and
fourth generation immigrants, their extended families, again, unlike
his sister.

He said, "We had a long talk, Mum and I. She wants her
freedom."

"All right. If you're the family broker, tell her okay. How does
she seem?"

He breathed out heavily. "Kind of eager to get going on her new
life, to be honest."

"Have you met him?"

"I remember him coming to the house. Otherwise, no. He
doesn't want to meet me, or Zoe, until it's settled."

"That's okay. Maybe if your mother is comfortable, we can try
keeping the lawyers out of it."

"That's what she wondered too. She even had an idea that both
of you could use the same lawyer, the one you've had for thirty
years."

"Okay. Tell her okay, would you?" Everything was okay. "Tell
her as soon as I get back we'll get together and see if we can part
friends. It ought to be possible."

"It's *your* life, Dad," he said, after a while, suggesting that if
things got difficult he would be on my side.

"How's Zoe?" I asked. I wanted badly to talk about something
else, to stop feeling so muddled. I was glad of what was happening
but it was all going so fast.

"If I tell you, promise to act surprised when she speaks to you."
He looked like his ten-year-old self, waiting for me to unwrap the
clumsily-tied-together birthday present he had brought me.

"She's pregnant, right?"

"Yes, and already she's sitting there smiling, the way they do."

I had to avoid his gaze in order not to break into the same foolish grin he had. I felt my eyes prickling slightly.

Eventually, he said, "What have you found out? About your family?"

"A bit about my father, and a whole other side of my mother, and about her family, and there are these cousins I mentioned."

"Is Mrs. Cullough a relative?"

"Sort of. It's a long story. I'll tell you the next time we go fishing." I meant it. I felt a surge of love for the boy, untouched by any of the feelings he usually engendered, puzzlement, irritation, the urge to bend him to my way of thinking and being. Perhaps he was too grown-up, and I had myself grown a little, perhaps by spending a week or two with Fred. Scott didn't judge me, just respected me as a father, and perhaps I should stop judging him.

"Which will be?" he asked. "I mean, when are you coming home?"

"Not long now. A few days. Now let's find Fred and go somewhere to eat."

"The place to eat around here is a pub in Paxford."

"How do you know?"

"I asked your partner, Mr. Grisham. And that's another thing. Mr. Masters has called a couple of times to find out when you are coming back."

"I know. I've talked to him. I'll call him again from London."

Zoe was pregnant; that was all I knew. In seven or even six months time I would be a grandfather, and that settled that. I wanted to be on site. Here I come, old Grandad himself.

I told Scott all about his grandmother's secrets, and he decided to be delighted, and thought it did make Bessie a kind of honorary grandmother, and I suppose I felt a tremor in that direction myself. I told him my plan to leave for London the next day, take Phyllis out to a restaurant, and possibly see my uncle.

Scott said, "Do you mind if I stay here for a day? I think a person ought to visit Shakespeare's birthplace, if he's nearby."

We were back in London in the hotel Grisham had booked for me. I needed two more days. Phyllis had to be told, and Albert, and the solicitor. Then I could go home and find out what they planned to call the baby.

We woke to a bright Saturday morning.

Fred said, "Time for you to visit Grandad."

"You coming?"

Fred said, "Yes, but I have things to do first. Time I went."

I said, "Don't leave me to your relatives. You can drive us."

"That's what we planned."

"Who?"

"Me and Grandad. He told me I had to bring you home before you went back to Canada."

Albert, on the phone, said, "Certainly, of course, love you to come, anytime. If tomorrow would be just as good, you say so. We don't mind. We *had* planned to spend this afternoon with my son-in-law. He's got a big screen. But we can do that anytime. Right? No. Come on. You know the way?"

I was looking at the map. "Straight down the A24, isn't it?"

"That's the idea. Just before you get to the A3 do a left on to the B279 and we're on the third turning to the right. You can't miss it. What time will you be here? We'll just pop out and do the shopping and all the regular Saturday errands first, so we can talk in peace. Don't rush. But what are we talking about? Fred is going to drive you, isn't he?"

Fred, listening, whispered, "Make it tomorrow. He wants to watch the cricket."

"Why don't I come tomorrow?" I said to Albert.

"No, no, no, no, no. Unless it's more convenient? All right, come for tea tomorrow, then. I'll get all the gang together. Yes. Come for Sunday dinner, too, if you like."

"We'll come for tea. What time?"

"Whenever you *like*. Hullo. Who's 'we'? Fred *is* still looking after you?"

"Yes."

"Be nice to see him, too. We don't see much of him."

I put down the phone and told Fred the other half of the conversation.

"I think I'll leave you to London, Uncle. As I said, there are some people I'd like to look up. One, actually. I have an agenda, too."

There it was, the invitation to ask. I wasn't very curious, because I wanted to concentrate on my own affairs, but I had grown fond of Fred, and it would seem indifferent not to seem interested.

I said, "Can you get to Cambridge and back before tomorrow?"

He said, "No need. She's here, in Ilford, home for the weekend. I — er — wanted her to meet my family. See you in the morning, then?"

And he was gone.

Phyllis was free so I got her to agree to come up to Leicester Square where I would meet her at the tube station. Be here at five, I told her, so we could have a proper supper or dinner or tea or whatever she called it now and she wouldn't be getting home too late.

I was on my own until Phyllis arrived. I thought I'd have a walk round the area but the sun disappeared as soon as I set foot outside, and it rained all morning. I tried not to mind but by lunchtime I was wet through and cold and fed up, so I had a sausage and baked beans and a pint of beer at a pub near the river, then walked back to the hotel. Now I felt the benefits of staying at a superior hotel, never mind the cost. I soaked away the gooseflesh in the full-sized bath, put on one of those complimentary bathrobes, ordered some coffee sent up and, like Albert, spent a nice couple of hours watching the horse racing, switching around among the channels to try to catch all the highlights. You don't want the palaver in the paddock, just the actual race, all two minutes of it. In between races I watched bits of a cricket match. When I was a kid, the cricket season ended, *then* the football season began, but now as long as there's money to be made you can watch anything at any time of the year. It's the same in Canada, watching the Stanley Cup played out in Dallas, Texas, in May, ice hockey in a temperature of thirty degrees Celsius.

The sun came back out and I walked down to Leicester Square Underground station where Phyllis was already waiting, probably had been for half an hour, so as not to keep *me* waiting. She insisted she'd just arrived, and we walked through to Leicester Street and the table I had booked at Manzi's.

I let her have her treat first. You could see by the dampness on her forehead that just being there again was excitement enough for her. I ordered a bottle of Blue Nun, a wine my elitist Toronto acquaintances have taught me to feel patronizing about (too sweet, not "crisp," served only at weddings in South Porcupine, etc.), but it was the first wine I liked when I was sixteen or seventeen. I liked it then a lot: that was the age when I couldn't believe that anyone honestly liked the mixture of battery acid and vinegar called red wine. I guessed that for someone who drank as rarely as Phyllis, and then mainly Guinness, Blue Nun would still be the wine of choice, and I was right.

She sipped it and looked at the label. "I love Blue Nun," she said. "Your mum and I used to drink a whole bottle at Christmas with the turkey. It goes well with plaice, too."

Like most of the English, Phyllis is a connoisseur of fried fish and we agreed that the only thing wrong with the fillets of plaice at Manzi's was that there was too much. She had a struggle to finish hers and afterwards she refused anything heavy and settled for raspberries and cream. "And coffee," she said. "They have lovely coffee here," she said. "You should try it." She picked her bag off the floor. "And now," she said, "if you don't mind I'm going to have a smoke. After a meal like that I'm dying for a fag."

"You smoke much, Aunt Phyllis?"

"One a day, and one in the evening, with the telly, and on special occasions. About twenty a week. I'm not worried about my health at my age. I tell everyone that I've managed to break the habit but I've still got the addiction, which a packet a week satisfies."

Watching her puffing away, shiny-faced with the warmth of the room and the food, I thought how easy it was to make people like Phyllis happy, for an hour or two. Dinner once a year at Manzi's ought to be on the National Health, for pensioners, anyway.

"Is it as good as you remember?" It was the best fried fish I had ever eaten.

"Better," she said. "Better for not expecting to see the place again. Thanks, Will, that was lovely."

I couldn't resist a small tweak. I said, "You knew all about David Cullough, didn't you?"

"I suppose I did, but I didn't *know* I did, you know what I mean? Mind you, I never saw much of him. And it was none of my business." She smiled. "It still isn't."

And that was that. Outside, the taxi was waiting, pulsing away like an old water pump the way those London cabs do. The lights of Leicester Square filled one end of the street but at this end the sights and the smells of Soho began. It all looked familiar from old English movies. I gave the driver the address, asked him to estimate the fare, paid him, and tipped him an extra ten pounds.

She said, "Tell him to go the scenic route," and laughed.

He said, "Piccadilly Circus do?"

"That's it," she said. "Show us the lights."

THIRTY-TWO

THE ONLY THING TO do on Sunday in London is read the papers and wait for lunchtime when you can eat roast beef and Yorkshire pudding like everyone else. At least, that's what I thought until Cora appeared in the lounge after breakfast where I was knee-deep in the *Observer* and chatted me up. (She was very good at her job.) Finding me at a loose end, she looked as if she was going to name the usual excursions, but, instead she suggested one I had never heard of, Spitalfields Market, near Liverpool Street. I shall be eternally grateful to her for pointing me towards it.

I like markets for the promise they hold that here you might buy, or eat, or just see something unavailable in Tesco's, or Marks and Spencer, or even Ikea, something which relies entirely for its attraction on my ability to see its virtues, unaided by any ad man. (I know, I know.) Now I have another idea for a tour I would put together for people like me, a tour that would make some of the world's street markets the real destinations, not merely the alternative attractions to the cathedrals. I'd start with London. Forget

St. Paul's, I would say, we begin with a daylong visit to Spitalfields Market ...

Go to Liverpool Street Station and walk along Bishopsgate, turning right at Spital Square. Have a cup of the best coffee in London at Valerie's, and then start walking. First see what you can find for the folks at home spread out on the stalls of what is the new Spitalfields. To start with, I was assured by a couple of knowledgeable-sounding girls that there are ladies' Italian leather gloves lined with silk to be had for a third of the price you would pay in Bond Street. They are possibly stolen, and you, yourself, are continually warned to keep your wallet under your shirt between purchases; if that bothers you, stay home, because it's perfectly safe otherwise.

Dozens of stalls, catering mainly but not exclusively to women, lead on to Old Spitalfields, the original market, where the first inhabitants sold their clothes to each other to pay for gin, and their descendants are still at it. At some point you will stumble over Petticoat Lane, Middlesex Street (you can look it up on Google). Now find Brick Lane, a long street lined on both sides with Indian restaurants. Take any side street and walk along a housing development of about 1820, once swarming with thieves and prostitutes, now lovingly and pretty successfully restored by lawyers and television producers to its original condition. I thought I had come across one address where the old days had survived, updated for the age, as a shop front advertising "S and M", appeared, but it turned out to be a restaurant serving sausage and mash with a name that had come happily to hand like found poetry.

Don't bother with a guidebook. Write it yourself. There are plenty of places in the area which offer a vantage point from which you can invent eight hundred years of history. A building advertises that on this site in the thirteenth century there stood a hospital "taken down" in the eighteenth century to be replaced by a hospital of the kind that Magwitch lay in at the end. Now it is a church school, though you won't hear many hymns along Brick Lane, I think. Not *far a way is a medical centre that caters to today's homeless. Don't move; now is the time to speculate about what you are seeing. Hitler tried to destroy this neighbourhood, for long London's home of the underclass, but rows of tidy little houses survived and became desirable to the young rich who work around the corner.*

There are plenty of other buildings, churches especially, that survived the Blitz; some even survived the later blitz of developers, and with any luck will be there forever, so it is fascinating to see the juxtaposition of the very old and the new and imagine the Londons of the eighteenth, nineteenth and twentieth centuries. There is enough left of each to see the whole, several alleys, for instance, so narrow, twisting and dark they seem still like ideal places for a mugger to serve his apprenticeship. Some of these buildings, the churches, testify to the genius of men like Hawksmoor and Wren, and some are just the remains of the warehouses and factories of the nineteenth century, horrible, but worth preserving as reminders of the working conditions in the factories of the day.

What will the modern buildings seem like in their turn? A familiar speculation. There is one, a huge glass-and-iron cone, pointed at both ends like a fox's turd, which was recently voted by a society of architects "The finest new building in the world," and perhaps it is, to a society of architects. On the other hand, even to a society of architects, the new Lloyd's building surely will never escape looking as if it had been born with its intestines on the outside.

Coming out of St. Mary Axe, the home of the dung-shaped building, on to Leadenhall Street I crossed over to have a look at Leadenhall Market, to add it to my collection of markets. It is an agreeably vulgar structure, a kind of Christmas arcade painted mainly in red and gold, lit up like a chandelier, and filled with shops and restaurants for people who enjoy getting and spending, people whose trade is money, people who make nothing else.

Coming out of Leadenhall Market, I turned towards the station and made another happy discovery. All of the major buildings had brass plaques lining the doorways, giving the names of the tenants.

I wondered how our new partnership would look on a brass plaque and got a surge of glee when the name, *"Masters and Prentice,"* came to me, a small gift I could take to Jack. Then a plate caught my eye, just like the others, except that it said, "Strictly no smoking in the doorway." Walking along Bishopsgate, I saw that half the doorways had the same notice. Perhaps such signs are all over, even in Toronto, but I'd never seen one and I was delighted. Ignoring the obvious, I fantasized about what someone, an archaeologist in, say, five thousand AD, picking over the ruins of a civilization that had been destroyed in the Third (nuclear) World War would make of it:

The plate is made of brass, a metal still in use then, about three spans long and a span wide. It is inscribed, in the English of the day, "Strictly no smoking in the doorway." Nothing is left of the doorway itself, reduced to dust by the inferno, but later diggings yielded enough evidence to show that such plates had once been common. We speculated that in the religion of the day the doorways of their temples were particularly sacred and that "smoking" as they called it, was akin to desecration.

It was well past lunchtime, time to meet the family, and I caught a taxi back to the hotel. Fred and his girlfriend, Daisy, appeared, and we watched the entertainers in the piazza for an hour before we took off.

I liked her name but talking to her was hard work. She began by asking me if I thought that Canada would become a republic in the near future. I said I didn't think so but if it did no one would notice. Then she asked me if the Canadian Senate wasn't just as anachronistic as the House of Lords, being unelected, unrepresentative and, really, just an old folks' home for whatever establishment had just lost power, or lost it in the nineteenth century, and I said the main difference was that half the billionaires in Canada were trying to buy their way into the House of Lords, whereas I'd never heard of a single Englishman trying to get into the Canadian Senate, so apparently the House of Lords had more cachet. But there were no bishops in the Senate, thank God.

On she went, pecking away at this topic and that in her adversarial Cambridge graduate (Upper Second) way, getting right up my nose until I realized that all she was doing was trying to be nice to a possible future uncle. It was like being involved in an advanced class in conversational English as we tried and failed to find a topic we could develop. But that was Fred's problem.

Albert lived in a semi-detached maisonette in Worcester Road, in Raynes Park, three up, two down and garden front and back. There was a path around the side leading to the back garden and the bike shed.

Albert was waiting for us, pretending to be parking his car. He was keeping a space for us; otherwise, as he said, we'd probably have to park three streets over. He took us through to Lottie, who was with Olive in the kitchen, and through the kitchen into the garden, where, daring the sun to go in (it actually stayed gorgeous all day), Albert had erected a trestle table with a sheet over it for a cloth. On this was set out the afternoon tea: cucumber sandwiches, fish-paste sandwiches, egg sandwiches, cheese and tomato sandwiches, sausage rolls, sliced bread and butter, pots of jam, wedges of pork pie, cold tongue, ham, Dundee cake, sponge cake, seed cake, jam tarts, lemon curd tarts, biscuits and trifle. There was more, but that's all I remember. There was lemonade and orangeade, and when the meal was well under way, beer appeared. It all looked like one of those street parties that the neighbours put on together when the last war was over.

There must have been twenty people in the garden, and I finally realized that it had all been planned since the funeral, probably. One by one, Fred introduced me to four cousins — three women and a man — and their spouses, and to his own generation, children in their twenties, few of whom had brought partners. My male cousin, Bruce, an air-conditioning engineer, was almost exactly the same age as me. Another one, Hazel, was married to a man who owned two pharmacies. Nearly all their children had been to university, including a lawyer who went to Oxford, so what you had on the lawn was that part of England that had prospered in the last thirty years, from working class to solid bourgeois in two generations. And there in the middle of them was my Canadian son, Scott, looking enormously happy to have found his extended family.

I, too, was bowled over by the attractiveness of them all, and spent part of the time silently cursing my parents for keeping me away from them. There was no cold shoulder here. They were all pleased to meet me, and welcomed me into the clan. By the time we'd reached the sherry trifle we were exchanging addresses and assuring each other of the availability of beds should I or my kids ever visit England on holiday, and, of course, if any of them should want to visit Toronto. No one, all afternoon, mentioned my mum and dad.

At one point I noticed Fred in earnest conversation with his grandfather. I guessed what they were talking about. I cornered Fred almost immediately and asked him. Was Great-Great-Uncle Jack gay, or a coward, and thus the family skeleton?

He said, no. Grandad said he really was missing in action. Fred had been asking after the wrong name. At the turn of the century a lot of first-born sons were nicknamed "Jack," whatever they were christened (this one was a Joseph), just as all fair-haired girls were called Daisy, even if, like his (Grandfather's) own mother they had been christened Caroline.

I said, "You'll have to go back to Durham to find out."

Fred said, "I think that's a job for the next generation."

Now, happy at the warmth of the family's welcoming of Daisy, he wanted to drive me back to the hotel, but I could see by Daisy's face that she still had a mouth full of topics, so I insisted he stay and look after her while I took the train to Waterloo, saying I wanted to walk back across the bridge. Scott stayed at the party, going round his relatives one by one, copying out their addresses and telephone numbers in his diary, insisting they all visit him in Toronto.

On the train I wondered again if I'd made a mistake by emigrating, just like when I smelled the sea at Coombe Regis. Of course I compared myself with my engineer cousin. His two kids, including the lawyer, would have a lot in common with mine, and I'd do what I could to get them together. And thinking about *that*, I realized, *really* realized, that my kids were Canadian, North American, more American than European, if you like. Their mother researched her birth mother and learned she is a third generation Canadian, descended from Loyalist Americans, Scotch, Welsh and, she claims, Ojibwa Indians, though it's trendy nowadays to claim some Indian blood, and I never saw a blonde Indian. So if I searched my memory, I could find plenty of times when my children obviously regarded me as "old country." In twenty years I'd be a funny old man with a comic accent who knows how to make airplanes out of paper. It would be a bit strange to be classified by your own grandchildren as "grampa from the old country." Maybe by then I really would be ethnic. I always thought of ethnic as anyone not English, all the other odds and sods. It's like, once upon a time, the English travelled round Europe observing the foreigners, but never being foreigners themselves, never being observed, they thought. Soon the English in Canada would be just one of the waves of immigrants: first were the Vikings, then the French, then the English and the Irish, then the Loyalists, and so on. That's if the Indians, who really were first, and the Inuit, let us stay.

THIRTY-THREE

THEN, WALKING ACROSS WATERLOO Bridge, thinking of this but mainly of what a happy afternoon I'd had with my new relatives, I got to thinking that it often turned cold in Canada on Labour Day, like it was supposed to, the last weekend before school. The leaves were turning, so that even as you drove north for a fall "experience" as my son's old girlfriend called it (she was a bit spiritual) you knew that summer was over. It was woodsmoke time.

And so, if the idea weren't silly, I'd have said that after only a few weeks away I felt homesick, and feeling homesick, I felt much less muddled. Because when it came down to it, there was no point in weighing the advantages of one against the other, or trying to decide whether I'd made the right move all those years ago; the real question was where was home? And Zoe had answered that one.

I watched television for a while and fell asleep on the bed in front of the set. When I woke up, I wasn't hungry because I'd been stuffing my face all afternoon, but I needed to mark that it was dinnertime, so I walked through to the Aldwych to a very swish coffee shop in a very grand hotel where I got exactly what I wanted, a Welsh rarebit with a glass of wine. Cost about four times what I would have been charged in Toronto, but the ambience was worth something.

The next morning Fred appeared for breakfast. Daisy had gone back to Cambridge, and a contented and now apparently un-bored Fred wanted to know if there was anything more he could do for me.

I said, "I assume Canada is off."

"Not completely, Uncle. I'd like to come sometime but Daisy's not very interested and we have another idea."

"Are you — er — engaged?"

"Er — no — but we are — er — going to be." He grinned, mocking me a little.

"Good luck."

"Thanks, Uncle. Where to, now? Let me take you somewhere."

"All right. Clapham. You know the way?"

"Indeed I do. We went through Clapham, remember, on the way to Coombe Regis. Now?"

"We have to be there by ten. Have another cup of coffee and I'll get the things I need from my room."

I had an appointment with Purrott, the solicitor, who I now intended to retain for myself. In his office, I told him the story of my mother and Bessie Cullough. He heard me through, and then said, "I haven't heard from Mrs. Cullough yet. In summary, your mother had been helping a friend with small gifts of money over the years, not so? Nothing taxable about that. But now your mother's friend wants to give you the guesthouse she has owned all these years. Not so? There may be some sort of gift tax liability there. I'll consult and let you know. I assume any fees I incur will be ...? Of course. Leave it with me, then. I'll let you know when I need a decision from you."

"Do you think they'll let me keep it? I mean it is my mother's unpaid taxes that have turned into an inheritance for me, isn't it?"

"These things are arguable, and I shall argue them for you. I think your tax inspector will eventually make an offer. It's often uneconomic for them to go after every ounce of flesh. We'll see."

"So you think I might get away with it?"

"Don't talk like that. You haven't done anything. But if you mean, free and clear, then, no, I don't. As you imply, legally, there is some doubt, and morally, too, I suppose, but that's not my concern. I would predict we'll have to negotiate something, and it might in the end cost you the guesthouse." He smiled. "But if I see any danger of you not getting enough out of it to pay my fee, I'll let you know."

"How long, do you think?"

"I'm sure I can keep them at bay for six months. After that, it will start to grind through the courts, or you will come to some agreement. Frankly, if that happens, I don't think there will be much left to inherit."

I explained the situation to Fred in a Chinese restaurant in Soho over lunch. "I'm not very concerned," I said. "I don't need the money. It would be nice to own Bessie's house but how could I run it from Toronto? Come to that, what's going to happen for the next six months? Bessie was quite clear that she's tired. She doesn't want to wait that long. I'll have to find a caretaker, close it up."

"Or a temporary manager."

"For six months? Would anyone I could trust take a job for that short a time?"

"I would."

"You? You?" I remembered a line I'd always wanted to use, "How could they send up a mere boy in a crate like that," then decided against it. "You don't know anything about it."

"I could learn. Bessie would be there, in the village. I liked her. Daisy thinks it would be a good idea."

And so the seed was sown and the idea sprouted and blossomed all before the fortune cookies and a bill for two hundred dollars (for a Chinese lunch for two!) arrived. It was a win-win situation. I was delighted to do something for Fred, and Daisy too. Maybe it would be for him the equivalent of what emigration was for me. He certainly wouldn't be bored. And if they *could* pull it off and the solicitor could save something from the tax man, enough to hang on to the house, what a nice base the Canadian Prentices would have for future holidays in England. (I was back in Canada before I realized that Fred had had the idea in mind long before he suggested it, ever since he had met Bessie in Wellborough, probably.)

"I'll phone Bessie from the hotel," I said.

There was another message from Jack when I got back to the hotel. I tried to return it but he was out. I thought I knew what he was calling about. When could we get started?

I phoned Bessie, and then asked the desk to find me the next available seat on a plane to Toronto. I thought a bit about the way it would be, working with Jack, and again I got a surge of glee when I remembered the name I had found for our new agency, my small gift to Jack to show him I had been thinking, too.

Cora phoned to tell me they had found me a seat on a British Airways plane leaving Heathrow at 3:50 the next day. I could check out at noon and have lunch at the airport.

The next morning I rose at seven, had one last English breakfast, and by nine I was packed and ready to start.

I plugged in my laptop and typed the title page:

"FINDING HOME"

BY

WILL PRENTICE